The Black Air

Jennifer Lane

The Black Air is a uclanpublishing book

First Published in Great Britain in 2023 by uclanpublishing
University of Central Lancashire
Preston, PR1 2HE, UK

Text copyright © Jennifer Lane, 2023
Cover Illustration © Sarah Dennis, 2023

978-1-915235-3-12

1 3 5 7 9 10 8 6 4 2

The right of Jennifer Lane and Sarah Dennis to be identified as the author
and illustrator of this work respectively has been asserted in accordance
with the Copyright, Designs and Patents Act 1988.

Set in 10/16pt Kingfisher by Amy Cooper.

A CIP catalogue record for this book is available from the British Library.

Printed and bound in Great Britain by Clays Ltd, Elcograf S.p.A.

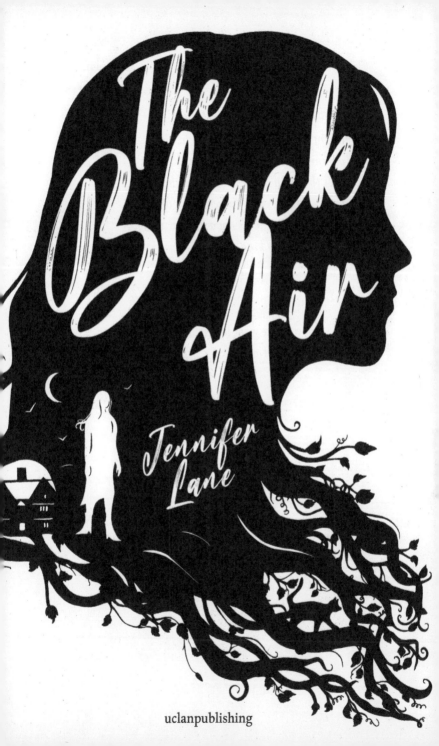

The Black Air

Jennifer Lane

uclanpublishing

I have gone out, a possessed witch,
haunting the black air, braver at night;
dreaming evil, I have done my hitch
over the plain houses, light by light:
lonely thing, twelve-fingered, out of mind.
A woman like that is not a woman, quite.
I have been her kind.

Anne Sexton, *'Her Kind'*

Women who are wont to practise enchantments...
do not allow them to live.

King Alfred, ninth century

Chapter 1

Long Byrne had a history of violence.

There had been two murder cases. In 1866, Mrs Meredith Fillstone had stared through her father's telescope at the moon for seven hours straight, mesmerised. She'd drawn herself a bath, ordered a new chandelier, then shot her husband and five kids with a hunting rifle.

She told the authorities that she had done it "to save them from the witches' influence". Or so the story goes.

Nutcase.

We've got a *lot* of them.

In 1958, a twelve-year-old girl had dreamt she was being eaten by the dogs of two witches out on the moor. They were tearing chunks from her arms, stripping off the skin from under her puffy white nightgown. She'd woken up and told her sister, who was sleeping in the next bed. When the sister didn't believe her, the girl had smothered her to death with a frilly cushion.

Nobody spoke about the little girl any more.

Long Byrne had seen two murder cases, but there had been more than two murders. There was the girl whose parents nabbed her when she got pregnant at fifteen.

They said she'd run away, but we all knew better.

Tawny lived for the thrill of this gossip, while I churned the old stories and legends over in my head as I read quietly in my bed at night.

Then there were all those girls hanged for being witches out on the moor on 31st October 1623. They were all murdered really, weren't they? Rose Ackroyd. Jane Hollingworth. All of them. Eighteen girls sent up to the gallows in long shadowy skirts.

Long Byrne at its finest.

Tawny and I were long-time Long Byrners. What did that say about us?

It wasn't that Long Byrne was cut off from the world. It just felt that way; nothing but a labyrinth of grey, stone houses – farm gates hanging off their hinges, roadkill-splattered tarmac between the hedges.

These are places you can't see on Google Maps until you really zoom in close. The kind where buses only go by twice a day, and where they sometimes have to close down the school because a crow has got into the air ducts.

It probably made us what we were today – big-lunged and hardy, like cattle or wolves. We weren't afraid of anything.

We were fearless, Tawny and me.

"Are you sure you can't see it?"

"A hundred and seventy per cent sure."

"But what if I have to turn around really fast?" she said.

I was lopsided in the doorway; my foot already out on the step. "We'll be late again."

The ladder in Tawny's tights poked out like a white worm stuck to a chalkboard. You'd have to be blind to miss it. She scowled at her reflection in the water-marked hall mirror that had probably been there as long as the house, and yanked her skirt down an inch further.

"Fine. Guess the whole school's going to be climbing my stairway to heaven."

I grabbed her college bag from the coat stand and started out at a trot.

I didn't know why I was in such a rush. It's not like we'd have been in trouble. OK, we'd have been in trouble, but only Miss Rillington's famous finger wag. You never got into serious trouble with Tawny around anyway. Even when she tried extra hard.

We pushed down the cobbled lane, boots gripping hard on the slope. The sun was already cresting the hills and lasering into our eyes. Through our squints, the light filtered everything into a pale gold that made Tawny's charity-shop red velvet blazer glimmer. Tawny and I had raided the charity shops on one of our trips to the city this summer, splitting my allowance straight down the middle so I could buy her a dress that made her look like Audrey Hepburn with boobs. I'd come back with a load of old-man jumpers that swamped me but Tawny said they made me look 'cute'. I was anything but: my face was pinched, pale and anaemic – someone had once nearly put pennies in my coffee cup when I was on a park bench.

My house – Alder Farm – was closer to school, so staying over at the Browns' attic apartment was never a good idea on a week-night, especially when you had to hop three stiles, jump the brook, and sometimes stop off at Pat's for a panini before arriving at school. That didn't stop me, though. It seemed like we spent half our lives hungover from tiredness, only dragging our pyjamas on at 4 a.m., and scaring ourselves silly with bargain-bucket horror movies, because we'd run out of chick flicks two summers ago. Now we'd started sixth form, my presence at the Browns' breakfast table had reached three times a week, and a good night's sleep was a fond but distant memory.

Since Mum had died, I was pretty much left to my own devices.

Just before we reached my farm, we passed Hollingworth House, the old creepy manor house where the Long Byrne witches had once lived. Nobody went there any more, but kids sometimes ran up the lane on a dare and prayed that no ghosts followed them home. We walked by the Slip, just before the high street. It was a dirt-track with a kissing gate into the wood, which led out to the moor and the craggy river where no one even took their dogs for a swim – they'd be swept off out to Garistone Lake in the blink of an eye. And besides, the locals tended to avoid the moor completely. It was too haunted.

From the path, you could see the old hanging spot; the gallows had long been torn down but the clearing where the witches had swung to their deaths was still obvious because nothing ever grew in that place. I remember when Tawny first dragged me there against my wide-eyed protests.

Nothing fazed her, especially not the ghosts of girls who'd been dead four hundred years.

We stopped at Maldew's Corner Shop to sate Tawny's liquorice cravings but I stayed hovering by the stack of yesterday's newspapers at the door. My eyes settled on the growing ladder on her thigh.

"What's up with you?" said Tawny. "It's assembly. You're not missing anything."

"You're functioning at minus five miles per hour."

She snorted. "*All right.* Not my fault you can't get enough of Miss Rillington." She tossed an Allsort into her mouth and sauntered out of the door. I hadn't had my morning coffee yet from the school canteen so I let out a slow breath, forcing myself to let it slide. You had to pick your battles with someone like Tawny, but somehow I knew I had to get to assembly even if it meant getting poked in the ribs by Tawny's sharp nails all day. My stomach whirled.

"I don't know," I said. "I just woke up with a feeling this morning."

"Oh, not one of your feelings again." Tawny rolled her eyes. "Remember, last time you had one of those you thought your stepmum had stolen your notebook with all your little stories in, but really you'd just left it in the hen coop?"

"Hey, one of these days, Alexa's going to do it. Anyway, come on."

The school steeple with its clattering bronze bell reared up, looming over a few stragglers. Even though the building tripled up as a primary school, high school and sixth-form college, there were still only a handful of muddy kids in each class, and no one quite knew how to teach Physics, so we'd had to learn that one ourselves. Every winter, a load of farmers got together and hired out the assembly hall for their Christmas disco. After New Year, the whole place reeked of spilt stout and old pigs. The ratio of swine to Long Byrne students was particularly high.

We stumbled through the side door and into the packed assembly hall. Everyone's clothes rustled as they craned around to look at us. My stomach knotted even tighter. All the grotty Year Sevens and sullen Year Tens were jammed in on bum-numbing benches. I was hoping Lower-Sixth would get off to a better start.

At the brim of the stage, on the lectern, Rillington was hawk-eyed under her grey bob.

"Mr Lawrence has asked me to remind you that smoking will not be permitted behind the sports block. I'm looking at you, Matthew Bridge."

She tried to ignore the clang of the door as we shuffled into the back row, but even she had to pause while Tawny kicked the bench and smacked her bag on the floor for maximum dramatic effect. I heard her distinctive tut. Despite the September heatwave, Rillington wore a long, clingy woollen dress. No one over forty should opt for skin-tight anything. She even had lipstick on – must be an important day.

"The hockey team has raised over a hundred pounds for the new sports kit," Rillington said in a monotone. "Give them a big round of applause, everyone."

There was a short spatter of funereal clapping. Some kids were already twisting their heads round to check the clock.

Tawny shook out her dark hair and widened her eyes at me. *SEE? Look what you got me up early for.*

I tried to stare straight ahead, but the kids in those rows were all straining for a glimpse of a girl with bright-blonde hair, sitting three rows in front of me, poker-straight. I could only see the back of her head, but something about those alert shoulders told me I hadn't seen her in Long Byrne before.

I nudged Tawny. "There," I breathed. Tawny squinted through the crowd. She locked on to the target. We shared raised eyebrows.

"And now," said Rillington, raising her head, "for something I know you've all been dying to hear about—"

"She's retiring?" hissed Tawny.

"Long Byrne High will be staging a re-enactment of the terrible events that make our village so famous. As you'll know, this Halloween marks the four-hundredth anniversary of the infamous hanging of the Long Byrne witches."

Everyone seemed to grow an extra vertebra. This was new. A bit of gore and gruesomeness before 9.30 a.m.? We held our breath.

Rillington put on a voice she seemed to think was mysterious. I despised her for it. "We all know the story of the witches. Even four hundred years later, people still come from all over the country to see where Rose Ackroyd and Jane Hollingworth were put to death out on the moors."

I started nodding before I caught myself. We knew all this. Even though I hadn't grown up in Long Byrne like Tawny had, I knew it all by rote. Mum had loved the story of the witches too and had often written about magic and mysterious things.

Tawny sat jangling her foot over her knee, looping a long glossy strand of black hair around her finger. If she'd had any gum on her she would have blown the biggest bubble possible and let it pop like a white bomb. Maybe she didn't remember the spells we used to make up like I did, but I could see her eyes fixed on the stage.

Rillington was drawn up tall and rigid with importance. *Go on*, I willed her. *Tell us something we don't know.*

"Long Byrne School is proposing a restaging of the events that happened, to find out what really went on all those years ago out on the moor. We're hoping some of you would like to get involved in the re-enactment. We will need a whole cast, a script and people to help with the stage lighting."

A crazed rumbling broke out. A few enthusiasts waved their arms in the air before snapping them down like they were on elastic.

The new girl's shoulders were still square and rigid.

Rillington smiled through thin red lips. "Don't worry, you don't have to sign up now . . . I'll leave a sheet here for anyone to put down their details. We've put some refreshments at the back if anybody would like to come and ask any questions about the re-enactment."

She might have finished by scattering rose petals. Refreshments? *Refreshments?* There was a round of applause, louder than I'd expected. I was impressed – she'd managed to infiltrate the Long Byrne School swamp of apathy with orange juice and biscuits.

We all unfolded ourselves and rubbed our arses. Tawny dug her elbow into my ribs, making me yelp.

"Is this what your feeling was about? A play?" she smirked but her eyes glittered.

I glanced over at the refreshments and saw the area was already filling up.

Tawny snorted. "Go on then, go and gnaw her ear off. You're witch mental."

I felt my neck get hot. "Am not!"

"You're signing up though, right? Your eyes are popping out of your skull. You know I'm in." She flicked her hair over her shoulder dramatically. "I was born for the stage."

I looked at Rillington wielding her red clipboard as she sauntered around the room, checking for unbuttoned blouses and dirty knees. I realised my fingers were hurting from gripping the bench. I shook them out.

"Maybe . . ."

Rillington shooed out Matty Bridge and his lot before they started a food fight. Along the back wall was a long table covered in a sticky plastic tablecloth stencilled with old crayon. There was coffee! Turns out she'd do anything to bribe us into a school play – not that she'd needed to make an effort; there was already an orderly queue forming in front of her clipboard. The idea of writing the play made my heart start buzzing too. It was a feeling I'd never had before. I'd been writing ever since I could remember – all scrawled in the back of notebooks and hidden under my mattress. I liked to read Mum's stories, the ones that she hadn't sent to her publisher before she died. Maybe one day I would finish them for her so people could still read her words. I longed to be a writer too – then I could get out of here once and for all. Now, she would never leave Long Byrne, but I would.

Could I really write something for the re-enactment? For everyone to hear? I'd always had a crazy imagination. I blushed even though there was no one there to see. I'd been eight when I told Mum about the gigantic purple cat that lived in our roof and that I would sometimes climb the rickety attic ladder to feed it with tuna sandwiches I'd saved from lunch.

"And why does it like to live in our roof, Cate?" she asked.

"It likes us. It thinks we smell nice."

"Oh, does it now? Does it want to have us for dinner?"

"No! It really likes us. The yellow cats with the spiky tails – they're the nasty ones. The purple one just wants to keep us safe."

She'd snorted and dropped the book she was reading; something really heavy and old, like a spell book she'd just unearthed from a witch's trunk. I could still see some dust in the ridges the title formed on the front cover. "Cate, you have the biggest imagination! What are you going to do with it all?"

I'd shrugged and said I wanted to check on the cat. Maybe I could start catching some mice for it.

"You'll have to find somewhere very, very special for all those thoughts. They might just get you into trouble one day."

What would she say if she knew I wanted to write about the witches?

My feet were itching to move to the line but Tawny was smirking at me.

"At least let me grab a coffee before class." I rolled my eyes and went over to pour myself a brew. Black, no sugar.

"You're hardcore, sweetie pie," she said, getting first dibs on the custard creams.

"You want one?" I asked, holding up the jug.

She pulled a face.

I put the pot down and took a big slug of scalding liquid. Tawny said coffee tasted like cat piss – how did she know? I'd once managed eight espressos before midday and had spoken fluent Spanish for three hours.

A cluster of witchy-devotees had followed the headmistress, mainly a bunch of goths who fancied themselves the reincarnation of Rose Ackroyd. The Witch Groupies. We'd grown out of that years ago, although I'd kept the outfit. Tawny looked at these girls with a crumple of disdain, but she couldn't hide her excitement. The last time Long Byrne High had put on a play she'd got to play Nancy in *Oliver!* and had performed a memorable, gutsy death scene. I still regularly thought about that last rattle of her dying breath as Bill Sikes lunged in for another blow – I think we all did.

Tawny put her head really close to mine and I got a waft of her strawberry shampoo. "Who do you think she is then?"

"Who?"

"New kid," she said, jerking her head to the right. "Think she knows what she's let herself in for?"

I looked over to where the girl was hovering at the door. Her hands were knotted in front of her stomach. Her long blonde hair was a single glossy sheet, film-star straight. There was a coolness to her gaze that reminded me of catwalk models pretending their outfits weren't cutting into their waists. She looked like she wanted to bolt out of the room to a place very far away from witch hysteria. If I could just go over and ask for her name—

"'Ey up," hissed Tawny.

I wheeled my head around to follow her gaze. Pad Mitchell and Jamie Duxbury were hovering by the Viennese Whirls, looking at us like they'd struck gold.

"What are they staring at?" I followed their eyes.

"My stairway." Tawny bared her teeth in a feral sort of grin, kohled eyes flashing, and seductively stroked the white line on her thigh with her index finger. The boys looked away quickly, knocking their teeth on their plastic cups. She turned to me. "You got a marker pen?"

I had a quick rummage in my bag. "Biro."

She whipped it out of my hand. "Give it here."

Tawny cocked her leg up and coloured in the white space with the sharp pen tip. Her skirt rode all the way up and I tried to keep an eye on Pad and Jamie, but they'd already diverted their attention to the blonde girl. She was now surrounded by Year Twelve boys – a grim fate.

Tawny jerked her head up and pretended to sniff the air.

"Uh oh. She smells fresh to them."

That was the trouble with Long Byrne: everyone had known each other since they were four years old. Occasionally parents made their kids mix with the kids in Stoutbridge to lessen the threat of inbreeding, but there were still a fair few extra nipples and toes here and there despite their efforts. Any new blood got honed in on like a rabbit in a fox den; I knew that from my traumatic first week at Long Byrne High and my chest flooded with sympathy for the blonde girl.

Rillington had extricated herself from the Witch Groupies and was heading our way. I took a step forward but Tawny thrust the Biro at my chest and said, "I'm going in!"

"Wait, I—"

But before I could finish, Tawny was dragging me across the hall towards the new girl, her full hips swaying.

"Hi!" She grinned and I saw the girl's eyes flicker with shock. Not surprise. I'd be shocked if Tawny turned her smile on me for the first time too. "Go on, the lot of you!" Tawny shooed the gaggle of boys away by crashing into them. They redirected their feet in a confused way, like they had just been tasered.

"Hi?" the girl said.

She sounded like she came from somewhere very far away from Long Byrne – which wasn't hard. Maybe the city, or one of the posh-knob schools up in Hillbury. Her voice was crisp and low.

Tawny pressed on. "So, we couldn't help noticing that you're new, and we're wondering how that feels."

The girl blinked twice. "Sorry?"

"Well," Tawny let her shoulders fall dramatically, "newbies tend to feel one of three things – complete terror of the local predators; superiority; or total violation. You haven't been violated yet, have you?"

New girl bit her lip. "Not that I'm aware of."

"Fantastic news! You've got plenty to look forward to then." And with that, Tawny thrust her hand out at the girl. "I'm Tawny."

"Bryony." She shook it. Not looking terrified, just perplexed.

"This is Cate." She gestured to me grandly; the magician's assistant. I gave a small wave. Bryony nodded as if we were swapping cards at a business meeting.

"Need someone to take you to class?" Tawny asked.

"Um, I'm actually meant to go to the office to sign some papers."

"Great, it's on our way."

I couldn't tell what Bryony thought of her sudden entourage, but she allowed herself to be steered out of the hall like a celebrity being escorted to her next interview. I saw her take a long sideways glance at Tawny before her green gaze met mine. Before I could smile, she focused intently on the floor.

Pad and Jamie looked at Tawny approvingly, saluting a leader.

"So you've just moved here? Where from?" said Tawny, touching the new girl's elbow in the Tawny Way. Bryony didn't flinch.

"On Saturday, from London." Her gaze didn't leave the floor. She sounded unsure about the location.

I could feel Tawny's gush swelling in her chest before she let loose. *Here it comes.* It was coiled up and waiting to spill from her tongue. I prepared my eardrums for a bashing.

"Really! Did you really? Whereabouts? In the centre?"

Bryony moved her lips silently, conjuring up the words, seeming to look at something very far away before finding herself again. "In the suburbs, really." As she spoke she played with a bracelet on her wrist – a dark brown piece of woven leather cord tied in a tight knot. A delicate silver charm shook to and fro. It was pretty, though I couldn't tell what the charm was, and she clung to it fiercely. Tawny babbled on.

"Oh my god, you lucky thing! Did you go to the theatre a lot? I'd go every night of the week."

Bryony shook her head. "Mum and Dad don't really do the theatre."

Tawny swished her hair back. "More fool them. I'm a Scottish Play sort of girl. Right? I'll bet all that witch stuff in assembly was super weird to you."

"Maybe a little bit?" Bryony summoned a small smile, which glanced off her chin quickly.

"It's what we're famous for." Tawny let her eyes do a full roll in her head. "Cate's obsessed with the witches."

"We *both* used to be," I corrected. "It's a legend in this area; people get really amped up about it."

"I can tell," said Bryony.

"Tell her," Tawny elbowed my arm.

"I mean, it's kind of silly but Long Byrne lives and breathes the story of the witches. It started with two girls – Rose Ackroyd and Jane Hollingworth. They were really close but, one day, there was a big fight and people saw them cursing each other in the street. All hellfire and literal sparks flying. People didn't like that, not at all – so they hanged them out on the moors on 31st October 1623. You should see this place on Halloween!

"There's this view that witches were these hunched-over old ladies with warts and too many cats, but Rose Ackroyd and Jane Hollingworth were just two young girls, only sixteen."

I looked for Bryony's reaction – her face had become stony. I faltered.

Tawny grinned. "Sounds like you're still pretty into those witches, Cate."

"Anyway," I continued, ignoring her, "we've been taught it since birth, really. There are books about it in the library, with all the grisly facts. When we were kids, we used to make up spells and rhymes. Cringey rhyming couplets, that sort of thing; but the witches were more than a legend and people still think you can see them out on the moors today, roaming around in search of revenge."

"That's the spirit, girls," a voice came from behind us. We spun around. Rillington. She was holding that clipboard in front of her again. "In fact, I'm surprised I don't have your names on my sheet. Cate, I could use your help with writing the script. How does that sound?"

All the blood in my body rose to my cheeks, leaving my limbs light and fuzzy. "Yes, Miss. That sounds good." My feeling from this morning was back. I wanted to do this more than I could put into words.

"Great, I'll put you down." She turned her body and raised an eyebrow. "Tawny, I'm guessing that there's no keeping you away from something like this? You'll have to audition like everyone else, of course."

"Oh, but of course." Tawny grinned. "It's only fair."

"Excellent," Rillington murmured through gritted teeth, jotting both our names down. "Bryony, don't worry. I don't expect you to take part if you don't want to. Unless . . .?"

Bryony shook her head quickly so her pale hair quivered. "I'm OK, Miss."

"Right then," Rillington tapped her fingers against the

clipboard with a *crack*. "On with the show, as they say. Have a good day, girls."

We watched Miss Rillington walk away and Tawny burst into a fit of silent laughter behind her back. "Cate, she loves you back."

I scowled in answer and I saw Bryony give me the ghost of a smile.

We had ended up in the entrance hall. The space had a perpetual air of gloom that could only ever come from echoey old towers with cobwebs that shook in the rafters where no one could wiggle a feather duster. In one corner was the bell-pull for the steeple, a gnarled grey rope that we'd all been dared to pull at some point in our Long Byrne High years. It was an initiation ritual made near-impossible by the careful watch of the school secretary, Mrs Waddington, who sat at her desk nearby.

"Well, here you are," Tawny announced, her grin in place as she squeezed Bryony's arm for good measure. "You'll fit right in, promise."

The girl nodded distractedly, looking straight ahead at the bell-pull, twisted in its knotty curl.

I left for Philosophy, but when I looked back from the end of the corridor Bryony hadn't budged, but stood looking at the rope before her.

After second period, Tawny met me in the canteen, with her hair coiled up on top of her head around a paintbrush. How did she even do that? My hair wouldn't do anything except hang limply by my ears. It only ever looked good after

Tawny had got her hands on it. She huffed dramatically, gesturing to her bun.

"What do you think?"

I looked up from *The Black Plague in Britain* and raised an eyebrow. Telling Tawny she was hot was like giving Shakespeare a B+ in English Literature.

"I think you need some style tips from Rillington."

She laughed. "I'm barely letting you have that one. You made me get up way too early for Rillington's witches today."

"I'm sorry," I said, deadpan. "You know I have a colossal soft spot for weirdos, Tawn."

"Well, I suppose we've all got to feel connected to our vibrant village past somehow." She widened her eyes; a saint. "I mean, you know I love a play but does anyone ever talk about anything other than the witches?"

"You used to think it was interesting though. You used to love the drama of it." I said, "Eighteen girls just decimated by a ridiculous old law like that? By superstition?"

"Hundreds of people die every day, Cate."

"Well, *I'm* interested. Everyone here is going to see this play. Besides, I could do with some excitement around here."

She held a hand to her chest, eyes round. "I'm not enough for you?"

I yanked the paintbrush out of her hair and watched it all tumble loose in a black spiral. She laughed easily. I kept my gaze on her for a second as she tossed her hair back over her shoulder and scanned the room intently for any straying eyes. I wished that kind of confidence was infectious.

Tawny went up to the sandwich counter and bought a

Twix for herself, a carton of milk and a cup of instant for me. The smell of the cheap coffee already wound through the room like burning film strip. It tasted just as bad. Tawny dropped the carton of milk in front of me saying I needed to "stop with the black coffee; you're not a goth." I saw the milk was an Alder Farm bottle and I smiled, wondering which of my cows it came from. I reckoned it was Pansy. Tawny twisted off the milk top and dunked her Twix finger in it, slurping off the chocolate as I protested half-heartedly.

The room had filled up around us but there was a notable omission. "I wonder how Bryony is getting on," I said. "It must suck to move somewhere new when you're sixteen."

"Ahh, imagine moving though. A whole new life. I'd call myself Magenta and you wouldn't have to get up at two a.m. to be a farm bitch any more."

"You know, Tawn – being a farm bitch isn't such a bad thing."

"Getting a life isn't such a bad thing either."

I scoffed, but there was something about Bryony that made me fill to the brim with questions. Why would anyone move to Long Byrne? And, especially, why someone like her?

I leant into Tawny. "Maybe she could join our covert gang."

"The third and final member," she nodded sagely. "Our coven would be complete."

When Mrs Waddington rang the steeple bell for third period, we scraped our chairs out from under the sticky tables that all had bent legs and graffiti from 2003.

The rest of the day slid by with no more excitement than

Mr Bentham arguing with Matty Bridge about 'the beast with two backs' in English Lit and sunbathing with Tawny behind the gym before the bell released us back out on to the cobbles.

The moon was shining brightly as I brushed my teeth before bed. It lit up the fields and the hills that seemed like mountains in the half-light. I'd never admit it to Tawny but Long Byrne was quite beautiful if you caught it at the right moment.

I spat out a mouthful of toothpaste and glanced back up. Something had caught my eye in the lane below. A person with bright blonde hair was walking silently past the farm using only the shine of the moon to see their way. They took the left-hand fork past our farm and carried on up the lane. But no one ever used that lane. That was the way to the old Hollingworth House. The place where the witches used to live.

Bryony?

What was Bryony doing walking up to the Hollingworth House at 10 p.m.?

I watched until she was out of sight; the blonde hair lost in the height of the hedgerows. It made me bite the inside of my cheek uneasily.

I put the toothbrush back in its holster and found that my last thoughts before I finally fell asleep were of witches.

Witchcraft and fear were all around – you couldn't escape it. If you had a birthmark, you were a witch. If you had so much as a lisp, you were a witch. But if you kept to yourself, minded your own business and were perfectly normal, you were probably a witch too. People glanced over each other for warts and pimples in the churchyard.

Villagers didn't look you directly in the face for fear you'd give them the Evil Eye, a look so cursed that even the worst of devils were afraid of it. Young girls and the sick wore it on talismans around their necks to frighten away the hooded figure at the end of their beds.

Ghosts, goblins, ghouls – in 1612, the supernatural was interlaced with reality. Some people were more in touch with it than others. Maybe some people still are.

The History of Long Byrne: Demons on the Moor,
Dr C. Munir

Chapter 2

I've heard farmers are supposed to leap out of bed at 4.30 a.m. grinning, fully dressed and already covered in sheep shit. This has led to my belief that any farmer must have been knocked on the head as a baby.

Yet here I was.

After everything that happened a few years ago, Dad had gone down to the farmers' market in Stoutbridge and paid someone a fortune to teach us both how to shear sheep and just about milk a goat with our toes, but his eyes glazed over when we got round to hen-plucking. Like all the worst bits, that usually fell to me.

Farmer Cate Aspey. Teen Tractor Girl of the Year.

When I wasn't at Tawny's, I'd rise like a Disney princess at 5.30 a.m. This was long before Dad or Alexa had even stirred in their cosy double bed. By then, the chickens had popped a few out and the cows were shuddering with excitement by the gate for their feedbags. Farm life had its advantages. I liked the way their breath rose in smoky tendrils to meet the hay dust floating in the barn. People said not to name cows in case they all collapsed from foot-and-mouth or had to be shot through the head in the case of first-world famine.

But I didn't listen. My Vera, Pansy and Myrtle were top-notch ladies.

Of course, they weren't just my girls. There was Robyn – Tawny's little sister – there to look after them most days. I did three mornings a week and she did four, but she was just a kid doing what she could for twenty quid a week and Alexa's cucumber sarnies. I wouldn't draw breath for one of those.

I tried to imagine Tawny holding a shovel and gave up.

Tuesday was clear and dawn over the hills was the colour of skin stretched taut. A pair of owls still hooted at each other in the trees not so far away, by the Slip. In front of me there was the barn at the end of the concrete yard – big enough for the animals, a hayloft and a crumbling tractor – the hen coop, an acre of field and a smaller storage shed filled with oats and enough grain to keep the chickens fat until Armageddon. Standing in the back doorway, my breath let out the faintest ghost in front of me as my cup of coffee warmed my hands. It might not have the same kind of glamour and razzmatazz that Tawny was all about, but this – the farm, the air rolling in from the moor – it had its own kind of beauty. Things weren't all bad.

Pansy mooed loudly.

"Morning, you big muppet."

I rubbed my hand across her nostrils. Pansy flared her lips at me and nudged my fingers with her purple tongue. "In a sec," I said, and went to start off in my usual order.

5.50 a.m. Plenty of time to do the rounds; probably even a few minutes to revise for the History test I had a feeling they'd spring on us today. I was on-track for an A* and was going to get one even if I had to do it around my udder-squeezing schedule.

I hung up the feed sacks on one of the old dripping hooks by the barn door and went over to the indoor pen to let the cows out into the yard.

Out of habit, they'd all lined up by the trough at the door so I dropped my milking stool on to the concrete for the first performance of the morning. Three full udders swung heavily in front of me. When we'd bought the farm, Dad said he wanted it all done 'properly', which meant 'old-school' with blisters on your fingers, kicked shins and definitely no machines. I was surprised Robyn and I didn't carry pails on our shoulders while doing a jig for him.

Vera was up first.

"All right, girlie?" You're meant to announce your presence with animals – as if they hadn't heard your earth-shattering gravel crunch across the yard or smelled your shampoo a mile off. Cows deserved more credit. I tied her to the post and gave her udders the morning rub down – it only took her twenty-four hours to look like the Creature from the Black Lagoon again. Then I did my favourite cow-thing – I leant in, putting my head on the big tan patch of her flank and felt the whir and chunter of her four stomachs as milk shot into the pail. It was like listening to a world from inside the womb.

It was warm and cosy here, and I suddenly wished I was curled up in bed with a pen and notebook, a habit I'd got from Mum. I didn't have a single picture of her where she didn't have a book or pen in her hand to scribble down something on a napkin in between feeding me baked beans, loading the car or chatting on the phone to her publisher about a new book deal. In some of my memories, she had a purple pen or a green one.

"A different colour to show how I'm feeling," she'd grinned and booped my nose with it, leaving a violet dot on the tip that I crossed my eyes to see. I liked being marked by her and wondered what mood the purple pen stood for. She wrote everything down and turned it into a story; something mind-boggling that the critics didn't know how to take, but the books flew off the shelves anyway. I thought of the pen and battered old notebook on my nightstand, and my mind drifted until Vera brought me back to my senses with a hot nudge on the ear.

No fuss or hassle today. I worked through them one by one. With a pat on the arse, I let them out into the field and glooped all the fatty milk into the churner for the dairy guys to pick up in their rickety blue van.

The chicken coop stood next to the barn, painted terracotta to go with Alexa's plant pots that she watered when she could be bothered. The close hustle of warm feathers and hushed clucking inside the hutch made it my favourite place on the farm. I hadn't named the hens but they were my Chicks.

"Hello, lasses," I whispered and was greeted by excited squabbles and the scratch of long-nailed feet on wood.

My fattest hen always took the spot closest to the door. She was black and glossy with a red crest and watchful yellow eyes, and always let you tickle her chin if you gave her first dibs on grain. I slid my hand under her and found a single egg steaming from production.

"Good on you, woman."

I collected the eggs one by one, slipping my hand under eleven feathery bottoms until my canvas bag felt heavy with hot swirling yolks. Seven today. A good haul.

I ducked out of the shed. My phone said it was 6.56 a.m. and I breathed out a sigh that evaporated into the lightening air.

Glancing out towards the paddock, something stilled my chest.

The old Hollingworth House had always made me look twice. Over the hill from the paddock gate, the house reared its gloomy face. You could see every arched window, every dark rowan tree lining the driveway. If you squinted hard enough you could probably see the golden chandeliers inside. Although it was made of the same grey stone as the rest of Long Byrne, even our own farm cottage, there was something else to it. It looked darker than the rest, like the whole place was waterlogged; like it was leaching all the moisture and goodness from the land.

I walked over to the fence, squinting into the low morning light. On the second floor, in one of those arched attic windows, there was a light on.

At first I didn't know whether I'd imagined it – maybe just the pinkish dawn seeping in. But there it was. A light hanging from the ceiling, clear as day. Long and dangling, like a hangman's noose.

I felt drawn to the house but I couldn't put my finger on why.

My knuckles were white on the fencepost. Why had Bryony been on her way up that lane last night? What had she seen there?

Behind me, one of my hens let out a cry and squabbling broke out from the hen house, making me jump.

I shuddered.

The top floor light clicked off.

"At ease, Chicks," I called across the yard, my voice a little higher than usual.

"People'll start to think you're crazy," someone said.

I spun round. Robyn Brown was standing next to me with a sack of feed across one thin shoulder. "Well, *crazier.*"

"You should start your stand-up routine with that one," I said, rolling my eyes.

She grinned and I reached out to shove the heel of my hand against her forehead, holding her in place. I was short but Robyn, at thirteen, was even tinier. She'd always been a scrawny-arse. I wondered if one day she'd have Tawny's swinging hips – weren't sisters supposed to look alike?

Robyn was practically a lifesaver – she helped to muck out the cows, feed the chickens and sweep the yard almost every day of the week. If anyone was the chalk to Tawny's cheese it was her, and I loved her for it. Whenever I stayed at Tawny's, Robyn did all the milking too, without complaining once – in fact, I think she liked the chance to get out of her madhouse and put her head on Vera's belly, just like I did.

Alexa didn't mind. In fact, I think that without a doubt she'd have preferred Robyn Brown as a stepdaughter.

Robyn grumbled, pushing against my hand and straining

towards me. "I always forget how freakishly strong you are."
I let her go and we both looked across the field for a moment.
The window in the Hollingworth House was dark now.

I scraped my wellie on the floor to loosen a clod of mud.
"What are you doing here, anyway? Today's your day off."

"You know me. I can't get enough of it."

"Well, I've pretty much done everything."

"That's OK, I'll just go brush up or something."

Her curly hair was scruffed up in a ponytail. She looked
like she'd been awake all night; big hollows nested under her
eyes and she squinted as if the sun was actually trying to hurt
her. I wondered what she'd been up late reading this time.
Probably Tolstoy, or Nabokov at least. I didn't say anything,
though. Robyn and I had an understanding: I wouldn't mention
her sleeping problem if she didn't mention all my stuff. Where
would we even begin?

Alexa called her a good egg. I called her mental, but anyone
who'd do this farm stuff for fun and a few pennies probably
had to be a little bit mad.

Robyn let the sack of seed flump to the floor. "What were
we looking at anyway?"

"Nothing," I shrugged.

"You're talkative today."

"Must be the fantastic company."

She scoffed. "I'll be in the field if anyone needs me.
Someone's got to do some work around here." Thumping me
on the shoulder, she turned away to lift heavy machinery and
wield power tools, no doubt. She'd probably do it for free if we
asked her.

I left the house at 7.20 a.m.

I'd have coffee number two at school.

The place was clunking with the unoiled brains of summer. It was only the second week of September and people were already bogged down in a fug of sums and stacks of revision cards, trying to kick-start the cogs back into action. Everyone who'd been looking forward to the return to school was now sitting bleary-eyed at whacked-out library computers, trying to decipher SparkNotes.

The memories were like wheat heads being stripped away from us bit by bit. Lounging in Tawny's back garden with our faces shoved in glossy magazines. Feeling the blisters between our toes where our flip-flops caught. Tawny would rub sun cream on my shoulder blades, telling me I should eat a couple of burgers, her slippery fingers doing this wiggly thing down my spine while she sang 'Let's Do the Twist'. The sun-bleached streaks were already fading from my hair, leaving it the old flat mousiness I was used to. I'd even taken to wearing jumpers early – although Kayleigh Whittard was still in shorts.

After break, in Psychology, I was doodling on the cover of my A4 pad when Bryony walked through the door. She didn't look like she'd seen the sun all summer. Her face was immaculately white – no sunglasses tan line across her nose, or crispy giveaway at the tops of her ears. There was only one spare seat, on an awkward corner desk – right next to me.

She sat down slowly and methodically, as if performing a risk assessment. How long would it take to reach the window if someone set fire to the whiteboard? Were there any stray banana skins? Quietly, she put her Biro at a right angle to her notebook, snapped the magnet catch on her bag back in place and put her hands in her lap.

For the next thirty seconds, I panicked wildly about whether I smelled of hay. I loved the scent of it and how it nestled its way into all my favourite vintage jumpers, but reeking like a farmyard in front of the new girl wasn't exactly what I'd had planned.

I slid my eyes over to her and could barely keep my questions inside me.

"Hey," I said.

A pause. "Hi." She looked at me sideways.

"How are you settling in?"

"Not too bad, thanks."

I watched her smooth out her black trousers. She was dressed for a job interview, not a crappy hour-long drone from red-nosed Miss Draycott.

"If you need to catch up with Psych, I can lend you my notes. We've not done much yet, though."

Her mouth twitched and she slanted her eyes to look at me. "Thanks, Cate."

"That's OK. Any time."

My stomach bubbled, as if I'd just found out a celebrity followed me online. She'd remembered my name. The feeling settled nicely in my chest. Her hair still looked movie-star soft and I had the crazy urge to reach out to touch it, but I clenched my fingers to stop myself just in time.

"Right, everyone. Books out, please." Miss Draycott had entered, bundled up in several scarves, with a glowing nose.

"Thomas Acton?"

"Yes, Miss."

"Caitlin Aspey?"

She called the register to a clatter of pens and bag rummaging. Then the world seemed to change.

"Bryony Hollingworth?"

There was a collective swivel of heads. Someone's pencil case crashed to the floor.

"Hollingworth?"

Bryony's shoulders tensed beside me and I watched her hair fall forward to hide her face. I quickly closed my open mouth.

"Woah woah woah," said Matty Bridge, grin in place. "We have a witch amongst us?"

"Settle down, class. That's enough."

But everyone was out of their seats, crowding around our double desk like she was an exhibit in a freak show. A witch on trial.

"Is it true, Bryony?"

"Should we watch our backs, Bryony?"

"I knew there was something weird about her," sneered Kayleigh Whittard.

"That's ENOUGH," Miss Draycott screeched. "Back to your seats this second."

But no one listened to a word of Draycott's lesson; their eyes were too busy scoring marks in the back of Bryony's head. I was speechless, my pen slack in my hand.

So, Bryony was a Hollingworth. And last night she'd been returning home.

Tawny's house was something else.

It was a big old one behind a row of tumbledown terraces, maybe Victorian but I could never tell with those grand sorts of places and the date had chipped clean off the mantle – acid rain, or something more dangerous and particular to Long Byrne. I could just imagine a sour-faced family sweeping about the place, their noses in the air while maids and butlers in starched black uniforms scuttled after them with a dustpan and brush.

There were three storeys – all lofty ceilings and plaster cherubs – each floor with more rooms than the last, getting smaller as you climbed the stairs. The whole place smelled like coffee – the proper kind, not the rubbish stuff in the teachers' staff room. Tawny's mum blasted it out twenty-four-seven, and you ended up a caffeinated wreck just by breathing it in at the doorstep. Like second-hand smoke, but tastier.

The Browns lived on the top floor, although we knew we could all pretty much go where we wanted. Mr Shilcock, the landlord, had even turned a blind eye when Tawny picked the lock to the basement to stash a supply of Gordon's gin. Their flat was small, but you can't be too fussy when your dad runs off with all your money and a makeup artist half his age.

As we traipsed in from school, Mr Shilcock was fixing a radiator in the downstairs hall. Steam fogged up the floor-length mirror and made all the walls streaky. It was so hot and I wondered why he hadn't taken his shirt off. He was small with peppery-coloured hair, a triple chin, beige shorts and sandals . . . On second thoughts, I was glad his shirt remained buttoned.

Tawny snapped on her smile. "Hi, Mr Shilcock."

A spanner clattered loudly to the floor. "Oh, he-hello, dear."

"Any luck with it?"

He looked puzzled, through a sheen of sweat.

"The radiator," she clarified.

His chins give an ominous wobble. "It's getting there."

We all stood there for a beat.

"Say hello to your mother for me, won't you?"

We stomped upstairs and were nearly at the top when Mr Shilcock started wrenching the spanner again.

Tawny snorted.

"Typical Shilcock. You'd think my mother drugs his Horlicks or something. He can't get enough." We went into Tawny's room and I immediately went into search mode. Half of my clothes were lost in amongst the mess. Robyn was sat rigid on one of Tawny's cushions, working through the year-eight booklist Rillington had given her. Star-pupil treatment. Her corkscrew curls had been loosed from their farmyard ponytail and she looked vaguely like a thirteen-year-old again. She tried to trip me up as I came in and I kicked her on the shin.

Curled up next to her was Ginger, her beloved black and white cat – Robyn had always loved the name long before the cat actually came along, so now the big black-and-white boy was stuck with it. He took it well.

I put on one of Tawny's long silky robes, the ones she bought at the flea market and had to wash ten times before she could prance around in them. They were always lying around as if a disorganised Arabian dance troupe had taken over the place. I rummaged through the rest of them for a vest top that might be lost for ever. It was my comfiest one but god only knew where it could be.

"I kind of feel bad for her."

"Who?" said Tawny, flopping down on the bed. The walls were a deep sunset red so it looked like she was swimming in a fancy Hollywood cocktail. The shelves were lined with pictures of old movie stars in heart-shaped plastic frames we got free from magazines: Theda Bara, Clara Bow and a load of twenties starlets I'd never heard of, though Tawny could give you their full, tragic life-story. And then there was Laurence Olivier dressed as Hamlet on her desk, ruff and all. She fancied the pants off Sir Olivier. I couldn't say I saw the attraction.

"Bryony."

"She was kind of tempting fate coming here, don't you think?"

"How do you mean?" I said, reaching under the bed and feeling only sticky toffees and dusty socks.

"Your last name is Hollingworth and you come to live in the only town in the world that's *obsessed* with Jane Hollingworth? What did she think was going to happen?"

"I don't think it's fair. It's not like those girls were actually witches; they were probably killed because they annoyed an old white man or they emasculated someone's firstborn son."

"That's a big word," Tawny mocked. "Maybe the world just didn't like them because they were a little *too* close, if you know what I'm saying."

My face flushed and I turned quickly to look behind the desk. "The whole world knows what you're saying."

Tawny held up her hands. "The 1600s just weren't ready for attractive young witchy lesbians."

"Who's a lesbian?" asked Robyn, looking up from her book sleepily.

"The new girl, Bryony Hollingworth."

"Oh, shut up, Tawny," I said.

On the window sill was a photo of us from when we were thirteen: we had matching plaits and there was a bruise on my left knee where I had fallen out of the hayloft fixing a broken slat. I had my own copy of the photo wedged inside an old notebook of Mum's that I liked to look at on nights when I couldn't sleep.

"Tawn, have you seen my stripy vest top? I haven't seen it for weeks."

"It's in the wash. I've been wearing it to bed because it really shows off my boobs."

"Oh," I said, blinking. "No worries. I'll get it tomorrow."

We fell into our routine, sliding out of our boots, curling up in our favourite places: Robyn by the door, me at the foot of the bed and Tawny sprawled by the window catching any possible drop of sun.

She had a French dictionary balanced on her forehead.

"I can't think."

"Open the window."

"No, I just can't think."

"It's a hard life."

"Shut your hole."

I threw a rubber at her and it landed with a hollow pat on her stomach. I looked at it sitting there calmly, wondering how Tawny ravaged her way through bumper packs of Celebrations and never gained an ounce.

"I mean, I can't stop thinking about witches," she said.

"Since when were *you* interested in them?"

She pouted. "Since one graced us with her presence."

I bit my lip, Bryony's bright hair and green eyes in my mind. "Should I really write the script? Do you think it seems wrong to do the re-enactment now, in case it hurts Bryony's feelings?"

Tawny's eyes sparkled under the rim of the dictionary. "Honestly, you know what I think. You're a massive nerd and the whole thing will be entirely embarrassing. But you'll get all the Brownie points from Rillington that you've always dreamt of."

Robyn chimed in. "I don't mind doing an extra shift or two if you need the time to write?"

I smiled at her. She had inherited all of the Browns' allotment of kindness.

Tawny ignored her. "Do you think she has family secrets, like there's a locked room you get the key to when you come of age? All sex voodoo and bones?"

"Sex voodoo?"

"And bones," she grinned at the ceiling. Robyn shook her head so her curls quivered. I thought I saw her eye twitch. "Shut up, will you? You're giving me the creeps."

Tawny ignored her again. "Alexa could probably do with some sex voodoo, don't you think?" She let the dictionary flump to the floor so she could see my reaction.

"Thanks for the image, Tawn. Actually going to puke now."

"Sure your dad's proper into it." The Tawny Grin was in place.

"Yep," I winced, "just keep on digging, why don't you?"

She snorted and even stony-faced Robyn hid her head deeper behind *Lord of the Flies*.

"Aw, come on. You know I'm just messing."

But as I tried to do my homework, I couldn't stop thinking about Bryony all alone in the Hollingworth House with her charm bracelet, writing her gently sloping words with a pale hand, and the tremble I had seen on her lips today in class.

Up on the moors, eighteen girls were hanged for witchcraft – consorting with the devil, cursing cattle and bewitching innocent young men with their red eyes.

Things were different back then.

Or at least we'd like to think so.

In Search of the Long Byrne Witches, P.J. Hebden

Chapter 3

On Wednesday morning I let myself into the farmhouse then rounded the kitchen door to grab a Thermos of coffee. I was glad it was Robyn's turn to muck out, as I was shattered from talking late into the night and dreaming about strange things rustling in the hedgerows. Alexa was standing at the breakfast bar, her sleek blonde bob already fixed in place. She must sleep in a cryogenic chamber to wake up looking like that.

"Morning, love," Alexa smiled, rustling a bag of croissants into a dish.

"Hi."

I'd had to nip home from Tawny's for my English notes and thought I was doing a good job being the queen of stealth when I'd first opened the front door. Apparently not. The kettle had just boiled so I ladled Nescafe into my flask and, working fast, topped it with water right to the brim. Alexa knew better than to interrupt my coffee routine so we stood awkwardly in the kitchen with its cheap white tiles and Formica work tops, scrubbed clean by Alexa's sturdy ex-nurse hands.

My first sip of the morning was like heaven. I swear I was a crack addict in another life.

Alexa was on safe ground now.

"Sleep well?"

"Fine, thanks," I shrugged.

"Are you sure?" she said. "I heard you up at least three times."

I wanted to shake my head in disbelief. Surely she knew I'd been at Tawny's last night? Instead of reminding her of what kind of step-mum she was, I said, "Sounds like you're the one having trouble sleeping."

She shook her head, ignoring every word I said, as usual. "You should go back to Dr Trelfa. She'll give you more of those pills. Put you on a repeat prescription."

"I'm fine."

"It's all that coffee you drink, Caitlin. You should think of your electrolytes ..."

I met her gaze coldly and took a defiant slurp from my flask. It was scalding but Alexa got the message.

She shook her head. "Take these through to your father, would you?"

I looked at the fresh pastries, all symmetrically arranged in the wicker basket. A little tub of jam was nestled in the middle like a tiny raw mouth. A desperate Alexa gesture.

I looked up slowly and reached her eyes. "I'm going to be late."

Alexa didn't need to glance at the clock. It was well before eight and she didn't bother raising an eyebrow. Classes didn't start until nine. "It would be really great if you did."

She held them out like she was handing me a plate of gold.

Dad's office was at the front of the house where the living room should have been. He insisted he needed maximum space for his thoughts. Apparently this involved the maximum oxygen supply too, so every corner of the room was rammed with big sagging spider plants and ferns that smelled perpetually wet and decaying.

I knocked on the door and received a sharp, "Yes!"

As a kid, I remember looking around the playground, terrified, when it was his turn to pick me up. I worried I would never be able to find him. He was tall and balding with wrinkles that stretched all the way up his forehead – just like everyone else's dad. How was I going to tell all the dads apart? I sometimes wondered if I shaved his hair off, would the wrinkles carry on all the way up and over his head down to the back of his neck? Wrinkles are what you get being Professor Mark Aspey. Dad gave uni lectures in Philosophy via webcam, and had all his emails in neatly stored folders on the sidebar. He never ignored the blip of his screen as it tingled with the latest research, or students sobbing into the night. Not exactly the farmer type. I don't think he even knew where pork came from.

"Alexa's store-bought brain food," I announced, plonking the basket next to a drooping Monstera. Dad had never eaten breakfast before Alexa elbowed her way into our lives. Just a coffee, like me, to get the synapses firing.

"Thanks, love."

"Dad, get away from the computer. You're starting to get square-eyed like Mike Teevee. Or a goat."

"What was that, sweetheart?" he said, not looking away from the screen.

"Nothing."

I hovered in the doorway for another few seconds. "Dad? Can I ask you something?"

He turned his body away from the screen before his eyes left it. "Of course, darling. What's on your mind?"

"So, they're doing this re-enactment of the witch story at school and I – I wanted to write the script for it."

"That's wonderful news. You'll be great at it."

"Thanks . . . it's just that there's a girl at school and she's related to the witches. She must be like a great-great-great grandniece or something. I know Mum had planned to write about the witches." I paused. I didn't tell him about the feeling I'd had on the day the re-enactment was announced. "Do you think it would be weird if I did it?"

He sat for a moment, thinking; brow crinkling even deeper. "I think that a long time has passed since those witches were killed. They deserve their story telling, don't they? Perhaps by someone who understands what it's like to be a sixteen-year-old girl herself."

I nodded. "Maybe you're right."

"I think that's what your mum would say. Why don't I try and look out some of her notes. She had folders and folders of papers . . ." He trailed off. We both knew he hadn't had the heart to throw anything away.

My stomach flipped. It had been years, but even the smallest mention of her was a catalyst for all kinds of strange reactions in my body. "OK. Thanks, Dad – that would be great. I think I'll do the play."

"Wait," he said, as if startled. He wheeled his swivel chair away from his desk and began rooting in a drawer that needed a hefty tug to open.

"Here! I knew it would be in there somewhere." Dad held out a mahogany fountain pen.

I gulped down the salty taste in my mouth. "Is that Mum's?"

"Her favourite," he smiled with a small breath of a laugh. "I'm sure it would love to write about the witches again."

I nodded and backed out of the room before I could let out the whimper in my throat.

In the hall I could feel caffeine swooshing through my veins, opening up all the tiny capillaries in my fingers. Sunlight curled in through the pane of coloured glass in the front door and made my skin look like it was moving underwater.

The pen felt cool, almost icy, in my grasp. Its smooth body and sharp golden nib hadn't been used in a while but I wondered if, when I used it, it would take my handwriting in the same curved, careful lines as hers.

I tucked it in the secret compartment of my bag.

It was far too early for school, but staying home definitely wasn't an option.

Robyn was turning into the front yard in her overalls, yanking her hair up as she trotted along. Her skinny arms went in above the elbow and she looked small, even for thirteen. Shouldn't she have a growth spurt scheduled about now? To Alexa, why Robyn wanted to help out at Alder Farm was a complete mystery. "Young girls should be singing in their hairbrushes, not brandishing pitchforks." She obviously didn't know Robyn at all.

Robyn saw me and slowed her pace. "What's the hurry?" she said.

"The whole kitchen's on fire. I'm making a quick getaway."

Her eyes went wide. "Really?"

"No." I raised an eyebrow. "Guess."

She grinned sheepishly.

"She's bad again, huh? Ah, well . . ."

"Just another day in the Aspey household. Make sure Alexa remembers to pay you, OK?"

Robyn nodded. "I'll do the cows first."

"You're too good to them, Rob," I laughed.

"They're high-maintenance ladies – someone's got to keep them in check." She sprang off to go a-milking then stopped suddenly, mid-step, her back tense.

"Everything OK?" I asked.

Robyn was watching something past the paddock in the line of hedges that bordered the Hollingworth land. Catlike.

"Yeah. I thought I – yeah, it's fine." She shook her head like coming out of a trance and ricocheted away to the backyard.

I turned right out of the gate and headed for the Slip.

I could have made my way through it with my eyes closed. The ankle-deep tangles of roots, the oak branches you ducked under, and the swampy bits you had to remember to jump over or you'd lose your favourite shoes. It was a long narrow walk, just wide enough to stand two abreast, closed in by thick, old trunks that crumbled when you touched them. The sour smell of turned-over earth and moss clung to everything, dark and still.

Some people used to call the Slip a 'holloway', which meant it had been there for many hundreds of years.

If you carried on through the trees, you were out on the moor. The Witches' Moor.

My big horse chestnut tree was ready and waiting as always, its arms stooped low for the perfect foothold. Someone had shaken it loose of all the early conkers, and the ground was littered with the empty spiked cases, soft and white on the inside like marshmallow.

The leaves would change any day now. I had a sixth sense about these things. That would really be the end of summer.

I swung myself up to the second set of branches so I could see the river – a wide strip of flowing steel – racing itself across the fields. Even in July it had shaken off swimmers with its cold iron glare. I wouldn't dare anyone to go near. I couldn't go out on the moor without thinking of Mum and what had happened there.

No one could see me up here in the cloud of leaves, not even if they walked within four feet of me. I took out a notebook, found the next clean page and opened Mum's favourite pen.

For the past two days, I'd thought about little else. The idea of the re-enactment had been rolling around Long Byrne like a ball everyone was trying to get hold of. Just to be part of it felt like you could join the witches' legacy.

Hubble bubble, toil and trouble.

As I wrote with Mum's best pen, it was like the white page was a visor against everything else around me. I could be in the middle of a murder trial and not even notice what was going on right next to me. Even the familiar surge of the river was just fuzzed-out background noise.

I'd found my favourite spot years and years ago. Probably

one of those days when Tawny was up at a dance recital or piano lesson. The thistledown was out, so it must have been the end of summer. Dad was trying to get us all to have dinner "as a family" even though Alexa still called me Catie and had only finished moving her stuff in the week before. Mum's picture was still on his bedside table; her collection of gem stones and pine cones freshly dusted by the front door.

I'd left and gone exploring. The horse chestnut tree had seemed warm and welcoming and I was up in its cradle before I knew it.

Down the Slip, this was the place I could be alone, undisturbed. Not even Tawny was here to roll her eyes. I felt free.

As I wrote, I breathed in deeply, taking in all the woody scents. All the hundreds of years-worth of magic stored under the moor, just waiting for someone to find it. I shivered to think that there was something deep-rooted out there and I tried to channel the magic out through my pen. Here, I felt a little bit magical myself.

The loud crack of a twig made me start back into myself.

Someone was coming from the moor through the undergrowth with thick-soled boots. Probably a dog-walker or a gruff old birdwatcher. I wished I came with a Do Not Disturb sign. I stayed very still as they passed below me in the morning light glinting gold in the leaves. Out of the corner of my eye I saw a flash of blonde hair. My head snapped up.

Bryony?

I was sure of it. Coming back from the Witches' Moor.

At eight in the morning?

I craned my neck but couldn't quite see the shape of her. The footsteps coming through the Slip were too quiet to be that of a man, surely. I went to call out her name but the word didn't come out, as if saying it was a curse.

Hollingworth.

It wasn't until long after the footsteps had died away and the wood was silent again except for the river that I put my notebook away and headed back to Long Byrne in time for the school bell, still feeling the pen's power beneath my fingers.

There are different ways of telling every tale. We all have our own versions – the fact, the fiction and the only half-believed. But if you want the tale that the Long Byrne Parish records tell, the real story goes something like this.

Rose Ackroyd and Jane Hollingworth were the town beauties – they ran races down the hidden village pathways like the 'Slip' and won the hearts of the men by dancing at the Midsummer Fair. Rose was the bastard of a maid at Hollingworth House, and Jane was the sole heiress to a large fortune. They cleant their teeth with willow bark and rubbed meadowsweet on their wrists out on the moor. They'd link arms and whisper down the street together in their own secret language.

One day, as the trees were turning, the pair had a huge row in the town square. Something about a lover, or a lack of one. No one was quite sure, but in the heat of the moment, Rose and Jane cursed each other, swearing one another to the pits of hell where only the pock-ridden plague was welcome.

'You rotten thief! I'll turn your guts – you traitor!' Rose screamed.

'Not before I send you to Hell!'

Shortly after, things in the village went sour.

Farmers found their harvests covered in blight. Cows' udders turned black and the milk was tinged pink with blood. The villagers knew something was not right. Dark magic was afoot and the people of Long Byrne went to sort things out once and *for all. They stormed through the Slip and over the moors, where someone had seen lightning flashes without a storm, ready to seize the girls.*

But when they found them, there was more to be reckoned with than they could ever have imagined.

The girls were out on the heath, their voices battling against the crash of the river, bating each other with ferocious familiars; big, black-headed dogs with white eyes as wide as dinner plates.

When the villagers gasped and made earthly cries, the vast hounds dissolved into the air like ash. The girls seemed to snap out of a trance, as if they'd been possessed by the Devil. They were left panting on the moor, waiting for the villagers to take them away.

Six months later, the girls were led up to Byrne Moor and had their necks snapped by eight loops of the hangman's knot.

More deaths followed. The townspeople were obsessed, and anything out of the ordinary was blamed on local girls. Girls with their white caps, long hair, and flowers behind their ears – every secret whisper they made was heard as a curse.

The Ackroyds died out, or left; unable to bear the stigma and pain caused by the villagers. The Hollingworths fled and vowed never to come back to this place of wickedness.

But the Hollingworths returned.

The History of Long Byrne: Demons on the Moor, Dr C. Munir

Chapter 4

The Hollingworth House.

This was unchartered territory. Only the bravest of us had gone down there. Pad Mitchell had been near for a dare when we were thirteen but wouldn't tell anyone what he'd seen, no matter how many Wispa bars we bought him from Maldew's Corner Shop. Looking around at the neat silver birches and the floppy white bindweed on either side of the track, I knew Pad had just sat in the woods for an hour smoking spliffs and come out thinking he'd seen a ghost.

And now, here I was.

I'd found my courage and asked Bryony if she wanted anyone to come over and help her with Psychology. I had my fingers crossed deep in my jeans pockets and had forced back a smile when she'd said yes. Secretly, I thought a trip to the Hollingworth House would be good as some research for my script. But I had another motive that I kept even closer to my chest.

The house itself was even more imposing close up and the three storeys of rough grey stone and iron window frames made me gulp. Bryony got out the key for a Yale lock – not the big rusty chain I'd been hoping for – and pushed open the door.

Stepping over the threshold, I felt a shudder run through me. So much had gone on in this house – the place where all the legends originated. Every creak of the overhead beams and the floorboards below us might be muffling a hidden cry for help. Everything was cooler inside, like we had just entered a crypt, and I had to reassure myself that Hollingworth House wasn't filled with the cold flowing gowns of seventeenth century ghosts. When Bryony locked the door behind me, I thought there might be a series of bolts and shackles behind it that would prevent me from ever leaving. But there was only a very normal-looking lock and I bit back my disappointment.

"Auntie?" she called. No one answered.

"Where is she?"

"She'll be down in the cellar – she's always tinkering with something down there."

I let out a long hot breath that I didn't realise I'd been holding and stepped inside. What would an old lady be tinkering with down in a creepy cellar? I decided to push that thought way, way down.

"Are your parents here too?" I asked.

"No, just me."

The blank way she said this made me shut my mouth.

The walls were painted a warm, old-person magnolia and the frilly orange stair-runner stuck up at odd angles like it had been recently hoovered. There was the smell of potpourri assaulting me from the window sill. On a wooden ledge by the door was a wodge of handwritten letters tied with a piece of string, each addressed to *Miss B.M. Hollingworth* in different coloured inks and envelopes. I hadn't even thought about her friends back home, like she had just materialised in Long Byrne with her suitcase at her feet, not looking back. The letters looked bursting with news and pictures; some were covered in heart stickers and doodles of cute little pigs.

She looked at the bundle, her face a perfect blank, and turned away. "Auntie hasn't ventured into the realms of the internet yet." I couldn't remember the last time our Wi-Fi had decided to work, either. Tawny and I should snail-mail each other too; it would probably be quicker. My eyes widened as I remembered my best friend. I fished inside my pocket and saw the stream of messages awaiting me – each one had more and more capital letters than the last. The excitement of going to Bryony's place had given me temporary amnesia. I sent a reply.

Sooooo much work to do. See you tomorrow, luvs xxx

She'd understand.

"Would you like something to drink?"

I wondered wildly if Bryony was offering me booze. You just helped yourself at Tawny's.

"Um, no, I'm good, thanks."

She kicked off her boots and hung up her jacket. I did the same, standing on tiptoes to reach the peg. Her long pea-green coat looked so elegant next to my old jacket that always smelled faintly of cow shit.

"Come on in."

I only hesitated for a second then followed her along the hall.

The house could have been a museum of 1950s kitsch. Where were the iron manacles? The creaky vaults? Every vase in the hall had a doily and all the lampshades had pink tassels, like sleeping jellyfish.

I looked to my left, into a long living room with antimacassars on the backs of the sofas. There was something carved into the mantelpiece and I narrowed my eyes to make out its faded shape. Then all of a sudden it hit me, the drag of panic in my stomach. I jumped back from the door like it was cursed.

The Evil Eye.

It was a long oval shape with a simple dark-painted mound hewn inside it to represent the pupil. It looked like it had been done with rough tools, the outline blurred and indistinct.

When we'd first moved to Long Byrne and I was a nerdy little kid who'd just found out about the Long Byrne witches, I had stacks and stacks of magic books from the local library. Dad thought there might be something wrong with me. Maybe he thought I was sick; I can't remember what he said but he took me to see a doctor. But that was a different story. I tried to remember exactly what all those crumbly books had said – the Evil Eye was a terrible symbol, something so evil it terrified everything in its gaze, even dark spirits. A big mystical peeper wagging its finger at anything that tried to sneak by. It was sometimes used as a talisman to ward off demons . . . or witches. It was both a symbol used by witches to work dark magic and a symbol of protection used to frighten off darkness.

But whichever way you looked at it, it meant that something bad was nearby.

I'd never seen it outside of a book before.

How many times had I doodled it in the corner of my notepad? On the poems I wrote? All the crosshatched shadows and sunken pen marks where I'd pressed too hard and torn a hole in the page. There it was, glaring and sullen beneath the row of family portraits.

Why did the Hollingworths have one in their home?

"Everything OK?" asked Bryony from the landing, and my heart skipped a beat.

"Yes. Yes," I said, a little more strongly, and followed her slowly up the wooden staircase.

I told myself it was nothing. It was just a carving that had been there for ever. It wasn't like Bryony had put it there.

Up on the third floor, Bryony's room was painted pale blue and bordered with a pattern of watery irises. I stepped gingerly through the doorway. Cardboard boxes stood Sellotaped and sturdy behind the door, and several frilly cushions were stacked up next to the bed like puffy building blocks. There was a big old architect's desk under the window; the polished wood shining orange in the sunset. She'd barely unpacked except for a pile of books and a polished silver microscope.

I blinked back my disappointment. There was definitely nothing gothic or mysterious about her ironed lace curtains. This was just some place she was staying. Temporary.

It didn't even smell like her.

Although I hadn't realised I knew what she smelled like.

Bryony put her school bag on the chair and ran her hand over the books sitting there. There was a kind of stillness to her – processing everything around her as it happened, watching it all unfold, then making her move like a white chess piece.

"I need to carry on with these at some point."

She flipped open a page of the top book and my stomach dropped.

The books were all about the human body, all sinewy Leonardo Da Vinci drawings and cross-sections of arteries. My eyes widened and I noticed a scalpel lying at a stern right angle to the microscope on the desk.

She followed my gaze. "I'm getting a headstart in Biology."

I just stood there, my arms feeling dangly like a scarecrow, my knees quivering. For some reason, my mind was back downstairs in the living room. She laughed and it was the first time I'd seen her teeth. Straight and white.

"You look terrified!"

I couldn't help grinning too. "You led me out to the countryside to dissect me – the perfect horror story."

"Hope you're not squeamish." She gestured towards the books and sat down on the bed. "I'm really into all this at the moment. Always have been, I guess. Dad's a doctor so endoscopies are just normal, after-dinner conversation."

"What's that?"

"When they put a camera up your . . . back passage."

I laughed, but the ooze of gore from the books was making me cringe and I wished she'd close the cover.

"I thought you lived on a farm?" she said. "Surely there's a fair amount of blood and guts there though, right?"

A few years ago I'd had to kill a chicken. A fox had sneaked in off the moor and bitten a chunk out of her but left her still alive. I'd kept her warm, wet her beak, then snapped her neck – a clean break. She hadn't run around the yard like they said she would. A headless chicken can stay alive for up to eighteen months after it's had the big chop. Or so they say. But this one just slumped in my hands like a dropped feed sack. I was supposed to be a farmer, but the thick sweat of blood on my hands still made me nauseous and I hadn't touched a KFC since.

I ignored the question and nodded towards the books. "These all yours then?"

She nodded, tucking a wedge of hair behind her ear. "They're Auntie's, but I got them as a moving-in present. She knows I wanted to be a vet when I was little."

I winced at the picture. "Or a mortician."

She looked at me, then at the picture and I felt my neck burning. I could feel myself getting jittery like I did when I'd not had a coffee in a couple of hours.

"How long have you been here?" I said quickly.

"I got here on Saturday. Quite the trip." She scrunched up her mouth. "Auntie wanted me to settle in as quickly as possible. You know, get into the spirit of things. But things here are . . ." Bryony trailed off with a wince. "Well, everyone knows each other. Everyone's in each other's pockets all the time. Don't you find that? How do you even deal with that?"

"Don't worry, you'll get used to it. When we moved here, I was twelve and don't think I'd even seen a tractor before."

She frowned. "I thought you said you'd always lived here?"

The pause in the room felt heavy. I stumbled around my head for something to say.

"Well . . . it feels like for ever. Four years is a lifetime."

"I suppose," she nodded slowly, watching me. "I've lived in London all my life. I don't think it was enough time though."

Dare I ask the question?

"Why did you leave then?"

She shrugged. "Had to."

I knew the feeling. I bit my lip, throbbing with questions. She turned back to her desk and closed the old volume. "What about you?"

"Huh?"

"Why did you move here?"

That jitteriness swelled in me again – someone was holding my heart like a mouse by the tail and its legs were going full-speed to try and get away. Bryony watched with her pale-green eyes slightly narrowed. Her left hand was around her wrist, rubbing the tiny silver charm on her bracelet. She seemed to be more than waiting; she seemed nervous.

"Something bad happened," I said. "Back home, there were so many people asking questions. Day in, day out. So Dad and I got out of the city, started fresh up here. Bought the farm, thought things could be different. New place, new life." I was gabbling and I realised my shakiness was adrenaline spurring me on. "So, this is home now."

"And, *are* things different?"

"Yeah, some things are. I shovel cow shit a lot now."

She smiled, watching me closely. "And you have Tawny."

"Yeah," I nodded. "I have Tawny."

"You guys seem super close."

"I know her better than anyone."

"I bet that gets tiring," Bryony half-grinned and I sat up a little bit straighter.

"She can be a lot but she's just Tawny to me."

She looked at me, nodding appraisingly, still swirling her thumb back and forth on her wrist. She seemed to have more questions but didn't say any more.

I felt uneasy, desperate to move on. I picked out my textbook and sat crossed-legged on the floor. "Shall we get started then?"

Bryony raised her eyebrows.

"Psychology?" I said.

Bryony nodded; swept the gory books out of sight. I rolled up the sleeves of my jumper and turned to the chapter we were studying in class but I glanced up and saw Bryony's eyes fixed on my forearms. I looked down, thinking I had ink all over me but I only saw my bare arms.

Bryony's eyes were fixed on them, her eyes wide.

"Cate, your . . ."

I looked down again and wondered what she saw. My skin had a translucency to it that showed the blue flush of my veins and, OK, maybe I could do with a meat and potato pasty to make the nobbles on my wrists not look so big, but I was just how I always was.

I yanked my sleeves back down and Bryony looked away.

"Shall we?" I said, tapping the book with my Biro.

By the time we'd gone over Freud's sexy (or was it sexist?) bullshit, my mouth was dry with long words. The sun had tipped into a deep greenish-blue and there was a quiet sighing in the house. It felt like the roof was un-tensing its shoulders for the night. Bryony seemed to grasp Psych more after our one-on-one session. She agreed to take my notes for the night, pretending she could read my scrawl.

Bryony fiddled with her pen and stared at the microscope on the desk.

"Thanks for not being like the others."

I stopped trying to buckle my bag. She said it so quietly, at first I thought she was humming to herself. But she went on.

"For not saying those things. You know, about my family."

"That's OK," I said.

"I didn't realise we were the local monsters up here." She smiled but I saw the hurt in her eyes. I very much doubted she was jumping for joy at Rillington's poorly timed re-enactment.

The moon was just beginning to form itself in the sky. A thin white crescent waxing through the tall window.

"Don't worry. Seriously. Next week, there'll be something new for them to talk about. Kayleigh Whittard will be up the duff or whatever."

"Yeah . . . four hundred years though. I guess there are some things you just can't escape." She shrugged, smiling calmly. The evening light was playing on her eyes. I sprang up suddenly and my knees clicked.

"Why would anyone want to come to Long Byrne anyway? What were you thinking!" I laughed, but I was curious and wanted to push it. London was a far cry from somewhere like this. This was nowhere. You had to have a very good reason to step foot here.

She grinned. "Desperation?"

"Insanity?"

"Dysentery?"

I snorted. "What?"

"I don't know – fresh air might be good for the bowels!"

"Gross."

I thought of all those letters downstairs. Who were they from? Would there be a love letter? She was probably itching to read them all, but she'd spent the evening with me. Here we were laughing over something completely ridiculous. I couldn't help feeling slightly lightheaded with giddiness.

When it was time to go, she walked me to the end of the drive. I'd kept my eyes forward as we'd gone through the hall, not letting them flicker into the darkened room by the door. The night was crisp and cold and you could hear the Thursday-night bell practice ringing out from the church in Stoutbridge, all the way over the hills. Bryony waved as I made my way to Alder Farm. I turned back and saw her hair, white-blonde and ghostly in the moonlight, getting further and further away.

They used to check girls for extra fingers. Moles as fat as flies behind their ears, white patterned scars on their forearms. The Devil had a way of scoring his marks on young women who'd barely had their first period. When the witch-hunter came to town, you locked up your girls or handed them over if they were oh-so-very wicked.

This was back in the days when they taught you the Sun went round the Earth and people thought that leeches could cure just about anything from diarrhoea to a broken heart.

Official reports say Jane Hollingworth was clean. Not so much as a freckle. They still hanged her first.

"They must have seen something in her eye.

In Search of the Long Byrne Witches, P.J. Hebden

Chapter 5

"Where were you? I texted you, like, *fifty* times."

"I was zonked, sorry," I said.

Tawny widened her eyes. "You? Tired? There's a first."

I shrugged. "Should I come over tonight?"

"I'm never speaking to you again."

I rolled my eyes. "I've got my toothbrush in my bag."

She grinned.

It was lunchtime on Friday. Finally: the weekend. College was already taking its toll and I'd been up for the cows at quarter past five this morning. Tawny and I were sitting at our new spot by the salad bar in the school canteen. I felt fiercely territorial and hooked myself around the table legs as soon as we sat down. Tawny had actually growled at Laura Harvey for putting her bag there the other day.

I was writing the re-enactment script and she was bent over the desk, working on a pastel sketch of what looked like a squashed grape. I tilted my head and realised it was a purplish vulva. My eyes widened involuntarily. Maybe I just didn't get 'art'. I looked at Tawny's smooth pale skin, clenched around the mouth as she worked. Most of the Long Byrne kids were red and blotchy, like they'd always had a bit of farmer in them. Joe Fuller had a chunk gouged out of his cheek from a horny bull calf. You couldn't get more country than that. But Tawny's skin, it was like she'd stepped out of one of our glossies, or one of those Photoshopped audition photos in *The Stage* magazine she got delivered once a month. She'd end up in there one day, that was for sure – she wouldn't even need airbrushing.

Tawny said my skin just looked shiny . . . but in a good way. Maybe shiny was OK in her universe. I liked to think the ghostly hue of my skin was from being studious late into the night. I'd just aced the pop quiz in History – the late nights were paying off.

"So, what do you think the costumes will be like?" I said.

Tawny's eyes flared in excitement, pupils dilated even in the bright September light. "For the re-enactment?"

"Mmm."

"I'm wearing a corset no matter what. I'll max out their budget. Rillington seems all aboard though. I've not seen her so excited since the mobile library came to town." Her eyes sparkled.

"You'll probably have to make it yourself. What a shame you have a seamstress for a mum."

"It's like it was all meant to be!" Tawny wiggled her eyebrows suggestively.

I rolled my eyes and she cackled into her painting. I sometimes tried to picture what we would have been like as kids together. Our parents would have dressed us in matching headbands, taken us to feed the ducks before school and I'd have made her a friendship bracelet from a do-it-yourself kit.

Bright yellow with cheap plastic beads. When I'd lived in the city I didn't make bracelets for anyone. I didn't even have a kid sister to force one on. There was Mum, but I'd never made anything for her except smiley macaroni faces and silly little stories in rainbow Crayola, to try and be just like her. Her stories had been sold on the shelves of big bookstores. They still were, actually. I'd once written a story about a fish who tried to jump over the moon and she'd stuck it on the fridge. All five pages.

I'd tried to shake off my city accent – maybe I used to sound a bit like Bryony, until Long Byrne got under my skin.

Tawny spoke suddenly. "What do you think, Robyn?"

I looked up to see Robyn passing our table with a tray of Long Byrne's paltry lunch options, heading towards an empty table across the hall. She looked translucent under the fluorescent strip lighting.

Robyn hesitated then asked, "About what?"

Tawny grinned. "This re-enactment. Want to be my understudy?"

"No, thanks," she replied in a clipped tone that made me raise my eyebrows. Robyn usually tolerated Tawny's bullshit.

But Tawny didn't even notice. She had her face scrunched up, seemingly wondering what the next step was with the vulva, when I saw Bryony walk in. With a quick scan around I clocked there were no tables left.

Tawny's head snapped up reflexively.

"Hey! Bryony!"

She kicked our remaining chair out eagerly next to where Robyn still hovered and it swayed precariously on two legs before landing upright again. Bryony grabbed her bag tighter on her shoulder, like she'd just turned down a dark alley.

"Come and sit with us!"

"Are you ... sure?"

"Don't be silly," said Tawny and, with one swoop of her arm, the table was clear. She leant forward as Bryony sat, Tawny's dark hair brushing the Tippex graffiti. Robyn stared at Bryony, her small delicate jaw fixed and set as if she had been carved out of wax. She reached into her bag and brought out a Tupperware pot. I noticed Robyn's eyes flick to my own empty tray and back and again.

"You sitting too, Rob?" I asked, uncertainly.

But she didn't say a word, just shook her head so that her mass of curls moved, and headed to her table as if its location was hard-wired into her feet. I followed her with my eyes. Tawny was looking at Bryony but with a very different expression. She didn't even notice her sister leave.

"So, how are you finding *that* lot?" she jerked her head towards the busy canteen.

"What do you mean?"

Tawny raised her eyebrows, stacked with meaning.

Bryony shrugged. "I haven't really noticed."

Tawny nudged her with her knee. "Just ignore them. They love drama here," she said, her eyes flashing again and she shuffled in even closer to the table.

Bryony didn't say anything. She was perfectly composed, her hands cradled in her lap as she considered her knuckles. I noticed her nails were bitten down to the core – even worse than mine.

"It's fine. Honestly."

I wondered what it could possibly be like to leave London at sixteen to come and stay with your wild country aunt who tinkered around in the cellar and left you to walk around the moors in the early hours of the morning.

I wondered if Bryony was lonely.

As if she wanted to put some distance between us, Bryony moved her chair back an inch. It squealed like a rabbit caught in a snare, a sound that reverberated around the canteen. Her body went rigid and the whole room spun to look at her. The stricken look on her face made some of the more feral Year Twelves stir.

"Oi, witch!" Pad Mitchell yelled from the window sill.

Bryony jumped but didn't take her eyes off the table in front of her.

The room fell silent.

Everyone's heads snapped his way like padlocks twisting open. He had his hands cupped round his mouth, letting each word clang off the metal canteen trays.

"Get your curse out of here – you're making me want to chuck up my lunch!"

The whole room stayed quiet. I expected Tawny to launch herself at him, but even she sat there wide-eyed. All at once a riot of noise burst out: grumbling, laughing, shrieking. It felt like a bomb.

Pad leant back, satisfied, and was engulfed by his mates. I saw them give Pad triumphant digs on the arm. In the crowd I searched for help and made out Robyn, sitting on her own, a book in her hand. She was staring hard at us, a frown clustering on her forehead. She saw me looking and hid herself behind *Lord of the Flies*.

We looked at Bryony through our lashes. Our table seemed very far away from everyone else.

"It's fine." Her voice was small and crisp, a defiant glint in her eye, but she dipped her head, disappearing behind her hair.

Tawny huffed. "Don't worry, he'll be hanging from the rafters when Rillington hears."

I winced. A bad choice of metaphor.

She leant in close. "How about we come to yours after college? I can show you my audition for the re-enactment. I've got three ideas but you can help choose one. Besides, we don't want to be around these weirdos, right?"

I watched Tawny's hand fall on Bryony's arm. How could she possibly resist after that?

All along the lane, purple-tasselled reeds made it feel like summer again. The daft white bindweed stuck its floppy trumpet heads out of the hedgerow. It was still warm and crickets had leapt down from the moor to fill the lane with croaky strings.

The sky shocked me like it always did on warm evenings – big brash explosions of pink and orange blared over the hills and made our hands and faces seem to glow like neon lights. The sun was already falling, dragging the day down with it, but Tawny was *up*. She was buoyant. Jabbering along the path, swinging her hips. I could sense her quivering as we headed up the Hollingworth drive.

Her eyes swept the staircase, the rugs, the dark-paned

windows, the packet of letters that still stood unopened by the door. If we'd left Tawny alone for a minute she would have run her hands over everything, like she did with people – reeling them into her arms like trout. I looked around too, pretending this was my first time inside.

I let Bryony lead the way but I had the sense that the old house seemed to be watching me, making me feel guilty about lying to Tawny last night. I clutched my bag for protection. Why hadn't I told her about it? I watched Bryony's sleek blonde hair swaying with her body as she walked up the stairs in front of me.

Tawny hadn't noticed the strange eye in the living room and I felt a shiver run through me.

Bryony's room looked exactly the same, even the pencils on the desk were still at right-angles, as if this room was only for show and she really slept in the garage or the dusty cellar. She struck a match and lit a scented candle on the window sill so the evening air blew around the smell of vanilla and musk. Tawny took a deep breath, absorbing everything. She'd obviously been looking for a clue into Bryony's psyche, maybe as I had been, but she found nothing to satisfy her intense gaze, just the microscope, scalpel and books full of horror. She flared her eyes in exasperation although the gesture was so infinitesimal only I could tell. I knew all her secret nose scrunches when something wasn't going as she'd planned, and the way she straightened out her skirt when she was nervous, and how she ate buttery toast and a spoonful of chocolate spread straight out of the jar for breakfast. I felt like I knew everything about her.

I wanted to know more about Bryony, about where she came from and her weird, slightly nauseating, interests.

"Where's Mrs Hollingworth?" asked Tawny.

"Auntie's busy."

Tawny turned her expectant eyes to Bryony, but Bryony was looking at the photos by her bed. There were dozens of them tacked in neat lines so they formed a dark wall over the headboard. These were new. Had they materialised from the letters last night?

"Your friends?" I asked. She nodded and Tawny waltzed over to stick her face close to the wall.

"Oh my god, they're adorable. Is that your family? 'Course it is, they look exactly like you. Are they your brothers?" Tawny jabbed her finger at the chest of a boy in the snapshot, like a child prodding a new and interesting sweet. Bryony looked so happy in the pictures – her grin seemed to cover her whole face. The girl in the picture did not look like Long Byrne Bryony.

She made a small noise, her lips tight, and her hand wavered around her left wrist where the plaited leather bracelet dangled. I looked closer for the first time and saw the charm was a dainty silver feather. The little point of the feather pressed into Bryony's thumb as she squeezed it and I imagined the dint it left – sharp and hollow.

"They're well fit!" Tawny cried. "Especially him." The boy in the photo had a cheeky grin and a smatter of freckles on his nose. I couldn't tell how old he was, maybe our age, a little bit older, but his eyes were the same clear green as Bryony's. There was another boy next to them who looked around nineteen or twenty; his chin was angular and he had a deep tan. Everyone in the photo was smiling on a summer holiday – the Eiffel Tower rising up behind them.

Tawny shimmered. "My favourite place in the entire world." Ever since I'd known Tawny she'd wanted to be a dancer on the French stage, and have a bloke with a curly tache who'd paint her. As far as I knew, the furthest away Tawny had ever been from Long Byrne was a trip to Cornwall when she was eight, and I didn't think Mrs Brown was about to have a windfall any time soon.

"Bryony, I hope I'm not being rude, but we want to know everything." Tawny put an arm through hers and guided her to the bed. They sat down in unison. I hovered by the door, watching the small single bed ripple around them. I let my school bag drop to the floor but they didn't seem to notice.

Bryony looked awkward and I found myself running to her rescue.

"What are your family like?"

A smile flickered in the corner of Bryony's mouth. "Well, they're mainly OK when they're not screaming and divorcing each other."

"Urgh," said Tawny, rolling her eyes and dropping her head back in disgust. "Parents."

"I volunteered to get away from the house for a while. Sam, my brother – the older one – is at uni in Scotland, so he's managed to get out of it all. But I said I'd come and stay with Auntie until things blew over. It took three trains and a bus, with a suitcase and a rucksack. They're not happy about it, but you know what mums are like."

She seemed to look at me directly as she said it and I held her gaze, feeling my cheeks get hot.

"I'll bet they think we're all flat caps and whippets, yeah?" Tawny grinned.

"They . . ." I could see the tact running across her face. "They know that it might be a bit different to what I'm used to." I thought of her in a three-storey Georgian house, like the ones Americans thought all English people lived in. And it actually turned out she'd been in private school, at which Tawny and I boggled our eyes to each other. I thought of my holey shoes and the own-brand washing-up liquid that Alexa bought.

"Next you'll be saying you holidayed in the South of France." I forced a smile and tried to make my voice sound less like I'd just fallen off the back of a tractor. It was weird to think of Bryony in this way, so different from the rest of us here. Living in another world.

But Tawny was entranced.

"Oh my god, you did, didn't you!" She cackled. "This is perfect."

The tops of Bryony's ears were practically crimson, but she told us stories about the fishing boat they'd hired in Provence and how they'd spent a whole week running around the deck. Her brother, Euan, would pretend to steer and gave their mum heart palpitations. Her dad, the top surgeon, had turned off his pager and given them his full attention that holiday; he'd shown them how to gut fish, told them the names of all the greeny-purple parts of their insides and shown them how to slice and dice the fish into sushi, which he'd learnt on a big tour of Japan when he was a student.

"OK, all right, we get it. You're very rich and very beautiful. Now, how about you listen to me practise my soliloquy for witch auditions. We're in the right place for it, aren't we?" Tawny wiggled her eyebrows and didn't let Bryony's slightly open mouth stop her. "I'm making use of the occasion."

Family history. Lots of money. Not a broom or cauldron in sight.

I don't know who was more disappointed, me or Tawny.

I woke up engulfed by floppy cushions in Tawny's room. I felt the sequins studded into my cheek.

Her face was about ten centimetres from mine and I could just make out her hair stuck up at right angles. Only I had the privilege of seeing Tawny this way. Morning breath. No makeup. No razzle-dazzle.

My mind reeled from the night before. Tawny had made her eyes wide, all that violet-blue soaking in each crisp syllable from Bryony's tongue.

I pictured Bryony's long limbs tanned and bare as the sun caught them, the same colour as the boat's wooden deck. How she'd stretch them out until every inch was coppery with summer heat, and the coconutty smell of sun cream hovering in a haze around her.

It was a whole other life to mine. In comparison, Long Byrne felt like something crawling out from under a rock or from an empty crisp packet.

I checked my phone. It read *5.10*. No messages, not even one from Dad replying to my *Staying at Tawny's x* text.

Typical.

Peeling off the duvet, I disentangled myself in the gloom. My legs radiated pale blue with the morning light that seeped around Tawny's blackout curtains. I heaved myself up, ready to vault over her sleeping body, but I paused halfway over her – I thought she'd squirmed. One time, I'd heard her recite the entire theme song of *The Phantom of the Opera* in her sleep.

There was a pink towel in the bathroom, thick and musty on the floor, but it was the only one in sight. After a power-shower, the bathroom steamed up and left the mirror in a fug that smelled of talc and damp. I tried to do my mascara in the fluorescent light but it showed up the hollows under my eyes and made me look even deader than usual. I gave up and let myself out the door.

On the way to Alder Farm, my mind kept drifting back to last night. Tawny and I had listened to Bryony with wide eyes. Every time she laughed, Tawny had edged herself closer, as if she was trying to see the story forming in Bryony's head before she'd even spoken it out loud. They sat cushioned together in a single dip in the bedcovers.

I let myself in, changed my clothes, then went straight to the kettle. The thin skin under my eyes felt stretched taut, like if I pressed a pin to it my face would shatter. My mind was sluggish and thick like bog sludge from the moor – the sort of feeling that sometimes meant I had to take a day off school. When that happened, Alexa said I needed the day to rest, but I usually just laid awake in bed for hours and hours or went off and hid down the Slip. I could sleep when I was dead.

My first sip of coffee made my eyes water as it burnt my tongue but I was used to it now and I'd even grown to ignore the twinge down the left of my body as I pushed through my fifth mug of the day.

Mum had got me started on the coffee. Swirling caffeine highs, the wide-awake eyes, where everything seems to fog together and get ten times as bright. She used to drink gallons of the stuff when she was writing; "It gets me in the zone," she'd say with a wink. Mum was into Pilates, acai berries, gem stones – all the sort of stuff that Dad rolled his eyes at and put up with because he loved her. They both liked to tell the story of when they first met at an art gallery; how she'd got so excited over a Lucian Freud picture that she'd scalded Dad with her Americano.

She'd made a lasting impression. He still had the burn.

She was all about cleansing and calm, except for the coffee. It was her one vice. Every morning at 7.30 a.m. on the dot she'd blitz fresh beans in the coffee grinder and I'd listen for the tinny rattle as they whirred around then settled into bean dust, knowing it was time to get up and start the day.

I can still taste her favourite blend.

I went out to the yard and did my morning chores. The cows mooed at the sight of me and I gave Vera a hug around the neck, which somehow felt reciprocated. She smelled like sweet straw.

Back at the house, Dad came into the kitchen looking like a mole emerging into the sunlight. Had he been working through the night? After a second in the doorway, he switched on the kettle and stood back, musing about where the teabags might possibly be.

"All right?" I said.

"Hmm? Oh, yes! Fine, just fine." He opened the cupboard below the sink then closed it again. "How is the script coming along?"

I shrugged. "Not bad." I took another sip of coffee and it seemed to make the overhead kitchen light extra sparkly.

"That good, hm?" He cocked a smile and I couldn't help but smile back.

"No, it's actually going well. I feel like I've got the plot sorted. I'm just having a bit of trouble with the characters."

"Hmm," Dad said, opening the middle drawer next to the washing machine. "How so?"

I took another sip. "I think I need a really good reason for them to have argued out on the moor. It seems so extreme that they cursed each other."

"Maybe they were extreme people. Some people are more intense than others. What was it that Tawny said that time?" He winced as he thought. "Maybe they had big *Aries energy.*"

I spluttered and sprayed coffee drops all over the counter.

"Yes, that must be it."

"Have you had a look at your Mum's folder yet?" The kettle boiled and Dad just stood there looking lost.

I hadn't. Things had been so busy with school. Part of me didn't want to look in the folder at all because I knew the torrent of emotion it would bring up. Especially because of the upcoming anniversary.

I reached forwards to the cupboard on the wall to get a teabag for Dad. "I—" I began, but the kitchen light suddenly seemed too bright. It was dazzling. I lurched forwards, my mug falling out of my hand and landing with smash on the floor. Dad ran towards me and I clung to his shoulder.

"You OK? What happened there?"

"I'm fine, I'm fine," I said, my voice seeming to come from very far away. Dad was manoeuvring me into a chair. He looked me up and down as if noticing me for the first time: the baggy thighs of my jeans, the jumper with shoulder seams that almost came down to my elbows.

"Right, let's get some toast in you."

"I already ate," I said, a grumble coming into my voice.

"What did you eat?"

My pause betrayed me.

"Right then," he said. "Eggs it is."

I started to get up but Dad looked at me with a gaze I rarely saw.

"Sit," he said and began bustling about making scrambled eggs on toast. The very thought of them made bile rise in my throat. Mum had used to make them when I was sick, and they were always creamy, soft and light. Now, I wanted to gag.

"Here you go," Dad said, too cheerful. "Pepper?"

"OK," I said and proceeded to push the eggs around with my fork. Dad watched me between mouthfuls of his own breakfast. I dubiously ate a mouthful.

"That's it," he said, like I was a toddler pouting over my broccoli. He smiled encouragingly and I forced a second bite down.

Just then, Alexa's key was in the front door.

"A little help!" she called and we heard the car boot open, filled with the Big Shop. Dad sprang up but I stayed put. I heard them chattering in the front yard and made my choice. I grabbed my boots from next to the table and made my exit through the back door. The cows needed me and I needed them.

WITCHES COME TO LONG BYRNE HIGH

Pupils from Long Byrne High School will be taking to the boards this Halloween to re-enact the mysterious story of the local witches.

The hanging of the Long Byrne Witches marks its 400th anniversary this year. The tale, familiar to many, still sends shudders down the backs of Stoutbridge residents. It tells of two young women who were caught practising magic and worshipping the Devil out on Long Byrne Moor in 1623. Met with a mob of terrified Christians, the pair were hounded, arrested and ultimately hanged on the site of their misdoings.

To date, the legend has brought up to £8m in tourism to the area. The theatre production of the tale will be dramatised on Long Byrne village green. It will be accompanied by a Halloween fayre with rides, prize stalls and food vans, and is open to all ages.

Long Byrne High head teacher Anna Rillington, says: "We're very proud to be honouring our local history. While the events on the moor would never occur in today's more enlightened world, it is important to share the stories of our village and make people think more closely about the long-term effects of their superstitious actions."

Join in the action at Long Byrne village green from 6 p.m. on 31st October.

Jamie Threlfall, *The Stoutbridge Star*

Chapter 6

Rose and Jane. Jane and Rose.

Their surging lightning bolts and burning energy whirl around me, whipping up the loose hairs around my face. Their words are fogging up my irises until all I can see are whorls of flashing light and all I can smell is charred gorse. The legend fills me up then spills out onto the page through my pen.

What had happened up on the moor? What was the real story of the witches?

Did I really know?

The sky is shuddering. What had happened with those two girls all those years ago? What had made them curse each other up on the moor? Was it really just over some man? Or was there something more important? Their curses rebound through our little village like tips of poison. If you mention Long Byrne up in town, or in the paper, it is always 'the witch place'. There is no escaping it.

I closed my eyes, letting all the witch history form straight lines in my brain – all those strands of gossip, all those nights spent under the covers with a story book, my torch shining sickly orange under my chin. What did it feel like to be cursed?

It was after first lesson on Monday morning and the sun clung desperately to the last shreds of summer, but the clouds were rolling in over the moor. I could just imagine the grey strands of fog forming around the corn bristles in the fields. I'd spent all weekend on the farm, feeling the cold gather around my ankles, lugging sterilised milk churns out into the yard and fixing the fence panel that always managed to let the foxes in, so I was one big aching muscle from head to toe. Long Byrne had it in for me.

If Dad had remembered Mum's anniversary looming over us, he never mentioned it.

Now, in my free period, I was in our new canteen spot working on the script. Mum's folder was sitting next to me. I hadn't opened it yet – something in me had pulled back, knowing that seeing her handwriting would be hard.

I opened it to the first page and saw a Post-It stuck to a plastic wallet.

I hope this is helpful for you, love. Mum would be so proud of your writing. You'll have to tell me what you find in here! Dad x

There was a smiley face and a kiss at the end and I found the corners of my mouth tugging up into an involuntary smile. Of course Dad would remember Mum's anniversary. Perhaps this was his way of acknowledging it without having to risk the tears that came through talking.

The A4 ring-binder was stuffed with newspaper clippings of spooky happenings in the area. People with mysterious illnesses, disappearances, large animals spotted out on the moors. There were photocopies of long passages from library books, black and white photos of the hanging spot and a local artist's impression of the Hollingworth House. I hadn't known Mum had been so into the history of Long Byrne. I flipped a page and my breath caught in my throat when I saw handwritten spells, lists of herbs, moon phases – all in Mum's writing. I let my fingers trail down the page. It sent a shudder through me. I noticed with a frown that some of the news articles went back almost twenty-five years. Had Mum been collecting these since she was a teenager?

"Cate Aspey? Hello?"

My head snapped up and I slammed the folder shut. Miss Rillington, tall and forbidding, was standing above me; long-nailed fingers around a red clipboard. Up close she smelled of violet creams, like a fake Victorian tearoom or a garden centre.

"Is that the script I see?" She raised her chin as if peeking over an invisible fence.

I glanced down at my page then covered if with the side of my hand. "It is."

"Wonderful!" She smoothed her tartan skirt out beneath her as she sat next to me. I tried to guess her age but couldn't. Forty-five? Fifty-two? Seventy-one?

She looked me directly in the eye.

"It's fantastic to see you so absorbed by your writing. Keep it up! Have you thought about auditioning too?"

"For a part? Oh, no. I'm not really one for standing in front of people."

"Are you sure? Not Rose? Not Bryony?"

I jolted, crinkling the edge of the page with my fist. "What did you say?"

Miss Rillington straightened her shoulders and checked her clipboard. "I asked if you wanted a main role – Rose Ackroyd, or Jane Hollingworth?"

"Oh." My stomach unclenched. "No, thanks."

She looked vaguely relieved. "Not another starry-eyed girl hoping to tread the boards, I see." I noticed her hair was rumpled on one side, like she'd been scrunching her fingers through it. Perhaps her project was proving to be a little too ambitious.

"Right," I said, nodding a little shakily.

"I'm disappointed that Robyn Brown hasn't been swept up in the spirit of things. She refused point-blank when I asked her this morning. Such an eager girl usually . . ."

"Yeah. I don't think Robyn's keen on being centre stage either."

Rillington shook her head; a hopeless case. "Anyway. I'm so glad to see you working on this. Think you could run me through it?"

"What, now?" I asked in alarm.

"Just a brief overview," she made her voice light. "Nothing major."

"Oh, um, sure." Anxiety coursed through me like caffeine. "So, at the moment it starts with witch-hunters telling the local people to beware of witches and how to spot them. Then it goes to Jane and Rose meeting for the first time, when Rose comes to work at the Hollingworth House. They get on and share a really nice moment before they're interrupted by

Jane's dad. Rose leaves and Jane and her dad talk about the house and their duties, so we can see that Jane is upper class and Rose is lower class." I cleared the embarrassment from my throat. "Is this the sort of thing you were looking for?"

Miss Rillington looked at me, nodding slowly. "Yes, yes, that's exactly the sort of thing. Jane would have been a very different class to Rose so their friendship is an unlikely one, and it adds to their mystery." She patted her hands on her lap. "I like it, Cate. I really do. I can't wait to see it!"

"OK. Thanks, Miss . . ." I wondered when Rillington was going to leave me alone but she was looking at me, considering, lapping up my scuffed farmyard boots, my dark jeans that badly needed taking in around the waist. She was curious. Was she curating my life history? But, then again, she already knew about that; pretty much everyone around here did. My history was as easy to escape as the Long Byrne witches.

"Why do you even bother with her, Tawny?" I'd heard Kayleigh Whittard ask once in the changing rooms after P.E. "She's such a freak."

"Yeah, Queen of the Sob Story. Quick, someone get her on X Factor," smirked Thea Matthews.

"Seriously, Tawn – *why* do you hang round with her?"

Tawny had given the ultimate Tawny Sneer. "Because *some* people have a little more imagination than *you*."

The girls had scowled, lost for words. You didn't want to be on the firing end of Tawny Brown. I'd turned away to my locker and smiled to myself.

Back in the canteen, Rillington cocked her head at me. "I've actually heard from a few people, teachers and students alike, that you're quite the prolific writer." If I wasn't so anaemically white, I would have flushed. Rillington left space for me to talk but I stayed silent.

"Your mum was a writer, wasn't she, Cate?"

My stomach plummeted. *Here we go.*

"It's great that you're following in her footsteps," she continued and I gripped my pen – Mum's pen – hard. I nodded.

The canteen seemed quiet suddenly, even over Matty Bridge's blaring phone speakers and the clatter of trays on the counter. I could hear Rillington's slow, steady breaths as she examined me. It was like she was trying to draw some kind of truth out of me. What did she want to hear?

"Look, I just want to have some part in the re-enactment, OK? The witches sounded like they'd be fun to write about," I garbled.

Rillington didn't move. "Yes, I can see that. But why?"

I shrugged again. "The history. It's part of our history, I guess."

"Not yours though. You're not from here, are you, Cate?"

"I am!" I said indignantly.

"I thought you moved here from Manchester a few years ago, Cate."

It wasn't a question and I sank into my chair. I felt like the whole room had turned to stare at me, even though they were too busy sticking gum under the desks and flicking chips at each other.

"I did, Miss. What I mean is, I just feel like I've always been here."

Rillington set her jaw. "OK. Well, you know the story. I think you've made a great start. Remember, what happened back then was unforgivable and quite gruesome. But there'll be kids watching, so don't be too graphic. We want to make it about twenty-five minutes long so the Mums and Tots group don't start bawling. No swearing either."

PG rating. "That's fine."

"We don't have too long until we need to start rehearsals. Send me a draft of the script early next week and we'll go from there."

I nodded and pretended to start scribbling again, but she hovered.

"You're a bright girl, you know, Cate. You should be thinking about getting into a good university. There'll be people there who can help you."

My finger balled reflexively into my palms. "Help me with what exactly?" My tone sounded like a threat. Perhaps I'd meant it that way.

"What you've been through. They will be able to help you get back on track."

She might as well have slapped me in the face.

"I'm on track for all A-stars, thanks, Miss."

We looked at each other for a long second then Rillington raised her eyebrows and stood up. "We can talk about it when you hand in the script. If you like?" she added.

I made a non-committal sound, shrugging off her pity-trip. I felt too spiky now. Rillington looked down at her clipboard for an excuse to leave and strode purposefully towards the canteen doors without a goodbye.

I sat, blinking by the grey window. Something squirmed in my gut as the canteen slowly came to life around me again. It was the feeling I got when I looked at the Hollingworth House and like the day when the re-enactment was announced. It was an uneasy feeling – akin to foreboding. The thought of being here when lunch was served was too much for me, so I gathered my things and went to find a quiet stairwell. That would be better. I didn't want to be seen right now.

Making stuff up was my speciality. It's a bit like lying, but without having to remember who you fibbed to.

Maybe I made up stories and poems to be like Mum, but I didn't fancy my name in glitzy lights like she had. I remembered having to wear a smart dress and patent leather shoes that squeaked as I walked down the corridor. It was way past my bedtime but Mum wanted me at the award ceremony. "You're all the luck I need, Cate-pop." We'd got up stupidly early to catch our train down to London so I was fidgeting like any seven-year-old would. The event was in a huge hall that smelled like new clothes and dry ice. When they called Mum's name she swept me into a big hug and took me up onto the stage with her, carrying me against her hip even though I was much too big to be held like that. I stared at the back of the stage while she spoke into the microphone, feeling all those eyes on me. It was so strange to close my eyes against her shoulder and hear her voice reverberating off all the walls around me. It felt like a special place.

Back then, I wrote about my cuddly toys – especially my

stuffed rabbit, Raspy – and the adventures they all went on together. Now I wrote about the bitchy girls at school and the nasty things I wished would happen to their noses. I wrote about Tawny's Technicolor dreams on Broadway, sashaying across the stage in a feather boa and one of her Arabian dressing gowns. I guess I wrote a lot about Tawny.

But, most of all, I liked to write about how the wind on the moor made me feel so free and about all the people who lived before me; who once slept in my small bedroom at Alder Farm. Where were they now? Were they happy? Or were they dead?

Sure, I could write a script that people could act out – I'd watched enough of Alexa's soap operas to last me a lifetime. I knew what I was doing. I loved a good story.

When Tawny and I were twelve – just after we first met – we had the *best* make-believe game. We played it for hours and hours on the weekends. One of us would pretend to be the little girl who murdered her sister all those years ago, just like in the village stories. Long Byrne kids are definitely weirder than most – but Tawny and I were off the charts.

We got Tawny's mum Sandra to sew us a pair of matching nightgowns, all fussy 1950s lace and frills. I'd be the younger sister and Tawny would be the elder and we'd lie in bed side by side. I'd pretend to wake up from a nightmare and Tawny would howl like a wolf – growling and snarling, her dark hair all ruffled up in the mane of an angry beast. I'd take my pillow and yell, "DIE DOG, DIE!" at her and push it over her face. She'd struggle and squirm perfectly and then fall still. She was so still that sometimes I'd worry I'd taken it too far.

Then she'd take a big gulp of air and we'd squeal and cackle. Always a brilliant actress. We'd scream with laughter for hours and hours until Sandra had to come in and tell us that if we didn't stop we'd wake the dead. Then we'd shriek with laughter some more. Tawny swore her mum tried to drug us with sleeping pills once.

It was hilarious.

By afternoon the weather had finally decided to make up its mind and I sat shivering as I ate my lunch in the hall, my Thermos flask between my knees. Everything outside was dark, and the fluorescent hall lights blinded me, as if they'd been snapped on during an air raid.

Tawny found me later on and shook her head. "God, Cate, get a grip! It's still summer!"

"Yeah, and minus two."

"Sum-mer," Tawny said defiantly, crossing her bare legs.

Rillington had cornered her too and had rolled her eyes when she said she'd be auditioning for Rose. Of *course* she was. But it seemed like everyone had the impression that Bryony would be playing her great-great ancient ancestor. Couldn't they see how ridiculous that was? Bryony Hollingworth wasn't your average Best Actress. I saw her more as an usher. One of the Witch Groupies would be on the Jane Hollingworth role like a rash.

I shuffled off to Psychology with my flask clasped to my chest. Miss Draycott had rustled up a green wool scarf from somewhere, so she looked like she had been tangled in garden string. I took my seat by the window. Bryony wasn't here yet, but I knew she'd wait until the last minute to arrive – unnecessary social interaction wasn't her style. My mind had been racing with ideas for the re-enactment script for the past few hours, but Tawny had been telling me about Kayleigh Whittard's latest bloke and I hadn't had time to make any of my notes. Apparently he was six foot four and had seven piercings — that you could *see*.

My pen quivered in my hand on the desk – from cold or excitement, I couldn't tell. It felt like my eyes were doing a ritual dance. But maybe I'd just had too much coffee that morning. I had a few minutes before the register got called. With a furtive look at the class over my shoulder, I turned to the back of my notebook and decided to make a start.

I began to write.

"OK, class!"

My eyes jerked up. I felt like I'd been pulled from deep sleep in the middle of the night. My brain scrabbled to hold on to the ragged dress of Jane Hollingworth. I checked the clock. 1.50 p.m. Bryony wasn't here yet.

"Turn to chapter three. Mr Bridge, take that ridiculous hat off indoors: we're not in the Arctic quite yet."

Miss Draycott started up and Matty pulled off the red hat with flaps that tied under his chin. His mates snorted and tried to snatch it off him. Their low laughter rumbled around the room and soon half the boys were chucking the hat around behind Draycott's back. But Bryony still wasn't here. I watched the door, the murky off-lilac of prison wards and old peoples' homes. Institutional mauve.

"Miss Aspey, is there something wrong with your attention span?"

How long had I been staring at that door? Sometimes it happened, time just blotted out, and all I could remember was a dull murmur of thought, nothing concrete. I felt the colour rising up my neck and I read the title of chapter three. 'Primal Instinct'.

Matty cleared his throat and we all craned round at him. "Sorry, Miss – she's just looking for her girlfriend." He grinned and my stomach collapsed.

The class looked at him in awe. The rugby player. Straight white teeth. Summer tan. The joker. My skin prickled as laughter shrieked from all the girls on the back row – blonde banshees with inch-thick foundation.

Miss Draycott tutted. "That's quite enough from you, Matthew. You'll be seeing me after class. Now, who has read this chapter already, or is this going to be a very long hour?"

I let my chin sink into the hollow of my collar bone, rereading the chapter heading over and over again until my eyes blurred. *Primal Instinct. Primal Instinct.* The class still snorted, tossing their heads like wild cattle as the afternoon stretched on.

Bryony didn't turn up all lesson. She didn't answer my phone calls or my messages so I spent my final free period in the library, writing up the script to keep my mind busy. It wasn't perfect, I knew that, but by the time 4 p.m. came around, I had already pressed 'send'. There – done. A rush job. My fate was in Rillington's hands now.

Tawny caught me as I was heading to our meeting point

by the bus stop just outside the school gate. She linked her arm through mine and my elbow felt small and pointy hitched up on her breast.

"Did you see Bryony today?"

"No," I snapped. "Why?"

"Neither did I. Do you think she's sick? Sometimes I think she looks as thin as you, Cate."

I looked straight ahead, fixing my eyes on the purple fuzzy keyring on someone's rucksack. Not this conversation again. "I'm not thin."

Tawny sighed. "Oh, come off it." She nudged me so I almost lost my balance. "Maybe it's the move from London. She's caught a Northern bug. Can't deal with drizzle." She gasped suddenly. "Or what if it's the curse!"

"Don't be a prat, Tawn."

She held up her hands and lifted my arm with them. "Just saying, woman." But there was no stopping her now. All the way to her house, Tawny flitted about the road, coming up with more elaborate guesses about Bryony's absence, and by the time we were past Maldew's I half-believed Bryony had been kidnapped by Witch Groupies and was being held for ransom up on the moor.

The sky was getting worse and drizzle kept sputtering through, but by the time I yanked up my hood it had stopped again. I thought of the farmyard turning into a pool of mud, pond-scum and chicken crap – Robyn was in for a treat tomorrow. My Chicks would be going berserk as the rain hammered the coop for the first time in months, and Pansy would be braying for her feed bag.

But I couldn't focus on home.

Where could she be right now? I thought of Bryony's hair flashing in the Slip, each strand turned dark and heavy with the storm. Out on the moor, her boots turning a deep peaty red. Why had she been out so early the other day? Surely she wasn't hiding from someone, too – not wanting to go home?

Outside Tawny's front door, I turned to her. My mouth flapped open for a second.

"Spit it out then," she said, fiddling for her keys.

"Look, Tawn. I'm actually not feeling too good."

Her head shot up. "You look fine."

"Yeah, but I don't feel it. I'm going to go home, I think."

She huffed, looking at the grey clouds above us. "I can't believe you're bailing on me. What am I meant to do with my evening now?" A little line appeared between her brows.

"Sorry. I'll see you tomorrow, OK?"

"Sure." She turned away. "Whatever."

Get well soon, Cate.

I left her and doubled back along the road. But when I got to Alder Farm, I carried on going.

They say there are things that can protect you from harm: a circle of salt, a band of green agate, the branch of a rowan tree. They all keep harmful magic away.

Maybe Long Byrne never got the message.

The Lunar Rites of Lancashire, Melanie Hargreaves

Chapter 7

When I'd first arrived in Long Byrne, I had this rabbit teddy I'd take everywhere. He had dark fur that curled so tightly all over his body that his eyes became pinpricks, lost in a tangle of matted hair. I liked to feel his velvety paws between my thumb and forefinger. I rubbed them so often that his palms became barren and dark with my finger grease and the pads had disintegrated like shredded petals. I knew Dad thought I was too old for teddies, and I was – I was twelve years old with bad period cramps and a love of black coffee. But Dad didn't mention it whenever I brought Raspy downstairs every morning or slung him in my rucksack to go out playing in the yard. I didn't know Tawny yet – she would have plucked Raspy out of my hands and chucked him over the fence. He'd been a present from Mum when I was eight: I'd spied him in a museum gift shop on the way in, and begged and begged her to buy him; whining my way around the museum, letting my shoes scuff on the dusty tiles, until she'd finally given in. I'd whinged so much that my throat had gone hoarse and Mum named the rabbit after my new husky voice.

It was raining one day in Long Byrne and I'd been crying

like I did a lot back then after Mum died. I remember because my face felt taut and tired, sort of ironed out and pressed firmly around my ears. I'd taken my rabbit up to the hayloft where I liked to sit by the round window and listen to the pigeons cooing frenziedly in the rafters, smelling the tang of shit as it dripped through the hay. I didn't play with the rabbit. I just placed him near me like a watcher, where he could make sure I didn't do anything stupid. Like jump.

I'd been staring out at the Hollingworth House, making up a story where I was kidnapped by hooded figures and taken to the Manor. The people there – all stunningly beautiful, the stuff of fairy tales – told me that I had been taken at birth and I was actually one of them, destined for something greater than mucking out manure.

I'd been getting to the end of my daydream when suddenly everything seemed to go deathly still. The pigeons stopped their soft murmurings and all I could hear was the wind over the moor, thudding the rain against the roof. The Hollingworth House looked infallibly dark; so opaque, like it had grown itself out of the world's oldest stone. I stared at it, feeling myself pulled towards it, like I was looking into a deep black hole. My breath was trapped on something that I couldn't swallow. I couldn't breathe at all. I wanted to call for help, scream for Dad in his office, which seemed impossibly far away, but I couldn't pull my eyes away from that house.

I clutched my throat, feeling tears stride down my face.

Then the air rushed back into the barn. The pigeons went crazy, bubbling out of their nests and boiling down on to the ground. I gasped, clutching at my clothes in bunches and making a sound I didn't know it was possible for a person to make.

When I reached for my rabbit, he was in tatters. His face hanging on by ragged sinew.

I hadn't thought about that afternoon in a long, long time.

The Hollingworth drive was already dark, shadowed by trees as tall as pylons. Blackbirds rustled around the roots, kicking up leaves and dead things to cover their tracks. I thought of all the people who'd been dared to come up close to the Hollingworth House, who'd come to swirl their fingers across the pits and pocks in the old sandstone walls before rushing back to the gate. As I walked closer to the house, my stomach flickered with static.

How would I act when she opened the door? Maybe I'd make myself into a Tawny, my lips winched taut all the way up to my cheekbones. I tried to rearrange my face into a normal expression, but my phone was dying so I had no way of checking my reflection.

Pull yourself together, Cate.

If I glanced back over my shoulder, I'd see the yellow glow of Alder Farm kitchen, sweet-looking and wholesome on its own little hillside. Alexa would be filing her nails to precise right angles and listening to Radio 2. In front of me, the Hollingworth House looked like it had been left out to soak all day – a dollhouse festering in the bath. Bryony's light was off and my nerve started to waver.

I knocked on the large double door, my hands sounding

feeble on the wood. The Hollingworth House was dense and silent.

Darkness was falling around me and I couldn't help feeling let down, like someone had told me the twist to a film while I was queuing to buy a ticket.

I knocked again. What did I want? To sneak inside? Catching myself, I realised that all I really wanted was to be through that door. All I wanted was to see that she was OK.

All I wanted was to be near to her.

I cast a hard look around the drive and crept to the nearest window, to the left of the front door. A high-ceilinged living room I hadn't seen before sprawled out before my eyes, lit by a reading lamp on a lace-covered coffee table. A fireplace contained the embers of this afternoon's fire, winking and glittering under a small pile of logs. The mantelpiece was cluttered with photographs. If I squinted I could just see a photo of a tiny blonde girl sitting on a porch swing, her hands folded patiently in her lap. There was a tortoiseshell cat on her lap. She was smiling.

Then I jumped back. My cheeks suddenly numb.

The Evil Eye on the chimney-piece was glaring back at me. I'd completely forgotten about it.

The eye had a sly, lazy look to it.

Is that what I'd felt watching me? I shuddered.

I grabbed my bag tighter to me. I shouldn't have come here tonight. I clasped my throat, the memory of thick straw-dust in the hayloft was suddenly all around me. I wanted to be anywhere but here.

I had to get away from the Hollingworth House. Fast.

I spun around but there was someone coming towards me up the drive. I swallowed, my throat still tight and my breath ragged. No one could see me like this. I had to get off the drive. I threw myself into a copse of bushes beside the house.

I could feel the house behind me, looming over the driveway like it wanted to oust me from my hiding spot. I could almost feel the Evil Eye watching me with its vacant stare through the mullioned windows.

Stillness gripped me as the footsteps grew louder. Was that two people on the drive?

I squinted in the half-light through the moving shadows.

No, just one. The person in front of me swung her hips almost violently in the dim light and I knew instantly who it was. Tawny's frame came into view.

Not now, I hissed to myself.

Why wasn't I relieved to see her? Had she come to rescue me? Was she following me? Or was she here for something else?

Panic filled the pit of my stomach, heavy like falling sand. I realised I was shaking. *Deep breaths. Long deep breaths,* I told myself. The air caught in my throat and made me blurt out a cough. Tawny froze.

"Hello?" she called, narrowing her cat-like eyes.

I covered my mouth in case another cough came, rising into the air like a white signal.

"I know you're there," she said, menacingly, flicking her feline eyes through the trees. I was almost convinced she could see me, my hands stark white on a tree trunk. She'd always been a good actress.

A beat passed. She did another scan of the drive then

straightened herself up, satisfied. She carried on up the drive, her short velvet skirt swaying in time with her.

I didn't move, but inside my guts were squirming. I felt so ashamed. Why didn't I want her to see me? I tried to push down the strange feeling bubbling up inside me. She shouldn't be here; this was not how things were supposed to go. Although I had left her on the way home . . .

I was meant to be the one seeing Bryony tonight.

Tawny rapped on the front door, adding a few extra knocks for luck like she was entering a secret clubhouse. Seconds passed.

The door opened.

I craned my head forward, trying not to breathe. Who was on the other side of the door? I couldn't see their face, just the golden glow of light on Tawny's skin. Tawny spoke for a minute in a hushed voice then stepped inside.

I stayed where I was for exactly thirty seconds but I couldn't stop myself any longer. My anger was forcing me to move.

My boots didn't betray me as I sneaked back to the living room window where the lamplight was still spilling onto the wet grass, turning it into oily tendrils.

They weren't in there. My heart reverberated in my throat, and my toes clawed at the inside of my boots as I waited. Then I squinted and made out movement just off the room in the hall. Tawny's long dark hair swung into view in the doorway. She was smiling and chattering. Typical Tawny. Her curved shadow rippled across the chintzy furniture. I flicked my eyes over the settee with its shiny cover. The old-person's fringed lamp. The photographs on the mantelpiece. The Evil Eye.

I snagged my eyes away from it. I could see Tawny's lips babbling through the glass. But then she faltered, her face falling like when she messed up the words to her favourite *West Side Story* song. My breath fogged the glass in front of me. Why was she here? Did she think I was seeing Bryony without her and had come to check? Suddenly I realised that Tawny was being shown out. She was going to see me – crouched and loitering outside the old witch house.

Like a complete weirdo.

My insides dropped. I had to go. *Now*.

I hurled myself towards the trees faster than I'd ever moved before, not caring what obstacles hit my body, my head spinning as adrenaline pulsed to my temples.

The door clicked open behind me and I flew face-first behind an ornate plant pot. My hands skidded on mud.

"I'm sure it's nothing," said Tawny, but I couldn't see her from my position. "Must be my imagination. See you!"

I heard her step on the path, slower and more hesitant than before. The heels of her battered leather boots with the silver toe-caps clicked away and I closed my eyes until I could tell she was getting further and further from my hiding spot. My feet started to get numb.

She hadn't seen me. But why would she have looked?

Pushing my body into a stooped run, I didn't look back, although I was sure eyes prickled along the back of my neck.

Alder Farm came into view around the hedgerows and I had never felt such a rush of relief to see my tiny cottage with its battered front door and pepper-pot chimney. My dirty hands were shaking as I steadied myself along the farm fence in the dying light. Inside, a nice hot shower had my name on it; big deep gulps of wet air to wash tonight away. I'd sit down and write and forget about everything that had just happened. I'd write long, delicate words that all clipped together neatly and felt good to say in my mouth. I'd curl my toes around the metal bedposts and try to figure out the script, but –

Someone was sitting outside on the doorstep.

It would start out as just a feeling. An inkling, threading its way through the seams of your mind. The first symptom of a witch's curse.

After that it was only a matter of time.

People in Long Byrne said they felt something dark and almost liquid searching through their brains: the fingers of witches probing their dreams at night.

They said that Rose and Jane left no pillow unturned. They said that Long Byrne was full of the curse."

In Search of the Long Byrne Witches, P.J. Hebden

Chapter 8

"Robyn?"

Her small frame jerked as she heard my voice. Her eyes took a minute to focus and shrink back to normal size. The oversized hunting jacket she wore around the farm threatened to engulf her.

"What are you doing out here?" I said, my voice still jittery. "It's getting cold. Did Alexa lock the barn again? I keep telling her not to do that."

She shook her head. "No, it's fine. I've milked 'em all. It's in the churn for the guys in the morning." She kept on shaking her head until I thought she was going to self-destruct.

"Hey, hey, are you OK?" I tried to channel Tawny, reaching out to cradle her elbow in my hand.

"Mm-hm."

"Come inside, you look exhausted."

"It's nothing."

"Rob, you look *more* exhausted than usual."

She didn't say anything.

I bit my thumbnail. "Come on, let's go inside."

The coast was clear in the kitchen. I could hear Dad pottering around, bumping into plants in his study as he read essays and walked at the same time. Typical.

Rooting around behind the bread bin, I came out with a packet of bourbons and a handful of Viennese Whirls. Robyn nodded vigorously when I waved the bourbons at her then immediately fell back into her trance. I'd never seen her looking so put out. There was a strip of mud running down her cheek that she hadn't bothered to scrub off and her ponytail was askew. Her fingers fumbled in her lap like she was holding something slippery.

I attempted to lighten the mood and pretended to wipe down the counter top. "What's troublin' ya, missy?" But Robyn had probably been too busy with Jane Austen or Baudelaire to watch old Westerns. Rillington kept her well-stocked up on the classics.

I watched her take a nibble of her biscuit and set it down on the tablecloth. I couldn't remember the last time I'd had a biscuit; nothing sugary for years, except a mug of steaming cocoa. It had been our first night in the house, just Dad and me. The new farmers. We'd lit a fire in the grate and after a few minutes the room started to glow and shudder in the light. It was around Christmas and I was wearing brand new pyjamas with tartan Scottie dogs on them. Dad came in with two frothy mugs of chocolate. He'd got quite beardy by then; I guess neither of us had really been taking care of ourselves after what happened to Mum.

"Cheers m'dear," he had said, lowering himself onto a cushion on the floor next to me. "What do you think?" He'd looked around the room, seeing through the shoddy wallpaper that had been left to peel by the last tenants.

"I like it," I'd said.

"It needs a bit of sprucing up, I know. Will you give me a hand?"

"'Course. Do you know what I'm going to do first? Give you a shave!"

"Are you now?" he laughed and set down his chocolate. "Well, we'll see about that. I suppose it has got a little long."

"A lot long."

"Cheeky madam," he winked and clinked our mugs together.

The next morning he'd shaved off the fuzzy dark beard that had given him a crazy-old-man vibe and he looked a bit more like my Dad again. That was so long ago now.

Robyn looked small at the table. When she spoke, she spoke to the biscuit in front of her. "Cate, do you ever get the feeling something's not right?"

I frowned. "Is something going on at home?" I thought of Tawny chipping at Bryony's door with her white knuckles not half an hour ago.

She shook her head. "I mean, do you ever have a *feeling*?" She was looking at me from under her lashes.

"Rob?"

She looked so fragile. I wondered who she had to talk to. I didn't see her hanging around with many other girls at school. OK, I could say the same about Tawny, but Tawny could have the pick of anyone she wanted. Robyn was gentler than her sister; preferred cows to people.

I cleared my throat. "Yeah, sometimes I have a feeling," I nodded. "Sometimes the hair stands up on my arms in the middle of summer and I don't know why." I'd had that feeling when Mum disappeared. "Is that the sort of stuff you mean?" I added.

Robyn's eyes were back on her biscuit. She nodded slowly.

"I've always felt like that when I look at the Hollingworth House. Spooky, isn't it?" I let my mouth drag up into a half smile to hide the residual fear that still clung to my veins from my visit to the house. But Robyn's head snapped up.

"You feel it too?"

"Well," I said, measuredly, taking in her wide eyes. "It's a creepy old house."

She shook her head. "It's more than that."

The kitchen clock ticked the seconds away. I chose my words carefully. There was something in her voice that made me hold my breath.

"How long have you felt like that?" I asked, my knees not holding me up as strongly as they had a few minutes ago.

She yanked at her ponytail. What did Robyn have to be anxious about? "It's always given me the creeps, but a week. Maybe more." I felt a shudder creeping up my arms.

"That's about the time Bryony's been living there."

She nodded slowly to herself. "I guess."

I tried to shake off my unease, pretending the hollows under Robyn's eyes were just the effect of the kitchen strip light and not turbulent, sleepless nights. "Have you seen something there?"

She shrugged. "I don't know."

I thought about telling her how the house really made me feel. The time in the barn when I was just a kid. The way it loomed up at me every morning over the hill as if it were about to tell me my fate. The Evil Eye on the mantelpiece. I thought about saying where I'd just returned from. How would she take the news?

But Robyn was so small. She didn't need to hear that right now. "It's a big old creepy place, yeah, I know . . . but it's no spookier than the weird P.E. block on the other side of the field. It's just old."

She broke the biscuit in two so dark crumbs fell on the white cloth like tiny footprints in snow. "I know."

"You're thirteen—"

"I *know*," Robyn said, flushing and staring harder at the table, attempting to bore holes in the tablecloth.

"Then . . .? Rob, what would you like me to do?"

"I didn't want to be alone tonight," she whispered.

I worried my lip with my upper teeth. "What about your mum? She's usually home from town by now isn't she?"

"She's downstairs at Shilcock's."

"And Tawny isn't home either . . ." I said, without thinking.

Robyn frowned. "How do you know that?"

"A guess. She's usually messaging me all night if she's at home." I hesitated, fumbling for words. "There's always Ginger?"

She didn't say anything. Chocolate disintegrated slowly between her fingers. This was Robyn. Robyn who could pluck a hen clean and shift cow shit twice her weight – probably at the same time if she put her mind to it. I crouched down next to her. My knees clicked loudly.

"All those legends and stuff, they're just stories, Robyn.

Don't listen to what they're saying at school – I've heard them whispering all those ridiculous ghost stories." How much did I believe what was coming out of my mouth? "It's all a story: Rillington's even asked me to write the script – like a proper story."

"That's cool," she muttered. I saw her propping up the corners of her mouth in her best imitation Tawny Grin.

"Thanks. But, Rob, it's just a story made up to scare stupid people, and you're not stupid. You know that, yeah?"

"I know." She nodded slowly.

"Bryony's not some kind of witch."

Her eyes suddenly snapped up, wide and glaring. "How do you know?"

I jerked away. I was taken aback by the anger I saw there.

"Robyn . . . seriously, there's no need to worry about anything."

Her voice had a stony grate to it I'd never heard before. "Why don't you ask her what she really is? Hm?"

"Robyn?"

Her eyes flared wide. "I've seen her out there at night."

A chill ran down my spine. I remembered Bryony returning from the Witches' Moor early in the morning and the strange feeling it had left in my stomach. What had she been doing out there just after sunrise?

"Rob, what—"

She stood up sharply so I jumped. "I'd better go," she said, her eyes trailing away from mine. "Don't tell Tawny I was here."

"Hey—"

"I just came to warn you. About her."

"Wait, Robyn!" I called after her, but she was already gone, her skinny feet flying down the hall, out the door and along the dirt track.

Outside, the yard was pitch black. I went back in and stared at the empty kitchen chair before sweeping all the biscuit crumbs into the bin.

I couldn't sleep. Not after that. So, I did what I always did. I logged on to study, even though my mind wasn't exactly ready for Carl Jung.

An email popped up. Rillington. It was a direct reply to the email I'd sent earlier. Had she actually read the script already? Bile squirmed up my oesophagus.

Dear Cate,

Thanks for sending over this first draft. I think it's really taking shape!

Some quick feedback from me: I really like the 'spooky' elements you've included and the pacing of the plot – you've nailed it. If there could be a few more scary moments, that would be good too.

I think it would be great if you could focus on the friendship between the two girls more. It will help people root for them. At the moment, they both seem a bit lost but I know you can turn that around. Overall, I think you're doing excellently. I look forward to seeing what you come up with. How about you get it over to me by the end of next week?

A shit sandwich. Great. Basically, I'd have to look at the whole thing again. My stomach sank. Did Rillington not realise I had tests to study for?

Downstairs, the kettle seemed to take for ever to boil. I needed coffee like I needed sweet, sweet oxygen right now.

"Couldn't sleep either?"

I jumped as Dad appeared in the door. "Jesus."

"Sorry," he muttered and stood behind me in line for the kettle. "What's the matter?" he asked, seeing my face.

I sighed. "Just had a stupid email from Rillington."

"*Miss* Rillington."

"She didn't like the draft of my play."

Dad's shoulders drew back, forcing him to attention. Of course, he'd forgotten I was writing it. "Anyway," I said, "it's no big deal. I just didn't need it today."

He was thoughtful for a moment while I made a coffee for me and a herbal tea for him. "You know, when your mum used to receive rejection letters from publishers, do you know what made her feel better?"

"What?" I blew into my coffee, making a black hole in its surface.

"Ice cream. But also, writing the publisher into a story and making them the bad guy or die a really gruesome death."

"No," I grinned.

"I'm serious."

"That's ridiculous."

"I never said she was a sensible woman." He shrugged, supressing a laugh behind his mug. "Maybe give it a go."

I looked into my coffee. I'm not sure Rillington would make a natural sixteen-year-old witch in my next draft. "It's just . . . I don't know. I wanted to do this justice. I've never had a chance like this before."

"Hm," Dad mused. "When do you need it finished by?"

"End of next week."

"OK, well, that's plenty of time. You just need to get into the minds of these witches, right? They were just young girls, really. You're one of those."

"A witch?"

"A *young girl*."

"Why do I feel about one hundred and two then?"

Dad put down his tea on the counter and looked me directly in the eye. "Caitlin Aspey, you're a wonderful writer. Your mum would tell you to go for a walk, stroke the cows and figure those girls out. She'd also tell you to lay off the coffee."

I frowned. "She absolutely would not."

"Maybe not," he agreed. "But she would tell you to go back to bed. Off you go, love."

I nodded and left the room. I would get back in bed, but Dad hadn't said anything about going to sleep.

By the time I looked up from the script, pale strips of dawn light bled under the curtains and my eyes were a flickering film strip of witchcraft.

***

"OK, but you have to watch, yeah?"

"Yes, Tawny. We won't take our eyes off you," I said, biting the inside of my cheek to suppress a laugh.

We were outside the P.E. block in the pale September light. Tawny was scrolling through a playlist on her phone with Bryony and me in the perfect viewing position.

"I don't know if Miss Rillington was looking for a dance routine," muttered Bryony to me out the corner of her mouth.

I closed my eyes, gently mocking, "Just let her do her thing. She's choreographed it especially."

Bryony grinned and I flushed.

Bryony had been at our lunch table every day. Tawny and I had scooched over to make space for the new object of our attentions, and she quickly became something I didn't know how to function without. Her ethereal presence made me feel like I'd been welcomed into a celebrity's fabled inner circle. Maybe somewhere in my mind she'd always been there, just waiting for the right moment to position herself next to us like a mannequin in a store.

I hadn't said anything to either of them about the night outside the house; I didn't want to make anything weird – I didn't want Bryony to stop accidentally grazing my leg with hers when she got up for class. I liked her calmness and the way everything she did was assessed and weighed up in her mind before she acted it out. Every day she ate tuna salad from the canteen bar and dabbed her lips neatly with a napkin. Tawny used the back of her hand. I didn't eat.

People stopped to look at us, actually staring with open interest. I was used to Tawny swiping away any unwanted attention for the both of us with a wave of her magician's arm. She attracted guys like flies and swatted them away just as easily. I just kept my head down. But the girls stopped to stare at us too, even the teachers, and although I tried to avoid their glances, for some reason I relished it. It was like we were something new and glamorous trooping in each day – we were the quivering excitement of a firework display, or the promise of record exam results. People circled us, wanting to know more.

As we waited for Tawny to find her song, Bryony whispered, "How's it going with the script?"

In all honesty, I was spending every available second on it but I was nervous. I had tried to talk about it with Tawny but she said, "Jesus, Cate! You really are the heir to Crackpot's throne."

"OK . . ." I told Bryony.

"OK?" She tilted her head.

"I don't know," I said. "There's something missing and I can't put my finger on it. I want to really get into the world these two girls would have lived in but . . . I don't get it. What could have happened that led them to fight on the moor that day? What made them angry enough to curse each other?"

All the books said that Rose Ackroyd and Jane Hollingworth were best friends. They did everything together. They swiped cakes from the marketplace and stuffed them into each other's mouths on the way home, squealing with laughter. They hid behind trees, ready to jump out at people. They peeled apple skins together and threw them over their shoulder at midnight to see the first initial of their true loves.

They would have done anything to stay best friends for ever.

Sometimes in the dark, I put my hand very carefully on the soft curve of Tawny's hip. I played a game with myself, seeing how long I could keep it there before she turned over or mumbled in her sleep. I wondered if she did the same to me. Except I didn't have a hip to hold onto. I was sixteen and my body still looked like a boy's – I definitely hadn't been blessed by the boob fairy yet and my hair was shortish and limp, never growing more than a sliver. Maybe by putting my hand there on her hip I was willing some of that swaying waist and D-cup bra to find itself on me. But I hadn't had a period since I was fourteen and I used to have to sit down every thirty seconds in P.E. because I got so dizzy. They tell you that's what happens when you stop eating. Hey, turns out it's true.

Tawny didn't say much about it any more. She didn't offer me a bite of her jam sandwich or the second finger of her Twix. She'd sit with me in the nurse's office at break while I had to drink the vile sugary tea they gave me, or eat the pieces of chocolate they'd break off into a bowl so they could try and pump me full of glucose. She'd come to the hospital that one time when I'd fainted and smacked my head on the farm gate. Tawny got out her phone and we'd listened to Eighties power ballads full blast and wrapped each other in bandages and taken stupid photos. Sometimes while we waited for a nurse, she'd even hold my hand.

That's what best friends did. Didn't they?

Bryony looked contemplative. "Hmm. I mean, I don't know the story as well as you do – people in my family try to avoid it – but maybe something threatened their friendship. Jane's dad maybe. A boy? And it made them scared. Maybe they thought they'd lose one another. People do strange things when they're scared."

"It sounds like such a strong reaction though."

"Not when people really care about each other," she said, lightly. Tawny had started her dance to an upbeat pop song that had topped the charts last year and, to be fair, she looked fantastic. I wasn't so sure Miss Rillington was going to approve of her gyrations though.

"What if . . ." I started.

"What if what?"

"What if they really did care about each other? What if they cared about each other in a more-than-friends way?"

Bryony's eyebrows rose. "I suppose that's one way of explaining it. It would make sense. Lovers to enemies."

Lovers to enemies.

Yes, it made sense now.

I bit my lip. What had happened on each of those evenings holed up in the draughty Hollingworth House, sewing by cheap candles made from pig fat? All those hours alone, all that unchaperoned time out on the moors between the heather.

Something in my head clicked. I knew exactly what to write.

Rose and Jane had fallen in love. And something had come between them.

"If you want anyone to look over it," Bryony shrugged slightly and smiled again. I suddenly felt light-head.

"I knew you wouldn't be watching!" came Tawny's furious interjection. "Terrible, both of you. Terrible friends!"

A little note of panic quavered in my chest. "We were watching!"

"Sure. Thanks." Tawny huffed.

"You were amazing!" I said quickly, sensing a strop coming on. "You're guaranteed to get the part. Literally guaranteed."

Her eyes flashed but I was saved by a bunch of Year Elevens coming around the corner.

"Oh, look," the biggest one said. "Here she is – the High Witch." He spat on the floor about two feet away from Bryony's shoe. I tensed. "Don't get too close, she'll dissect your balls with voodoo."

The group laughed at this strange joke. Out of the corner of my eye, I could see that Tawny looked enraged but the red I saw was crimson.

"Have you even heard yourself?" I said, my voice high and reedy. "You're pathetic. Leave us alone or I'll dissect you myself."

"Oooooooooh!" they cooed in unison and I immediately regretted it, but I didn't need to retaliate as Tawny was already in their faces.

"Get away from us, you dirty little scrotes. Do you think anyone would want to touch you and your disgusting little bodies? Go and get a grip and stay as far away from us as possible. Got it?"

The boys took more notice of Tawny, and all I could do

was glare. They put up their hands in an 'OK, OK' gesture and made to saunter off.

"Steady on, ladies. Don't let your tampons fall out," one of them offered feebly as they turned the corner.

"Are you all right?" Tawny asked, flying to Bryony's side as soon as they were out of sight.

Bryony stood stock still. "Bryony?" I asked.

Her hand flew to her temple. "Maybe it was a mistake coming here. I'm sick of being thought of as a freak. You know at my last school I was Head Girl? I played hockey for the district. I was on track for top grades. And now, I'm a laughing stock."

"No, you're not," I insisted. "We are just surrounded by idiots. You're incredible." The last part came out in a whisper but she smiled softly.

Tawny swept Bryony into a big hug and said, "Look, you've got us, no matter what. Just ignore them, or they will feel my wrath, yeah?"

"OK," she smiled bigger and brighter but there was still a sadness behind her eyes. "Look, I'll see you both tomorrow."

Panic fluttered in my chest. "Oh, you're not coming to Psych?"

She shook her head. "I think I'm just going to go."

I wondered if my face looked as crestfallen as I felt. But then my mind flipped back to seeing her down the Slip at dawn. Would she go there again to clear her head?

"I've seen her out there at night," Robyn had said. I felt like I had so many questions for Bryony but I squashed them down. My head was so full of the witches right now, the characters in my script. I shouldn't be entertaining Robyn's sleep-deprived thoughts. Should I? Instead, I said:

"Oh. Well, see you."

"What are you up to this evening?" Tawny asked. I felt my heart skip a beat. Maybe Bryony would invite us over?

But then my chest hollowed out again when she said, "I'm helping Auntie with a project."

"No problem," smiled Tawny, shaking it off, her dance recital long forgotten. "I'd better be going too. Textiles needs me!" She squeezed Bryony's arm. "You'll be fine," she said and left without a backwards glance at me. Bryony and I were left by the P.E. block all alone.

"What about you, Cate?" she smiled, softly. "What are you doing tonight?"

"Oh." *I wish I was spending it with you.* "I'm probably just hanging round with Daddy dearest, as I'm such a doting daughter." I rolled my eyes.

"Is your dad meeting you from school?"

I smirked. "I was being sarcastic. And Dad probably doesn't even know I left the house this morning."

She smiled and shrugged. "Oh, right. Your mum?"

"Oh. Um. She's dead."

I heard the sharp intake of her breath.

I shook my head and held up my hands. "It's OK, don't be sorry. It was a while ago. Nearly five years ago. This Halloween actually. Morbid on so many levels."

"Cate . . ."

I shrugged. "I should really get going: lots to catch up on."

Bryony nibbled her lip, twitching the bracelet at her wrist between two fingers. "If you ever need to talk . . ."

I forced a grin. "Don't worry, I won't be bashing down your door. I've had time to get over it."

She nodded, reassuring herself, and said goodbye. I watched her leave, clutching a book close to her chest. Her long hair swung gently behind her in a fine wave. I'd still not asked her about the Slip or the night in the driveway. Wouldn't that be weird though? Both times I'd been hiding in a tree like Robin freaking Hood. But she'd been out in the Slip so early. . .

I opened my mouth to call her back, questions looping around the end of my tongue. I'd ask her about Hollingworth House, about the moor, about Robyn's strange words . . . But it felt as if my words were tied inside my throat, trapped there as if by a magic spell.

I wouldn't ask. I realised I didn't want things to change. I wanted it to stay Tawny, Bryony and me.

I went to class when she was completely out of sight.

The witches were creative.

When there was no rain, they danced – pushing and contorting their bodies into the shapes of heavy water and clouds. When there was a cold snap, they lit bonfires, sent up smoke into the skies – let the elements sniff out their wishes and send them back some fiery bursts of sun.

When the spirits gave them good crops, a beautiful sunset, a healthy child, they said thank you. Praise to the Otherworld! Here, have my flowers, have my fine jewels! A gift, a present! Here, take my hen's head. Drink her blood. It tastes like heaven.

Take it, take it all. Every last drop.

In Search of the Long Byrne Witches, P.J. Hebden

Chapter 9

That night, September really flickered its way into autumn. I felt the chill seeping under my bedroom door like bloodless fingers. I wished I'd stayed at Tawny's, where Sandra made Mr Shilcock blast the central heating all the way up to the top floor as soon as the leaves started to shudder.

But I felt unsettled. I wanted to be on my own tonight.

I'd stayed up late, writing – the sudden cold reminded me how close Halloween actually was. If there was going to be a play, there needed to be a finished script and I couldn't stop thinking about Rillington's email. In retrospect, maybe it hadn't been so harsh but I hadn't slept properly in days.

I mean, the story of these women being killed was horrible enough but the people of Long Byrne seemed to want more 'scariness'. With a flash, I thought of the Evil Eye carved into the chimney breast of Bryony's house; its stoic gaze and the shiver that had run down my spine when I had last seen it. The eerie feeling came over me again, making my stomach clench. The Eye had been used for centuries as a way of warding off evil. Perhaps even by people of Long Byrne when they saw the witches with red sparks flying from their fingers out on the moor.

I thought about what Bryony and I had said about the witches, about their friendship being something more . . .

I began to write.

[ENTER a dungeon with torches on the walls. JANE lies unconscious downstage]

ROSE: Unhand me!

GUARD: If you say so.

[GUARD throws ROSE to the floor. ROSE cries out in pain]

GUARD: What? Satan's lap not catch you?

ROSE: You're disgusting.

[JANE starts to mutter softly under her breath. GUARD laughs as ROSE notices JANE]

ROSE: Jane! Jane. Are you all right? Jane?

GUARD: Hold up there, what's she doing? Make her stop.

[JANE continues to mutter curses]

ROSE: Jane, don't. You'll only make more trouble. Please, stop.

GUARD: You make her stay back. Don't let her near me.

ROSE: Jane, stop!

GUARD: God, save us!

ROSE: JANE, NO!

GUARD: I call upon the Evil Eye. May it cast its gaze upon you, witch, and strike you down!

[JANE gags then falls motionless]

ROSE: Jane?

GUARD: She dead?

ROSE: JANE!

By the time I finished writing, the hawthorns outside my window were making shadows with the moonlight across my bed. Was the script going to be enough? With a sigh, I got up from my desk and stretched tall enough to crack my back.

I tried to spend as little time as possible in my room – the walls were still bare from when we'd first moved in. If it weren't for Tawny, I'd still be pretending that this whole thing was just a daytrip and I was actually going home really soon to the place where we had a red front door with a shining silver knocker, a fuzzy blanket on the back of every chair and a Wendy house at the end of the little garden. I even had a bag permanently packed – woolly socks, teen magazine, coffee sachets – the bare essentials, just in case Dad decided he'd had enough of muck-spreading and we had to get up and go. I was very good at pretending. I wondered which parent I got that from.

Alexa bought me picture frames, a lilac alarm clock, and a metal rack to hold my three pairs of shoes: farm boots, a pair of sandals and the tan school brogues Tawny had forced me to buy.

"What about a few more cushions?" Alexa had asked, and I'd looked at her in disgust but eight purple pillows appeared on my bed the next day.

"I just want you to feel at home," Alexa had said.

"Can't you see that I don't want them? Send them back!"

"I can't, love. They're out of their wrappers now."

I'd shoved them under the bed when she went downstairs, muttering, "Mum wouldn't have done this."

Through my thin curtains, a glaze of moonlight forced its way in and glinted on the covers. I wiggled my toes under the duvet, not feeling sleepy at all. I grabbed the torch I used as a bedside lamp, stuffed myself into my boots and headed out into the night.

September smelled like wet leaves. The metallic tang of the milk churns found its way to me across the yard from the barn where Pansy, Vera and Myrtle were tucked in amongst the hay bales. In the field, a skulk of foxes squawked but the stillness of the black air meant I couldn't tell how far away they were.

I gulped the night in. It was weird, in the years I'd known her, Tawny and I had never really been out at night. Yeah, we'd snuck out once or twice to see how far we could get before Sandra went ballistic, but Tawny was not a creature of the darkness. In sunlight she was something unforgettable, twirling so her skirt pooled out around her in the heather, swigging the neck of a Pimm's bottle in the midday heat.

I thought about going over there, curling up in her soft bed with all those cushions and red silk and bright candles, but the five-minute walk felt like a marathon.

Maybe she wasn't who I wanted to see.

Over the fields, the light was off in Bryony's bedroom. The curtains were still open. I wondered if she was asleep yet, or maybe she was shuffling through the coloured envelopes sent by her friends, like playing cards. Or maybe she was out. Out by the Slip.

The moor was a rolling sheet of darkness.

Was she out there right now? Where had she gone while I was taking Psychology notes?

I stared for a while and hitched myself up onto the rough fence. It tried to pierce my fingertips but mine were sturdy like a guitarist's from years of haymaking. I took a deep breath so the air stung my throat.

I felt light, airy: witchy.

I squinted past the Hollingworth House to where the hills met the star-pricked sky. I could see a small yellow-gold light on the hillside. A campfire? A torch? I craned my neck forward as if the extra three inches would make a difference to my sight. It seemed to be moving, jostling, like it was being carried.

I blinked hard and, when I looked again, the light was gone.

It was about then that I realised something was wrong.

The Chicks were making short sharp startled noises. I knew the sound well. A cat treading lightly on the henhouse roof. A buzzard circling way up above. I squinted through the black but couldn't see the predator. Peering around the yard I swept the torch back and forth in a triangular slice of light. Maybe they thought I was a wolf.

"Girlies, it's only me. Shh, sh, sh." I made my usual morning sounds that made them sit back obediently on their eggs. But still their noises came sharp and fast. I had the horrible sense I was being watched.

And then I heard the sound I was dreading. My heart froze.

A dull clunk.

Once.

Twice.

Something was inside the coop with them.

I wasn't about to put any more of my Chicks out of their misery. Moving silently, I went to the barn and unhooked a pitchfork. I gripped it hard, like shoving my keys between my fingers when I walked home in the dark in case someone jumped me.

A pitchfork could poke out more than someone's eye.

I pressed my heels down deeply. The cement absorbed my steps. I crept to the coop. I reached out and I yanked open the door.

Something inside screamed. I screamed back.

"Bloody hell!"

"Put it down!" she shrieked.

"Robyn! What the fuck?"

"Cate, put it down!"

I lowered my weapon. "I – sorry. You scared the crap out of me."

Robyn was curled with her knees drawn up close under the nesting shelf. Her cheeks looked gaunt in the torchlight.

"I'm sorry, I'm sorry . . ." she whispered, and then she started breathing fast, way too fast. Oh god, what did you do when someone hyperventilated? *I* was usually that person! What would Tawny do?

"Here, here, cup your hands around your mouth – you've got to breathe in carbon dioxide, OK? Robyn?"

She nodded and did as I said, doming her fingers and pushing the skin around her mouth so it was airtight. I rubbed her back and pushed her head down between her knees. After a minute or so, her breathing seemed to return to normal. The hens stared scornfully at her as if she was a poor relation who'd just stormed the ballroom.

"Feeling better?"

She nodded, taking a calmer breath.

I put my head down close to hers. "Robyn, something's really not right here, is it?"

She shook her head and I rubbed her back. I could feel every single vertebra through her woolly jumper.

Her voice quaked. "I have a bad feeling."

"Rob . . ."

"I – I just wanted to sleep somewhere safe. The hens help . . ." she trailed off. It scared me how small her voice sounded. "Mum's always out, I don't know where she goes, and Tawny thinks I'm going to mess up her room. No one knows I'm here, so I'm safe. No one can get me here."

I felt my eyes fill up with tears as I asked, "Who's going to get you, Robyn?"

She looked at me pleadingly and I dropped it. Instead I took her elbow in the Tawny Grip. "You should stay here tonight. With me. You're not in the right mind to go back home tonight."

"I don't know, Cate."

"What are you afraid of?"

She stared at me.

"Please, just tell me," I didn't like the note in my begging voice.

"I . . ." she started.

Just then, a light flared on in Bryony's room at the top of the Hollingworth House. Robyn jumped and her eyes flashed to it as if she was a moth in a cruel science experiment. I took a step back. I could have sworn Robyn's eyes turned silver when they turned toward the house. I couldn't see Bryony at the window but Robyn looked like she could see through the veil of two worlds.

"Rob?" I squeezed her arm tighter as if to dislodge her reply. Her eyes were still and glassy as a frog's as she stared back at me. It sent a shiver through me.

"I'm scared, Cate. Something's not right in this place. I've got an awful feeling and those terrible witches are all I can dream about. And – and . . . you're the only friend I have."

Even though Robyn looked like she'd seen a ghost, I couldn't help the flush of pride in my cheeks.

"Rob, I—"

"Don't you see?" Robyn lunged forward and grabbed my wrist. Her hand felt like a baby bird. "She's trying to get you and Tawny to join her. She told me so herself."

I looked long and hard at her. Her crazed eyes. Her dark-blue veins. What was happening to the little girl who liked to stroke cows and tend to the hens? Perhaps she really needed help.

"Come on, Rob," I kept my voice soft and low. "Let's get you a hot chocolate. Alexa keeps a jar behind the fridge."

I pulled Robyn to her feet and let her lean on my shoulder as we squeezed out of the hen coop. She came willingly, crumpled. Her footsteps sounded very small on the concrete yard as we walked to the back door. But someone was there to meet us.

"What on earth is going on out here?"

I had to let my eyes readjust for a second. I hadn't seen him out in the yard for nearly three years. He still had a work shirt on, rolled up at the sleeves but with the top button done up and glasses pushed up onto his forehead wrinkles.

"It's nothing, Dad. Go back inside."

"Robyn, is that you? Are you OK?"

She nodded.

"She's going to stay here tonight, Dad."

I watched her duck her head, embarrassed, and I gripped her elbow tighter. She'd appreciate it in the morning. At least she wouldn't be covered in chicken crap.

He made a fuss, filling a hot water bottle to wrap in a towel and rooting out a tin of fruit cake a student had sent him. "You're a working lass. We need to keep your strength up." For once I didn't feel the urge to sit in the corner and be quiet like I did when he was typing or had his professor pals over for drinks. He felt like Dad tonight. Maybe just a little bit, anyway.

Once we'd shooed him off back into the study, I let Robyn pick a side of the bed. She got in first and scooted over so that she was closest to the wall, pressing against it like she was trying to find a secret passageway there.

"You feeling any better?"

She nodded. "A bit."

"Has sleeping still been rubbish?"

"No surprise there."

"You know what would help?"

"What?" She sounded cautious.

"Pillow fight!"

I swiped a purple cushion from under my bed and whacked her over the head. She squealed and grabbed the other. Her hit was a lot harder than mine. We both pummelled each other with cushions, shrieking with laughter until we could barely breathe.

"Girls?" Dad's warning sounded.

"We're fine! We're fine!" we chorused and snorted into our fingers. I had a stitch. "C'mon," I said. "Let's at least try and sleep."

She looked at me, flushed, in the half-dark.

"Can you lock the window, Cate?"

"It is locked."

"But can you check?"

I nodded and made a show of lifting up the latch and bolting it again with a resounding clunk as a light rain began to patter onto the window sill. When she was satisfied, I saw her little body relax and sag into the mattress. She was asleep before I'd even untied my bootlaces.

I sighed. Robyn Brown was the best person I knew. She hardly made a lump in the covers.

I texted Tawny to say that Robyn was with me: *So she didn't have to get up so early.*

That night my dreams were full of things I didn't know I had in my head. It felt like they were playing out right before my eyes.

I didn't get a reply from Tawny until the morning (*She's way too keen*). It seemed that no one had even noticed Robyn's disappearance in the Brown household.

DISASTER STRIKES AT WITCH PLAY

Three Long Byrne High students are currently being treated at Stoutbridge General Hospital after events at a local play turned sour.

The young people had been attending the much-publicised Halloween fayre held on Long Byrne village green. A play marking the 400th anniversary of the deaths of the Long Byrne witches had been taking place when injury occurred.

Witnesses are unsure what might have caused the incident but ambulances were seen close to the scene.

Jamie Threlfall, *The Stoutbridge Star*

Chapter 10

When I was little, Mum used to make up little rhymes to help me go to sleep. Even before the caffeine habit kicked in I was an awkward sod and my mind point-blank refused to switch off. I'd have nightmare after nightmare about Disney villains chopping my toes off, or my teddies being blasted by aliens. I don't know what it was – my overactive imagination, or just bad genes. Either way, Mum would spend ages crouched down next to my bed, not singing, just saying things softly, which was almost like singing.

She repeated them again and again, until I knew them by heart and would say them over and over until the words didn't make sense any more and I was nodding off to the soft thrum of her voice. I knew all the old wives' tales she whispered.

An apple a day keeps the doctor away. Find a penny, pick it up, then all day you'll have good luck. Birds of a feather flock together. And the silly rhymes:

"Twenty-ninth of May,
Royal Oak Day:
If you don't give us a holiday,
We'll all run away."

I don't know where she'd got that one from.

My favourite was one she used to say every weekend when I came bursting down the stairs: "Friday's dream, on a Saturday told, is bound to come true, new or old." When Tawny had tried to tell me one she'd had about leaning too far out of a skyscraper to escape a giant lizard, I shoved my hand over her mouth and sang loudly with my eyes shut, just in case it came true. I'd had tooth marks on my thumb all morning.

Last night had been my first nightmare in four years.

The smudges under Robyn's eyes somehow looked worse today. She looked full-on vampire, rather than her usual sixty-five per cent zombie.

It seemed like neither of us had dreamt of kittens last night.

I made Dad give her a lift back to the Browns' house and then drop her off at school with me despite his protests of "so much work to do". My head felt like something was gnawing at its edges. I sat outside in the car with Dad and waited for Robyn to reappear. Tawny was still in the bathroom with only twenty minutes until the register. Dad wasn't prepared to wait.

I got out and nudged Robyn into the backseat.

"You're looking a lot better," I lied as we set off to school.

"That's the first time I've slept for weeks," she nodded as I stifled a yawn. Her chin stuck out defiantly – the conqueror of fears. Robyn's front tooth was chipped from where she'd smacked herself on monkey bars a couple of years before – it was so easy to forget that she was only thirteen. I'd seen her lift a half-bale of hay, ride a horse bareback, and was pretty sure I'd caught her with a copy of *War and Peace* before she was even twelve.

"Thanks, Cate."

Arriving at the gates, Dad nodded to us and muttered something about a paper he had to finish. Robyn headed off towards Form but before I could turn to leave, Dad called my name.

"Look out for her today, Cate. She doesn't look well. Do you want me to call Sandra?"

My eyes followed Robyn's skinny frame up the pathway. I knew I probably wouldn't see her all day once she dissolved into the crowd, and guilt stabbed my empty gut. Maybe I could tag her with Zombie GPS.

"No, it's OK," I said. "Best not to worry Sandra." Sandra may not be the most attentive parent but surely she already knew Robyn was looking a bit off.

Dad nodded but looked troubled and headed off, leaving me to hover by the gate. I craned my head down the high street.

I'd spent a good hour and a half writing up my Psych notes that morning before Robyn woke up, and planned to give them to Bryony before the bell sounded. We'd moved onto the Oedipus Complex – just another way for Freud to tell us we were messed up and needed to sit down and have a word with ourselves. I made my writing as clear and careful as possible, but next to Bryony's languid loopy letters, mine might have been written by a chimp with hand cramp. I'd blown on the ink three times to make sure it didn't smear then slotted it in my folder with a neat paperclip from Dad's stash. I knew every word on those sheets of paper now and believed Freud was a complete pervert.

I stood on my tiptoes. No blonde hair in sight. Where was she?

Then Tawny jumped on me out of nowhere.

"Can you believe it? Can you *actually* believe it!" Her eyes were wide and livid.

"What's happened?" I gasped. My thoughts automatically leapt to Bryony.

"They're giving us twenty-four hours to rehearse for auditions and I won't even have time to get a new dress. Argh! What kind of day *is* this?"

"What? They're doing auditions already?" My stomach felt cold. The script wasn't finished yet.

"Rillington wants the re-enactment doing on Halloween but doesn't seem to realise that's in, like, what? Five weeks? What did I tell you? She's a nutter."

"No one can do that in a month."

"Well, obviously!" She threw her hands up. "It's like she wants to give the entire school a mental breakdown by half-term."

The notices were tacked all over school – all Clip Art and bad witch puns. "It'll be cackle-tastic!" So much for premier advertising. But everyone stood in quivering knots around them as if the circus was coming to town.

"What's up with you?" Tawny said. "Face like thunder, you. You're not even auditioning. Oh, what I'd give for a normal life."

I rolled my eyes. "Need some Vaseline, much? It might help your head fit through the door."

"Oh har-de-har-har. By the way, thanks for returning my

sister. I saw her before. What did you do, poke her all night? She's looks *rough*."

Why don't you ask her? "Mmm," I muttered noncommittally and looked at the door. "Have you seen Bryony? She'll probably want to hear the news."

Tawny shot me a withering stare. "Aren't you going to offer me anything reassuring at all? I'm in bits."

I sighed and resigned myself to a day of self-absorbed Tawny wittering. I wondered if she even knew about Robyn. As families went, they weren't exactly Little House on the Prairie, but they got on all right. Only Robyn and I knew about how Tawny lost her cherry behind the May Day coconut shy last year to Simon Kerridge, a Year Twelve with back acne. Robyn had wrinkled her nose at the idea and hadn't tried to win a goldfish at the fête since, but she'd held her dutiful silence nevertheless.

I'd never had a sister, but having Tawny around was pretty much a deal for life. I thought of all Bryony's pictures beside the bed – all smiles and shiny blond beach hair. She must miss her brothers like hell.

As the day went on, audition hype kicked in. Girls screamed at each other in blind panic across the dinner tables. Phones vibrated loudly under desks and someone had dug out the Halloween decorations so big *Scream* faces and plastic spiders dripped from the banisters.

I still hadn't seen Bryony all morning.

Tawny had gone to corner a girl about borrowing some tap shoes, and I desperately needed a break from luvvie banter, so I lounged at our usual table, stretching out my arms, relishing the click of my elbows. The canteen was noisy, but at least you were allowed coffee in here.

Without warning, Bryony slunk into the seat beside me. My chest bubbled and I slanted my eyes to catch a glimpse of her skinny jeans and bottle-green coat, but I didn't let on. The questions that had been trapped before strained against my throat, like a pack of dogs pulling on their leashes.

I kept my head down. "Where have you been?"

"In class. Why, where have *you* been?" she raised her eyebrows, amused. She looked slightly flushed, like she'd just stepped out of a wind tunnel.

"No, I mean where were you yesterday afternoon?"

"Not here."

Helpful.

"You were bunking, I know. It's fine," I tried to shrug. "Tawny does it all the time. I just wouldn't have pinned you for the skipping school type."

She shook her head. "I wasn't skipping school. School makes me skip life."

I pondered this. It wasn't something I thought Bryony would ever say. She seemed too 'proper' for that. "That's one way of looking at it."

"I prefer nature's classroom," she smirked.

"Oh." I looked at her. So she did go out there. My dream came back to me and I stuttered, "I- I took notes in Psychology. You want them?"

She smiled. "I'll give you them back tomorrow. You're a star." She hugged me with one thin arm and headed off towards the library.

I stayed sitting there. I looked at the plastic chair she'd sat in.

Bryony Hollingworth smelled of coppery rain and smoked wood.

A sudden light appeared in my mind as if from a distant memory, but then I realised it was the small speck of light from the moor last night. It had rained last night.

It takes thirteen witches to make a coven.

Unlucky for some. Friday the thirteenth.

They'd stand in a circle: the witches. "By the power of Earth . . ." They'd invoke the elements: Earth, Air, Fire and Water. They'd raise the spirits of the dead. Then they'd call the Devil, to watch what he could do.

Thirteen witches. A ring of women all speaking in time.

Many people wonder how Rose and Jane did it, or whether they had a different kind of magic made just for the two of them.

In Search of the Long Byrne Witches, P.J. Hebden

Chapter 11

Auditions were held in the school hall the next day, so P.E. got cancelled and all the Year Eleven girls cheered. Tawny had had me up past midnight rehearsing lines with her even though she kept changing her mind and picking Oscar Wilde, then Shakespeare, then some weird pop ballad from 1982. Even Kayleigh Whittard and her gang looked flustered as they traipsed from class to class, practising tense dramatic scenes from *Eastenders* under their breath.

Term was going by so quickly already.

The day was overcast and gloomy despite the excitement thrumming through the school corridors. The trees on the playing field cast long spidery shadows across the floors, making the assembly hall feel like it was trapped inside a giant's hand. Even with all the surging adrenaline, the judging panel was a bit of a disappointment: Rillington sat in front of the stage with her papers in front of her and tick sheets resting on top like a cheerleading pageant. She wore a weird jazzy waistcoat circa 1979 and her hair was pinned up, revealing dangly earrings that tapped her jaw. A bloke from the local library sat slouched to her left, sniffling into a striped hanky and pushing his glasses back up his long nose. Proper Long Byrne stock.

Tawny had clamped me to her side for moral support. It got me out of reading about the bubonic plague.

"Why's he here? I've never even seen him before. You think he's taking it seriously?"

"And *you* are? Why not him?"

"You know I'm only doing it because it looks good on the resumé." But I saw her twitch the hem of her skirt down. I knew she'd tried out four different lipsticks in the loos before school. Her fingernails were freshly done in shiny witch black. "Bet he's just hoping someone'll get their kit off."

I rolled my eyes.

She gambolled off to get her spot in the wings while I sat to the side halfway along the hall, a few places away from the other gawkers. I made myself as small as possible.

My head was still hurting from my dream that night; a faint roll of nausea threatening to flop itself down into my stomach. I wondered if Robyn was faring any better. I did a quick recce of the hall and saw her shoved in a corner at the back. I raised my hand but she didn't budge her eyes from the bare stage. Zombie-trance. I guessed I'd be sitting alone.

People were shifting round in their seats, waiting for things to start. Where was the host dressed in a glittery suit? Wasn't there going to be a big drum roll to kick things off? My stomach gurgled loudly and I hit it, wishing I'd thought to take a cup of coffee from the canteen. Who knew how long this was going to take?

But then we were off.

"Tom Sheridan."

"Hannah Garstang."

"Ellie Murgatroyd."

Someone had memorised the first half-hour of *The Fellowship of the Ring*. Another girl sang 'Greased Lightning', complete with dance moves. A little Year Seven lad, forced into it by his mum, came out in a cassock and lisped his way through 'We're Walking in the Air'.

We all stared in horror as each act was even worse than the last.

Rillington's lipstick had started to wear off by the time she got to "Tawny Brown" and I thought I could I hear the hearty sigh in her voice. Tawny blasted onto the stage; arms swinging; grin in full-throttle.

"Morning, Miss!"

"Go on then, Tawny. Wow us. We need it."

I smiled to myself. Rillington begging Tawny for a favour? Tawny might not exactly be the headmistress's favourite Brown but at least Rillington knew she could rely on her for a show. The Tawny Factor was always good for school morale.

Tawny made sure she was exactly centre-stage then let a big breath out through her mouth. I saw the cogs working in her mind. Something dark settled over her face like a veil, like the character she'd chosen to play had cut and pasted itself over Tawny's eyes and mouth, covering them with an exact fit. The whole room seemed to sense it and even Kayleigh Whittard's crew sitting on the back row turned to listen.

"Is this a dagger I see before me?"

Macbeth. She'd opted for *Macbeth* instead. Good choice.

You go, girl. I wished I had a mini flag to wave.

Tawny's eyes turned wide and trembling, the perfect picture of a shaken Macbeth. Murderer. We'd read it out loud in class in Year Nine and Tawny had genuinely scared Jamie Duxberry with her Weird Sister cackle.

"The handle toward my hand? Come, let me clutch thee."

She stood stock still on the boards, not out of fear – she was perfectly in character. I'd never seen Tawny play a bloke so well. She went through the famous soliloquy with a flourish and twist of her hands. She was word perfect.

"I go, and it is done; the bell invites me. Hear it not, Duncan; for it is a knell that summons thee to heaven or to hell."

A moment passed. The crowd was hooked on her. She broke character with a knowing wink and the applause rose up instantly. Tawny turned her grin on us all. We were enchanted.

Rillington sighed loudly. "Oh, Tawny."

Tawny threw her head back and laughed. "Well, this lot seemed to like it." There were a few whistles and claps from the audience.

Rillington's eye-roll was obvious now. "You know where the cast list will be up, don't you?"

Tawny smiled even wider. "I sure do."

Nailed it.

She slipped herself off the front of the stage and plonked herself down loudly next to me. "Roll on, rehearsals," she whispered. "My get-out-of-class-free card." Half the room was already designing her costume.

"You were OK, I suppose," I muttered and Tawny grinned.

"Bryony Hollingworth?"

My head snapped up. Rillington was frowning at her clipboard. A hiss of trapped steam erupted from the hall as everyone began whispering at once.

"Bryony?" Tawny's head flashed to me. "Bryony's auditioning?"

My chest felt tight. I hated that I hadn't known. Why hadn't Bryony mentioned it? We'd spent hours and hours together over the past couple of weeks – *days, even* – why hadn't she thought she could tell us? Tell me?

Bryony came out onto the stage from the left wing, her chin held at the defiant angle I'd seen as she walked through the corridors trying to ignore the remarks and the stares. In the circle of the spotlight, her skin looked translucent.

"Well, Bryony," Rillington sounded like she was making small talk with a shy Year Eight. "What are you going to do for us today?"

"I'd like to play Viola in *Twelfth Night*."

"Another Shakespeare girl. I like where this is going. Off you go then, Bryony. Maybe you can knock Miss Brown off the top spot."

"Nothing like a bit of healthy competition, Miss!" yelled Tawny and people tittered. She leant back in her plastic seat with a strange smile on her face.

The room tasted feral.

Bryony's face twisted into a mesh of confusion. For a scared moment I thought she'd forgotten her lines, and embarrassment flapped in my chest for her. But then

I realised she was in character. I wasn't a Shakespeare fanatic like Tawny so the words seemed unfamiliar and, as I watched, Bryony transformed into something I'd never seen before:

"She loves me, sure! The cunning of her passion

"Invites me in this churlish messenger.

"None of my lord's ring? Why, he sent her none!

"I am the man. If it be so, as 'tis,

"Poor lady, she were better love a dream."

She stood in the middle of the stage, her hands clasped in apparent agony – Viola was obviously having a hard time deciding something. Bryony's eyes were pleading and for a split second I forgot she was a blonde, sixteen-year-old girl on a stage in a grey Northern village, and was caught up in the golden spotlight; I liked the way it dazzled her, how it made her something to be awed at. If someone had fired a flare-gun three feet from me I couldn't have looked away.

"O Time, thou must untangle this, not I;

"It is too hard a knot for me t' untie."

Bryony's stoic gaze was fixed on a spot at the back of the hall above all our heads. She didn't blink. It was like she was seeing another world hovering inches above our heads. She was stunning.

"Earth to Cate? Houston calling Caitlin Aspey." Tawny was clicking her fingers in my ear.

"Huh?"

I noticed for the first time the deafening roar of applause. The hall sounded thunderous. Bryony had finished. Her hand was clutched to her chest.

"Tawn?"

Tawny looked at me, grinning, and I saw there were tears in her eyes.

"I think I love her," she said and fell into a fake swoon across my knees.

I turned back to the stage and saw Bryony there again. The character she'd embodied so fully had fallen away. Her shoulders had regained their Bryonyness and the firmness of her mouth was back even though the spotlight stayed just as bright.

"Yeah," I said quietly.

Tawny fanned herself with both hands as if trying to keep the tears from falling and I watched Bryony as she nodded at Rillington and the library bloke, then took the right-hand exit offstage.

There were only a few more people to try out but no one was really paying attention any more. Tawny Brown followed by a shock display from Bryony Hollingworth – there was no competition. Rillington shooed everyone out, rustling her papers at anyone who got in her way. I was glad to be free – the hall had been starting to smell like feet. Tawny and I stayed back to wait for Bryony but she never emerged, having made her exit through some secret trap door.

Bryony's performance was the talk of the school. But not in the way I had expected. While people had stared in the corridors before, now they scowled. An awkward new girl swooping in and bagging the lead role? It had to be foul play. Surely Bryony had used her 'magical powers' to get the part. Long Byrne High felt like a mob with pitchforks.

At the bell for fourth period, Tawny and I found her in

the corridor with hands twisted in front of her, and we mobbed her like two super-fans wanting our tits signed.

"Bloody hell, woman! You didn't tell us you could do that!"

"You were fantastic, Bryony."

She gave us a small unashamed smile. "I used to practise with my brothers. If you messed up your lines you had to go and moon Mrs Twinton next door."

Tawny raised an eyebrow. "Well, that's one way of getting things done."

"You were fantastic," I repeated.

"And there was you saying you didn't go to the theatre. Lies! I should have been on to you, Missy," Tawny laughed.

We were walking towards the entrance hall. Miss Rillington went past us with a knowing smirk. I had an image of Miss dressed as Fagin, training Bryony up to be her best pickpocket in town. Robyn had better watch her top spot.

"Here," Tawny flicked her phone out. "Get a picture of us. The Golden Girls." She thrust it at me and my fingers fumbled. Bryony's face fell into an easy smile I hadn't seen her use in public before. Tawny put her arm around Bryony's waist.

"Hurry up, Cate! All this attractiveness won't last all day."

"Hold on," I stalled. "You know how much I hate your bloody phone."

I framed them both and took the picture. Their cheeks touched together, their arms crushed around each other. The dim grey light in the hall made their faces paper white as the flash blinded them.

Best friends for ever.

Tawny swiped the phone back off me. "Urgh, red eye. It'll do. Come on, I'm starving. Snack, Bryony?" They started off towards the canteen. It seemed like Tawny already knew Bryony had a free period now.

"I've got to get to English," I said.

"Meet you outside after?" said Tawny as she whisked Bryony away.

I held up my fingers, feeling like the lamest idiot ever as they walked away, and melded into the crowd.

Through the open double doors in the hall, the sky looked ready to pour.

Later, in the glow of Tawny's red room, she and I were both lying on our stomachs on the carpet. The walk back had been a weird one where I'd done a lot of nodding and not a lot of talking. Ginger was hunkered down amongst the clutter that had fallen from Tawny's desk, looking oddly alert. You had to be careful where you stood in there so you didn't get pierced by a kirby grip or a discarded coat hanger, but once you'd nestled into your nook it was quite cosy. Outside, the school traffic had died down and there were only a couple of hikers trundling along the cobbles on their way back from the moor. The sun was almost down and the orange light was shining through the red glass crystals on Tawny's homemade chandelier. All the clouds had lifted for the night, revealing a shimmering September sky.

Tawny looked up from pretending to do her French verbs. "Who knew, huh?"

I sighed. "She's something else, all right."

Tawny rolled her eyes. "'Something else'? Who even says that? I think you mean, 'I want to bonk her brains out, she's so good!'"

"Don't be gross, Tawn."

"I had my doubts for a minute there, I've got to admit. She's got that whole mysterious thing going for her. But she's really . . ."

"Really . . .?" I prodded.

She cocked her head to the side, staring at Ginger's black flicking tail. "Wonder if she's ever had a boyfriend. Maybe there are all sorts of layers of repression under there."

"You're painting a great image of your psyche here, Tawn. . ."

"I'm just saying. She doesn't even look at guys. Pad Mitchell proper wolf-whistled her the other day—"

"I'm sure she was thrilled."

"—from the top of the science block and she didn't even bat an eyelid."

"Being told she's fit by Patrick Mitchell must make her melt inside. Wolf-whistling makes me cringe."

"You're into Pad?" she gaped.

I turned my head to her and gave her my best withering look.

"You totally are, Aspey." She nodded decisively and went back to her verbs.

I was about to concoct a slamming putdown when the door flew open. Sandra burst in. We jumped. She was usually so carefully made up, sometimes with a glass of prosecco in one hand and a trashy novel in the other. But right now she had no makeup on. She looked pale and there was a pucker around her eyelids I'd never noticed before. It made me tense all over.

"Have either of you seen Robyn?"

Tawny frowned. "Not since last night, why? She gone walkabout?"

The look in Sandra's eyes made her pause.

"Has she gone walkabout, Mum?"

"I don't know. Most of her school books are still on her desk . . ."

"She's not been to school?" Tawny asked.

Sandra flitted to the window. "I don't know," she muttered. "Didn't you see her there?"

"She was there this morning," I said. "She's not at the farm?"

"I already rang."

Tawny made a movement like she was going to get up. "She could still be at school. The library's open late. Maybe she just forgot her bag today."

We all sat in silence for a minute, not knowing what to believe. Our eyes flickered back and forth in their sockets like our bodies were frozen to the spot.

Eventually I recalled every crime show I'd ever seen, in a flurry of magnifying glasses and plastic evidence bags. "OK. OK. Someone should stay here, but let's split up. Tawny and I can ask around. See if anyone's seen her."

"It's getting dark, Cate."

"I know."

Sandra's fingers were claws on her arms. "Where is she?

She's never late. I've never even seen her outside past six o'clock. Not ever. She's so small."

I cringed inside. I had definitely seen Robyn out late at night but she'd usually been on her way to Alder Farm. Could she have got lost on her way there? But that was ridiculous – the farm was less than ten minutes away and she walked there almost every day.

Robyn had to walk past the lane to Hollingworth House every day too.

A shiver ran through me but I kept quiet. The manor house wasn't evil, just as Bryony Hollingworth wasn't a witch.

The flat suddenly felt quiet. We waited. No one whacked a cheesy musical on. No one opened a packet of Minstrels. I'd never seen Sandra so still, her hand clutched around the house phone. Tawny sat with her jaw clenched, as if challenging Robyn to walk through the door. I could see the argument they'd have flying through her head.

"We were so worried! Think of all the stress you've put us through, you idiot!" I wondered how Sandra would ground her – Robyn never used her mobile, she didn't watch TV unless we were inflicting our bad influence on her, and she had had a sparkling blue tick on every piece of homework she'd been given since she was six years old.

Ginger prowled the window sill.

Miaow.

He sounded like he was pleading.

But the minutes ticked by and still nothing happened. Sandra decided to go out and look for Robyn, saying she'd check the school. Tawny was told to stay put but said,

"Don't be ridiculous, I'm coming too." Sandra roused Mr Shilcock and he said he'd sit guard by the door. Tawny and I went to the farm. Tawny looked out of place in the yard, amidst the potholes filled with sludge-water and the ever-present tang of manure. She looked around it like she was seeing it for the very first time. I saw the note of panic in her eyes, one that I didn't recognise, and it made her appear a lot younger than sixteen.

"You don't need to check in there," said Tawny, snappily, as I headed towards the chicken coop.

"I . . . I just have a weird feeling," I gulped.

Tawny tutted but then again, she didn't know about any of Robyn's episodes so why would she think I was being anything but deluded.

"Tawn, I need to tell you something. I don't think Robyn's been very well lately."

"What's new?" Tawny's eyes flicked around the barns and discarded milk churns. "She's been an insomniac since she was seven."

"I know, but I think things have been getting worse lately. Have you not noticed how she's been looking recently?" Tawny's mouth tightened as I spoke. "She's been to see me a few times, saying that she has a weird feeling."

"'A weird feeling?' What does that mean?" She frowned and drew herself up. "Why didn't you tell me?"

I looked at my best friend and felt myself recoiling slightly under her gaze. I'd never been on the receiving end of Tawny like this and it felt like the earth was going to give way beneath me. "She seemed scared."

"Scared?"

"Scared of the Hollingworth House. That something bad was going to happen." It sounded ridiculous as I said it out loud. "I tried to help her. But it didn't seem like she wanted me to tell anyone."

Tawny exhaled through her nose, leaving a plume of silvery smoke behind. "If my sister is scared, you tell me. She's not your sister, Cate. She's mine."

I hesitated. "I know that. It's just—"

"And now she's missing." Tawny turned away, shaking her head. "You should have told me. You've pretty much lied to me." I was left standing alone next to the coop. Tawny stomped away to search an unlocked shed. I stood for a second, took a deep breath and went to join her.

Dad and Alexa joined us and we searched the whole farm by the light of four torch beams but Robyn was not there. Over the hill, I couldn't see the outline of the Hollingworth House against the sky; its windows all dark, Bryony's light switched off.

Not at school. Coming home, said Sandra's text.

Tawny and I jogged back to the Brown house empty-handed.

"I'm calling the police," said Sandra as the clock hit half nine.

She got jerkily to her feet and took the phone into the other room. Tawny and I got into bed, but neither of us closed our eyes for a long time, and all I could think about was how bony my elbow felt against the curve of Tawny's waist, and Sandra's voice rising shrilly in the next room.

"I don't care how long it's been! She's thirteen! She has dark curly hair. She . . ."

I squeezed my eyes tightly shut. This is how things had been when Mum went missing. This was how things were before they found her in the water. I remembered lying awake that night in our rented holiday cottage while Dad threw things around downstairs, looking for any sort of clue. I'd hoped this was just one of the bad dreams she'd warned me not to tell.

I kept hearing Robyn's words. *I have a bad feeling . . .*

Come through the door, Rob, just come in. We won't be angry. We won't.

Sandra came through the door looking wild. "Get up, get up. The police are coming."

"We need to keep looking," said Tawny. She seemed filled with a new vigour, one that I'd only seen in the protagonists of Hollywood films. "Cate and I will go. You stay here, Mum."

"Yes," agreed Sandra, nodding over and over again like her life depended on it. "Yes."

Tawny grabbed my arm and dragged me down the stairs.

"Where are we going?" I asked.

"Bryony's, since Robyn was so scared of the place." Her eyes were like torches.

When we arrived, I had a stitch. The driveway to the Hollingworth House was so dark that we had to use our torches the whole way up. Tawny knocked three times on the door.

Silence.

"Why isn't she home?" muttered Tawny through her teeth, looking up at the top-floor windows.

"Want me to look around a bit?" I darted my torch to the bushes and trees of the front garden. Everything looked equally as terrifying in the darkness. Tawny did the same then went back to hammering on the door.

I spun my light into the living room of the Hollingworth House and my beam caught the carving above the mantle. The Evil Eye sat in darkness, looking out on the empty room. I took a step closer. There was something different about the eye. It seemed to be more intricate than I had originally noticed. I peered through the window, cupping my eyes to the glass.

The Evil Eye blinked at me.

"Argh!" I yelled, falling back from the window. My feet scuffled in the dry leaves below the window as I tried to push myself back from the house.

"What? What is it?" Tawny ran over.

"I – I—" No words came out as I looked from Tawny to the window. "I just – it was a trick of the light."

"Stop messing around, Cate," Tawny scowled and left me to get up.

"Tawny?" A voice came from behind us and we spun around.

Bryony was standing behind us in the drive carrying two tote bags of shopping over her shoulder. "What's going on?"

"It's Robyn," Tawny said. "She's missing."

"Have you seen her?" I cut in.

"What? Oh!" She shook her head. "No, not at all."

"We need to find her. Now."

"Wait, hold on. Let me help you look. Two seconds." She opened the door and put her shopping in the hallway, then said, "Where first?"

Tawny played with the edge of her jacket. "I don't know. I don't know where she can have gone." There was a faint trace of despair in her voice and I put my hand on her back lightly.

"There's the moor," I said. The faint sound of sirens started up far away and began to get closer. We all looked at one another.

"I'll go," said Bryony.

Tawny shook her head. "In the dark? Don't be mental."

"No, Bryony's right. We should look."

The worry in Tawny's face doubled until we said that she didn't have to come with us. She would go knocking on doors while Bryony and I, armed with a torch and the beam from Bryony's phone, would go to the Slip.

I tried to think of any of Robyn's friends or girls I'd seen her with – Shannon, or was it Chloe? I didn't even know. I might have made them up. It was so strange to think that I didn't know anything about who Robyn hung out with outside of the farm. We flashed our lights over the gnarled stumps and roots of the Slip, double-checking the shadows we saw there.

This was all my fault. She'd come to me, scared and alone, and all I'd done was tuck her in and tell her to go back to sleep; there were no monsters under the bed. Why hadn't I taken her seriously?

In my mind, an image swirled of a police hunt; trudging, thick-soled boots, combing the fields for scraps of fabric or until an Alsatian caught her scent.

Or found something in the river.

My stomach churned. I squeezed my eyes shut.

An image came of Mum in her soaked nightie. Her eyes puffy and staring, her skin smelling of wet stone and weeds. I prised open my own eyes.

I have a bad feeling, she said in my mind.

Bryony walked her solemn, straight-backed gait by my side, walking with such force that I almost felt like she was leading the way. That long curtain of blondeness caught in flashes of light as we moved. I swallowed, very aware of my sour breath and my pyjama pants tucked into my boots.

"You OK?" said Bryony.

"Yes. It will be fine."

I have a bad feeling, Robyn said in my mind.

I looked out for footprints in the mud. There wasn't much mud around under the trees – no rain got through the thick leaves, but slid off into the fields instead to make great pools of moor mud that reeked of peat. Nothing ever prepared you for the rotting greenness of the moor smell. It rolled off the heather so that you could smell the hugeness of it for miles around. You might have been a fox or even a wolf, sniffing that dead hare-stink or the remnants of scoffed stonechat eggs. Sometimes that smell came through your window at the very end of winter and woke you up with its creeping fingers. When had I last been up here? I always seemed to stick to the Slip these days. It seemed safer there.

We went through the gate and then we were out on the moor, where the trees looked slashed and torn with their red rowan berries. Bryony was always half a pace ahead of me. I was shorter than her but she never even tried to match my step. Maybe she was more nervous than her calm exterior betrayed.

I tried to focus on the task at hand, forcing down a slurp of bile. Could Robyn be out here?

I closed my eyes and took a deep breath, hoping I wouldn't catch the smell of thirteen-year-old girl.

"How did she kill herself?" said Bryony.

I stopped dead. My stomach plummeted.

"She's not dead. She's fine." My throat was dry.

She cleared her throat softly. "No, not Robyn, she'll be OK. We'll find her."

"Then why did you ask that?" My voice was high and strained.

"How did your mum do it?"

Her calm face was like she'd just asked me the time or where I bought my shoes. I felt my eyes go wide, straining in the corners. Did she realise this was the worst timing ever? My knot of vomit swelled.

"I'm sorry." She shook her head. "That came out wrong. I'm just curious."

"How did you know?"

"That she'd killed herself? Oh." She blinked – the only ruffle in her calm exterior. "I thought it was obvious. It's written on you."

"Oh."

An animal scuffled in the undergrowth, making my skin crawl.

"She drowned," I said.

Bryony nodded. *Yeah, obviously.* "It can be quite quick."

I kicked my boot against a stone. "They don't think it was."

"Ah," Bryony ducked her head, probably wishing she'd asked me about the weather. "I'm sorry."

And then all was quiet except for the crunch of our boots on old heather.

Could someone really have death written on them? I held myself tighter. I think I'd been afraid of that.

It had been five years ago. A family holiday. Watching the leaves turn on the Lancashire moors. Mum's idea – she was always dragging us to one beauty spot or another. Nature was her thing. Mum's speciality, and she loved to write about it. There was something about Long Byrne that grabbed her attention. Maybe she'd fallen in love with Jane and Rose just as I had. Maybe that was what got to her in the end.

She'd sometimes drive me out to the countryside and we'd go hunting for acorns and conkers. When we got home, she'd chip holes into them and we'd make necklaces, with them clacking around our shoulders and hitting us in the face if we turned around too fast.

I'd once pointed to a spindly sapling, weighed down with heavy red fruit.

"That's a rowan," she'd smiled.

"There's so many berries!" I'd wanted to snatch a big handful of them and smear them around my mouth.

"Rowan branches are meant to keep evil spirits away," she'd said. "In the olden days, people used to make their window frames from its wood so that if a ghost or goblin passed nearby, they'd get frightened and not come back again."

We'd snapped off a couple of the smaller twigs and put them in our pockets. I still had my bit of rowan in the shoebox of precious stuff I kept in the wardrobe.

Mum had drowned three days into the trip. Right here on this stretch of river. People called it an accident. Or a tragedy. Dad didn't call it anything at all – he never spoke about it. But it didn't stop him dragging us both to Long Byrne. At first I thought it was so he could feel close to her in a place she loved, but now I just think he wanted to punish himself every day for not noticing she was going to hurt herself. I wonder if he realised he was punishing me, too.

"It was a long time ago," I muttered. "The police report was inconclusive."

"How old were you?"

"Twelve."

"Did you know she was going to do it?"

I looked at her. "She didn't leave a note or anything. I had no idea."

Bryony nodded like she'd heard the story before and was just confirming the details. This was the first time I'd ever spoken about it with someone. Tawny always changed the subject or turned the music up louder – there was no space for sadness in Tawny's life: she only wanted the tragedies of Hollywood to occupy her mind, and my trauma wasn't something that could mar the world in her head. I wanted to tell Bryony more; I wanted to tell her that I'd never been the same again.

But that wasn't why we were here. Robyn needed us. I started walking with a renewed sense of purpose, focusing on where the torch beam fell before me.

A crop of bent-over trees stood up ahead, broken fingers blistered with years of wind. We made our way towards them.

"Robyn?"

"Robyn!"

No answer.

"This way," said Bryony, when the path forked, and I shot a sideways glance at her. We took the left-hand route, which narrowed so much that we had to walk one behind the other.

I waited for Bryony to apologise, or at least pretend to be sorry for asking those questions. But she didn't.

She stooped. "This'll be a good one." She held up a flat black stone. "I find that skimming stones helps sometimes."

I looked at her, trying hard to be annoyed. "Helps what?"

"It's all about the wrist," she said, examining the stone for imperfections.

I looked at her sideways. "Yeah, we used to do it all the time."

"You and Tawny?"

"Me and Mum. You wouldn't get Tawny out on the moor too long – not unless you bring a camera."

Bryony paused then smirked. "Harsh."

"She'd be the first to admit it," I smiled back. "You'd get Robyn up here like a flash though. She loves . . ." I felt something catch in my throat and I blacked out an image that was formulating in the front of my mind. I wouldn't let it come. Something was warm on my coat sleeve. I looked down and Bryony's hand was gripping my arm.

"I like talking to you, Cate."

I blinked. My breath frozen in my throat. "I like talking to you too."

"You should come and stay over."

I looked at her. Her eyes were so clear they startled me. I felt like she was inviting me towards something. I opened my mouth.

But then someone else spoke.

"Cate?"

Bryony and I were pale mirrors of each other. Our faces filled with dread. Something rustled in the gnarled trees up ahead. I held up my arm, telling Bryony not to move. Her eyes were narrowed, body frozen, honing in on the voice.

"Cate? Is that you?" And then there she was, coming through the gorse towards us.

"Robyn!" I ran towards her. "Robyn, are you OK?" I reached her but something in me recoiled.

Her face was streaked with mud and there was a dark stain on the knee of her jeans. Around her ankles was a silvery track of mucus left by a snail. But it was her eyes that got me. Her eyes were the size of dinner plates, staring and staring.

I snapped my mouth shut and mechanically yanked off my jacket. "Here, here you go. Shush, it's OK," I muttered. Her little body was so stiff with cold and fear. I begged everything in the world that she wasn't hurt and no one had touched her.

For the first time, I saw that she wasn't looking at me at all. Then a little quavering voice, so unlike Robyn's, came up from her.

"Get her away."

"What?"

"Get her *away*," and from the cloak of my jacket she raised her thin arm and pointed at Bryony.

Bryony stood stock still.

"No, it's OK, Robyn." I clamped Robyn to my side. *Shut up.* "Bryony's here to help too."

Robyn shook her head once. "No. No, she's not."

Her voice was guttural.

I looked at Bryony. A slight frown creased her skin. My mouth fell open, wishing to stuff all Robyn's words back behind her teeth. I tensed with embarrassment for Bryony, who stared at Robyn with a straight back and blank eyes. Was she thinking of London? Would she go back to her home with no witches or rumours and never see me again?

"I'll go and tell the others," Bryony said and she turned and ran, her hair a golden ribbon behind her in the night.

I looked at Bryony then at the small bundle of person under my arm. "What do you mean, Rob?"

"No," she shook her head again more forcefully, like it answered all elements of my question. Her shoulders began to shake and I clasped her to me. I suddenly realised how deeply cold it was.

"Come on, sweetie," I said, "let's get you cleant up." But my eyes were on Bryony's retreating back.

On the way back, Bryony now out of sight, all I thought about was the blinking Eye in her house and how my skin went as cold as Robyn's when I felt its gaze upon me. I took a deep breath of night air and pushed it all down. All that mattered was that Robyn was safe.

[ROSE and JANE circle each other, centre stage]

JANE: How could you? After everything we've done?

ROSE: It wasn't me – it's all a lie. Jane—

JANE: Don't lie to me. I can smell him on you.

[ROSE's distress grows]

ROSE: Who told you this? Whose lips did you hear it from?

JANE: Never mind that. You are a traitor.

ROSE: Jane, would you please just listen! I'm trying to tell you the truth of it.

JANE: You need not bother. I can see it in you. I can see the flicker in your eyes, those false tears. To be quite honest, I'm surprised you had it in you.

ROSE: Jane, please, I did not—

JANE: How could you have lain with another? We vowed to be together. We swore it last summer and we have sworn it every time we have shared my bed since that day.

[ROSE breaks down crying and falls to the floor]

JANE: You know what? You make me sick. I knew I should never have trusted you, not with your family.

[ROSE stops crying and looks up at JANE, her face hardening. She slowly gets to her feet as JANE says:]

JANE: False. Deceiver. Traitor. Who knows where your family came from? And now you want to drag yourself down to their level?

ROSE: Don't you dare talk of them that way. My family have done nothing but serve you and your ridiculous wants. I could curse you for what you have just uttered.

JANE: Curse me? Curse me! We both know you wouldn't know how. I am the only true witch around here.

[ROSE smiles]

ROSE: That's where you are wrong, Jane. That's where you are wrong. I will curse you for your wickedness and you will come to regret your words in this life and the next.

Chapter 12

After that, Robyn didn't come to work on the farm again. I didn't know if this was Sandra's influence or whether Robyn didn't want to be out on her own, although I suspected everyone had her under lock and key. The ten-minute walk from their flat to the yard was dark and, even though I'd have been there to meet her at the other end, she was still thirteen and skinny and . . . we couldn't let her do that any more.

"Come on, lovie. Just tell us what happened and we'll all be on our way."

A policewoman had to examine her at the precinct up in town and Robyn didn't come back to school the next day or the day after that. Neither did Tawny. School was terribly quiet without her – people looked at me like I was a lost arm missing the rest of its body. Alexa clucked and fussed about Robyn on the phone to her friends in Hillbury. "That poor girl. Her mother shouldn't have let her wander around. Just think – someone might have got to her up on that moor." Not that she thought twice about setting Robyn loose with a tractor.

Alexa bulk-made pâté sandwiches and ordered a carrot cake from Mrs Maldew. Bad choice, but she wrapped everything up in cling film and took them round to the Browns' on a tray with watercolour kittens on it. Sandra kept her talking in the living room for hours and Alexa came back flushed with excitement, like she'd been given the secrets of the universe. An invitation to the crime scene.

Tawny sent me long voice notes, hopefully while Robyn was out of earshot, saying, "OK, I get that she's under a lot of pressure at school and her brain probably imploded – did you know Rillington gives her extra lessons? I didn't! But it's been *days*. I don't get it. Why isn't she talking to us? What happened to her?"

But Robyn still wasn't speaking.

My teeth chattered as I milked Myrtle, watching the steam come up from her pink nostrils. The days were getting colder. I spread the hay-bedding, mucked them out, swept the yard and collected the eggs. Alexa made me cups of coffee instead of sandwiches. At least that was something. Dad left a note saying he was going to ask for a farmhand to help out so I could get a lie-in (ha). I prayed to every god in the book it wouldn't be Pad Mitchell.

With the extra farm work, I only just about had time before school to tug on my boots and scarf and head to the Slip to work on tweaking my script. 'Script' was probably pushing it. 'The-crap-I-was-churning-out' seemed more fitting. It might just about merit a 'Good Effort' sticker and maybe Rillington would be slightly happier with the changes I'd made. On Tuesday morning, I fired off the email to her. At least if the story was no good I'd never have to see it again.

But I'd have Rillington to answer to.

***

When Tawny came back in on Wednesday, people swarmed. Local celebrity status. I'd have been shocked if anyone had known Robyn's name the week before. Nevertheless, girls came in with bunches of flowers wrapped in brown kitchen string, and little teddies with hearts stitched between their paws. Unwanted Valentines' gifts.

"It's not like she died," Tawny said to me through a forced grin as we pushed down the corridor. She snapped the head off a droopy carnation as we walked to class. "This is the crap you leave tied to gates near a hit-and-run."

"They're just being nice."

"They could have brought me a fucking Lion bar. I'm starving."

"You could tell them it's Robyn's favourite."

Tawny gave a Tawny Huff. "Drama runs in our family. She did a pretty good job of following Dad – a nice little runner she did there." There was an edge to her voice. "If I have to tell another person that she got lost on her way home, I'll scream. And if she thinks she's forgiven she's got another thing coming."

"That's harsh, Tawn. She's not well."

She shrugged. "She shouldn't have done a disappearing act. Mum's still ballistic. She keeps making things – the sewing machine's going mental. You should come round soon though. She'll knit you a hat. Besides, Rob's been asking for you."

"For me?"

"Yeah, wouldn't say why. She's not saying a lot, which

is pissing irritating for the police, but she's asked for you. Reckon she wants to know how the cows are getting on without her or something."

"Yeah, or something."

"Cate, can I ask," she stopped walking and pulled me round to face her.

"What?"

"Why didn't you say something was going on with her?"

Saliva filled my mouth and I fought the urge to swallow. "I thought I could help her and she didn't seem to want to talk to anyone else. I was trying to be her friend."

Tawny shook her head sadly. "I'm really grateful to you and Bryony for finding her but . . . I don't know," she said. "She talks to you. She never talks to us." Her eyes were far away.

There was a knot in my stomach that felt dark and cloudy. Bryony had been hiding herself away in the library since Monday and I thought she might have forgotten about me and about her offer to stay over.

What had Robyn meant?

"She just didn't want to worry you," I said.

I didn't see Tawny again until after lunch. Work was starting to get on top of me and my eyelids were drooping in class. Miss Draycott even clicked her fingers in front of my face. Long Byrne High lacked a decent espresso machine.

At lunch there was a commotion in the entrance hall and I followed the sounds, along with half the school. Someone had knocked the old bell rope in all the fuss, and the clapper clattered around loudly inside it like a wasp trying to escape from under a glass.

Tawny was standing on her tiptoes in the centre of everything.

"What's going on?" I said.

Tawny clocked me. "Crackpot put up the cast list for the re-enactment. Said she's got the script sorted so rehearsals can start. I'm practically wetting myself here."

I stood stunned. "She's actually using my script?"

"Well, don't act so surprised. She did ask you to write it. And, by the way, you'd best have given me Rose."

"I don't really have—"

"Coming through, people, coming through." Tawny elbowed an eager Year Eight in the neck and surged through the crowd. I saw her glossy head held high through the forest of grasping hands all pulsing around the notice board.

In case we didn't already know, Tawny held up her hands and yelled, "Rose Ackroyd goes to Miss Tawny Brown! Cate, you're an absolute star!" She shoved her way back through the throng and twirled me round in a massive hug. I always forgot how strong she was from years of ballet and tap, and the smell of her berry shampoo threatened to knock me out. "I knew I could count on you!"

One of the Witch Groupies burst into tears.

"Oh, suck it up, sister," said Tawny. She squinted back at the list. "Look, you're a villager. You'll get a pitchfork and everything."

She turned around and grinned at me, making a hearty cackle. The perfect little witch.

"Who's playing Jane Hollingworth?"

"Oh. Didn't think I needed to check. Hold on."

She ducked back through the crowd with a few well-placed elbows.

"Take a guess," she yelled.

"She got it?"

My whole chest froze for what seemed like an eternity. Bryony. Bryony as Jane on stage, reading my words.

"Hells yeah, baby!" Tawny fought her way back to my side. "Oh my god, this is *perfect*!" She squealed as more disgruntled actresses fled the scene. "We've got to tell her, where is she?" Her eyes looked wide enough to crawl through as she tugged on my arm.

"Congrats, Tawny." Pad Mitchell was leaning against the canteen wall like James Dean with acne. "You'll rock."

"I don't need *you* to tell me that, Patrick," she flicked her hair at him defiantly but I saw the smile quirk up her lip as she led me down the corridor.

"Really? Pad Mitchell?"

"Why, what's wrong with him?"

"It's. Pad. Mitchell," I deadpanned.

"Oh give it a rest – you're hopeless." And she dropped my arm, sashaying away from me. "Bryony!" she called. Bryony had come out of the library and was immediately swamped by Tawny. "You got the part! You're Jane! You're Jane! We're leads together!"

Tawny grabbed her into a huge hug and tugged her around in a circle. I caught a glimpse of Bryony's face and she was grinning just as widely.

Bryony was playing Jane. Tawny was Rose. It couldn't

have worked out better, and yet my steps felt shaky on the school corridor tiles. I thought of Robyn in bed with all the sheet corners tucked in tight like a straightjacket.

"You coming?" Tawny jerked her head to me. "We need to *celebrate*," she grinned, wagging her tongue.

I watched her for a moment. Her skirt flaring out over her hips, one hand on her waist, the other around Bryony's shoulders. Tawny's eyeliner made her eyes startlingly blue.

"Of course," I said.

I knew Tawny's Lower-Sixth timetable better than mine. I'd recited it in the shower during the first week of term, to optimise chance meetings in the corridors. She was meant to be in Textiles, pricking away at cheap school-bought fabric. But instead I knew she'd want to go to the field with us. Tawny had been saying for years she knew where the Upper Sixth hid their vodka supply. I guessed it was time to test the theory.

We'd just turned the corner, when—

"Caitlin?"

Miss Rillington was rounding the door from the staff room. Her bob was razor sharp. She looked like she meant business.

"I was just coming to look for you. Mind if I have a word?"

I looked at Tawny, who shrugged. Bryony looked a bit dazzled.

"In my office."

Urgh. "Yes, Miss."

I went after her with a doleful look behind me. Tawny

winked and made a glugging motion as she scampered away holding Bryony's wrist. Bloody Rillington.

We went through the English block, past the library and up a well-worn spiral staircase. It creaked ominously beneath our feet, even though I weighed less than a pint of milk. Her office was up in the attic, all done out in fresh wooden floors and white-painted walls. It was a long, thin room with trophies in a sparkling cabinet. Wide, bright skylights along the ceiling were covered with leaves, forming papery orange shadows on the desk and floor, which made me feel like I was underwater.

"Do come in, dear. Have a biscuit." The equivalent of the Head Tilt. I sat down on a leather chair with hard wooden arms that knocked my elbows. She had a winged swivel-throne behind her desk.

She got straight to the point. "Is there any more news on Robyn Brown, Cate? I can't even imagine what Sandra is going through right now."

I let my shoulders slump. So this is what it was all about. Why hadn't she collared Tawny too?

"She's fine – I mean, stable, or whatever they're calling it. She'll be OK, she just had a shake-up. Alexa – my step-mum's – been around at their house a lot, so I think Sandra's been distracted."

Rillington shook her head, looking uncharacteristically lost. "It's amazing how these things can be stirred up in people. All these Long Byrne girls : . ." She sighed and cut herself off.

"Miss?"

Her face looked tight with concern. "The young certainly choose their moments to embrace tradition."

I blinked. The wooden arms of the chair felt like splints holding me up.

Rillington gave a fleeting weary smile. "But that's not what I brought you up here to talk about."

"Oh, right."

"It's about the script."

My insides shrank. Oh god. Here we go.

"I think it's wonderful."

She looked at me closely, maybe hoping I'd pant like a dog looking for treats. But instead I just blinked.

"I'm sorry I didn't tell you sooner – there have been a lot of questions from the police over the past few days."

Oh, right.

"I'd love to use it word for word. You have a real talent, Cate."

"Oh." Blink, blink. "Thanks, Miss."

"Of course, I might make a few tweaks – artistic direction and whatnot." She grinned widely and I didn't know where to look.

"OK. It was just a first draft anyway."

"A first draft?" she raised her eyebrows high. "I see."

My neck decided to flush violently. Perfect. "You can change it if you want," I said, "if I've missed out any of the facts."

She shook her head. "Ah, but this play isn't about the facts, it's about the girls, isn't it?"

"Yes, but surely the facts—"

"Caitlin," she cut in, "who do you think will be watching this play?"

I stared at her, feeling suddenly sullen.

"Pretty much all of Long Byrne?"

"Exactly. Not the BBC. We want something spooky for Halloween. You hit the nail on the head, and went one step further. You've done an excellent job of capturing Rose and Jane."

My tense shoulders settled slightly but my eyes flicked to the door. "Cool. Thanks."

She settled back in her chair and it swung slightly to the left. A small pendulum clock tinkled on the wall behind her and I began picking at the skin around my nails. Something about this didn't feel quite right.

"Are you sure you don't want a biscuit?"

I nodded. "I should get to class, Miss."

I stood to go but she leant forward sharply. "Is there anything you want to talk to me about, Caitlin? Anything on your mind?"

I sank back down, my elbows clacking on the wooden arms. Here we go again. She was about to play the Dead Mum card.

"No, Miss. I don't think so."

"Only, you seem to focus very clearly on Jane and Rose's ... friendship. You've got a very particular view on them."

What was she on about? I shrugged slowly. "I just think they were interesting. Everyone round here does, or they wouldn't have lasted so long. They're legend."

"Yes, but you focus very closely on their *friendship*." I saw the imaginary quotation marks spring up from her fingers, even though they were still firmly clasped around her clipboard. I wondered if she took it to the bathroom with her.

"Yeah, I think Rose Ackroyd and Jane Hollingworth had a very close bond. It might have been more than just friendship. Does that bother you, Miss?"

"Oh no, dear, no. I'm as tolerant as the next person." A fine red band had risen to the tops of her ears.

Some part of me enjoyed watching her squirm and I suppressed a smile. "It's just an interpretation." Had Rillington brought me up here to discuss my lesbian witch script?

She cleared her throat. "You could be a great writer, Cate. And it's great to see you've got such a close friendship with Bryony Hollingworth. Such a clever girl. A bit mysterious too, yes?"

I angled my feet to the door. The heat was rising in my face and all I wanted to do was leave.

"Has she ever talked to you about things at home – back in London, I mean?" Rillington looked at me with bright blue eyes; I had the distinct impression she could see every question forming in my head. She even learnt forward to get a better view.

"Umm, no, I—"

"Nothing about Euan?"

I shook my head slowly, expectantly, keeping my eyes trained on hers. But Rillington sighed softly, like she'd just finished a novel with an unhappy ending. "The girls in this village have already had enough sadness to last a lifetime."

When I was a kid, Dad always told me to ask as many questions as possible. "It's the only way she'll learn," he'd say to Mum. She'd roll her eyes and say, "I guess you're right." But when I tried asking about stuff – like why did the people at his parties ignore me? When was I going to get taller? How old did I have to be before I could be in his big-people classes? – he'd flick his newspaper out and say, "Cate, you're going to learn to ask the right kind of questions one day, and then maybe I'll answer them."

Bloody academics.

He still hadn't answered me, so I guessed I still wasn't asking the right questions. I didn't respond to Rillington's bait. She put down her clipboard and looked marginally less terrifying without it. "I know I've made you uncomfortable today," she went on, "but if you ever need anything . . ."

I considered her. Rillington in her freshly pressed smock with the buttons all shining down the front. Her dark grey hair neatly styled with a hot iron that morning. There was no Mr Rillington that I knew of. No kids.

Maybe she just needed someone to take under her wing.

"Thanks, Miss. I appreciate it."

"Take a biscuit for the road. Please? Oh, and rehearsals start tomorrow night. We've got to get everything ship-shape before Halloween, haven't we? Be there." She smiled.

I took a chocolate digestive for Tawny and left down the chilly staircase.

But she'd liked my script. A smile crept to my face and I couldn't help but keep it there for the rest of the day.

They say that on Samhain the walls between the living and the dead are at their most fragile. Halloween, All Hallow's Eve. There's only a whisper-thin veil that separates us from this world and the next.

Now, you dress up for Halloween. You put on your rabbit ears or your Red Riding Hood outfit. Halloween used to be about scaring away the evil spirits with Jack-o'-Lanterns, not bobbing for apples or eating your weight in sweets.

Maybe that's why they hanged the Long Byrne witches on Halloween. Maybe they thought they wouldn't have far to go into the next world – to Hell – so it was easier to get rid of them.

But what they didn't count on was that it would also be easier for them to come back.

The History of Long Byrne: Demons on the Moor,
Dr C. Munir

Chapter 13

Rehearsals started at 4.15 p.m. Sharp.

Rillington had us sit down in the assembly hall while Tawny tried to sneak crisps from her jacket pocket. There were about twenty-five of us – Rose, Jane, the love interest I'd conjured up – I'd called him Dick, just because I could – and a good stock of villagers, most of whom had colds and spluttered through their fingers. Rillington had arranged the benches in a rough circle so that we could all sit and "share". I wasn't entirely sure why she'd asked me to come, but Rillington mentioned something about prompting people's lines and "keeping Tawny in order". Perhaps Robyn would have been better at the latter, but then I thought of her quiet and alone in her bedroom and felt a pang of guilt for not having visited her yet.

"You all have a copy of the script – I've added a few parts that Miss Aspey had left out."

Everyone riffled through the pages.

"There's a song?" a Witch Groupie exclaimed, which set them all off. My mouth dropped open. I shot a horrified stare at Rillington. Tawny bellowed with laughter. I'd heard about creative licence, but this was ridiculous. Rillington wanted to make people tap their toes at a public hanging?

"I'm not singing!"

"Can I do the solo?"

"I don't think that's historically accurate."

The headmistress huffed. "Well, we do realise that, Josie. But it's not a cheery subject and we thought we might need some . . . pep, to bring in the crowds."

Tawny rolled her eyes. Rillington honed in on her. "Do tell us, Tawny: what are your grand suggestions?"

Tawny sprang up straight in her seat. "Well, Miss," she smacked both hands down on her thighs. "While a song is a stroke of genius – I'm sure we'd all agree – there are other ways to liven things up." We waited. "Like, we could have fireworks, lights! A bit of glitz. Some real drama." She sparkled, doing her best jazz-hands. The whole room murmured.

"Yeah, go on, Miss."

"There could be rockets for all the magic."

Rillington's nose crumpled slightly. "What do you think, Cate?"

I looked from Rillington's narrowed eyes to Tawny's dancing am-dram fingers. I stole a look at Bryony, whose eyes were trained firmly on the words in front of her. I nodded.

"Right. Well, Tawny, you *are* the expert. I suppose there'll be some fireworks coming out of the school budget. Cate, as you've agreed to this incredible plan, you're in charge of setting off the fireworks."

Only in a farming town would the headmistress trust the kids with gunpowder. I fought off a wince and Tawny winked at me.

After ten minutes of bickering, Rillington got us all in order for a read-through. I'd much rather have scraped tar off my eyeballs. There wasn't a lot for me to do but Rillington assigned me to the lighting, props and special effects crew. They scowled at me, probably because I was allowed to light the rockets.

Straight from the blubbery mouths of Year Nines, my words sounded stiff and brutal. The yard was getting dark outside. The orange lights of a backfiring van crossed the stage curtains in a ripple. I wished it would take me with it.

Rillington was on stage directions.

"'A dark wind rises. The girls are heard chanting.'"

Tawny began majestically. "On this night, and in this place—"

Bryony continued. "We call upon an ancient grace."

"Bring us light and love, all weathers—"

"And let our friendship never sever."

It was all the stuff I'd read growing up. I don't know how making stuff rhyme was somehow magic, but I was dredging up years of cheesy nineties TV reruns where girls shot lightning from their eyes and danced in circles made of flowers. A charm for a sniffle in a library book. A spell for rainy weather. A hex of boils for an enemy.

I muttered words that rhymed under my breath, imagining Alexa covered in warts, all her hair falling out in the sink. I'd taken out Mum's little box of gem stones and put them in a circle around my feet, protecting me from whatever was outside. Green malachite to ward off spirits; red jasper to ground me; lapis lazuli to clear my head.

Rillington nodded along to the script, flicking her eyes towards me every once in a while but I kept my face poker-straight. As far as I was concerned, the script was in Tawny's hands now, maybe even Bryony's if Tawny ever closed her gob. Bryony's eyes licked Tawny's face as she read the words loud and regally in her clear, ringing voice.

Bryony took up a thick sheet of white cloth from her side and used it to bind the pair's hands together. Fingers held together in the rope of the sheet, they were melded together, bound by the spell.

At the end of the page I saw Tawny look up at her and their eyes connected through the circle of bowed heads. Something reverent passed between them and I suddenly had to look away.

The play showed Rose and Jane out on the moors together, promising themselves to each other – friends for ever – making a sacred bond. How could they ever leave each other now? But then Dick came along and changed everything. The room was in stitches whenever someone said the name, and Rillington had to clap her hands for silence.

"I think we'll have to rethink that name," she muttered.

Stomachs were growling. A Year Eight girl sat with a face like a slapped arse. It was time to call it a night.

Outside, we watched our breath curl away under the stars like cigarette smoke.

"Well, that went well." Tawny's eyes were wide with delight as we began the walk home. I exchanged raised eyebrows with Bryony.

"Wish we shared your enthusiasm, Tawn."

She ignored us and grabbed my shoulders. "You'll help me learn my lines, right? You wrote the bloody thing – you should know! Mum's already started taking my measurements. Think my hips will be all right in a peasant frock? Cate?"

I rolled my eyes. "Shut up."

But I agreed to help out and we all walked down the high street together. Me and Tawny on the outside, keeping time with Bryony's steps in the middle. She was taller than us and I felt like a spindly bodyguard – the one who couldn't punch but could chase stuff. Tawny didn't break her smile. Was she glad to be back in pride of place in the eyes of the school, now that talk of Robyn's troubles had simmered down?

"So long, darlings!"

Tawny carried on alone straight up the road while the pair of us curved off to the left.

"God, I'm glad that's over," Bryony breathed out deeply.

"Year Nines make me want to stab my ears."

Our steps fell in sync.

"You didn't tell me you could act," I probed.

A faint blush came to her cheeks. "Yeah," she muttered.

"Did you have classes?"

"No, it was just me and my brothers messing around."

"Oh . . ." I didn't know what else to say. I opened my mouth to say something to fill the silence, but then Bryony surprised me.

"We act every day of our lives though, don't we?"

"How do you mean?"

The moonlight caught on her cheeks. "We pretend we're someone we're not, out in public – we play-act all the time – someone confident, caring; even happy." She gave me a small smile. Was that part of the act?

"Yes, I suppose you're right . . ." I clutched my folder tighter to my chest, the script clasped firmly and safely in the silver rings of the binder.

"It's easy on stage – you just need to channel the character. Maybe it's easier if she is your great-great-great-great-grandmother or whatever."

I panicked. Had I forced her into playing Jane Hollingworth? Had I pictured Bryony's long blonde hair twisting and blowing in the wind out on the moor; her mouth contorting in harsh-sounding words, hexes and incantations?

Of course I had.

"Bryony . . ."

But she looked at me and laughed softly and the sound of it set me off too.

Either side of us, the hedges were still heavy with berries. If I closed my eyes I could almost hear quivering field mice taking their pick of fruit in the dark, away from owl eyes. There was something soothing about their presence – just out of sight – preparing for the onset of winter. Did Bryony feel them too, or did she still think in buses, Tube stops and flickering city lights? We walked in silence and I wanted to ask her but couldn't. I wanted to ask her about Euan and Rillington's sad sigh. This was the first time we'd spoken properly since The Robyn Incident, but I didn't know what to say at all. Tonight she had belonged to Tawny.

We came to a halt outside Alder Farm. The light in the front room was on: Dad would be finishing a paper, in his dressing gown with the elbows worn down at the sleeves.

I hesitated at the gate.

"Fancy staying at mine tomorrow night?" Bryony said and I flushed.

"Yes, sounds great!" I cringed at my enthusiasm.

"Great." She turned her head to me and grinned. "Bring a bag to school."

I nodded and we stood for a beat of awkward silence. The front door was only fifteen paces away. Should I invite her in? The question hung between us.

"I'll see you tomorrow," she said, and the night air cooled in relief.

"Keep up with those lines!"

"You'll have to be my mentor," she raised an eyebrow.

I could do that.

They said that Jane was the village beauty. Rose Ackroyd had the hips, the dark sultry lips, but she was just a serving girl – a maid with dirt under her fingernails. She scrubbed the front steps of Hollingworth House humming songs the village boys had made up for her. They queued up at the gate to get a view of her bosom. Or so the court records said.

But it was Jane who stunned the crowds.

She would walk to the market once a week, her golden hair coiled up in a crown of curls on top of her head. She had a smile for every passer-by. Even the sourest washerwoman had a curtsy for Lady Hollingworth's girl.

Rose was her chaperone and, together, they walked arm in arm through the streets, turning every head as they went.

Which one started it all? Which one cast the first spell?

Were you born a witch, or did you become one?

In Search of the Long Byrne Witches, P.J. Hebden

Chapter 14

Friday passed in a blur.

We started General Studies classes with Mr Lawrence from P.E., and Kayleigh Whittard put her hand up to ask if the Prime Minister knew anything about aliens. She'd seen a documentary on Channel 5. Mr Lawrence went out for ten minutes and came back reeking of Pall Malls.

The sky was full of dark murmuring clouds, a bit like my head. I couldn't even concentrate on coffee – I glugged it back in the canteen without tasting it. I kept my head down, writing fake notes on my pad, nodding along with the group work we'd been set in English Lit. We got our marks back for a History essay. C+. My stomach flipped. How had that happened?

By the time Mrs Waddington rang the home bell, I was clawing at the edge of my sanity.

Bryony met me after class and we stopped off at Pat's for a Friday night panini – her treat. Tawny would be waiting at the school gate but I steered Bryony down the high street with the dizzy guilt of a thief. I did my best to nibble at the grilled cheese but it tasted like painted cardboard and I started shredding it up in my hands, even though Bryony was already licking her fingers.

"You don't want it?" she said.

"Umm . . ."

She nabbed it out of my grip and ate it so fast she had hamster cheeks and I almost wet myself laughing.

"Did ooh 'ell Owny?"

"What?"

She swallowed. "Tawny – did you tell her you were coming?"

It seemed like I didn't tell Tawny much these days.

"That's OK," said Bryony. "She doesn't need to know where you are all the time."

Then why did I feel slapped in the gut with guilt?

We got to the Manor and went straight upstairs. I forced myself to look straight ahead when we passed the door to the living room. Her room was neat and tidy and I wondered if she'd spent the night before cleaning it just for me. Had I been on her mind?

The whole house felt empty, as if there was no furniture or personal knick-knacks on the other floors, and I realised I'd never seen behind any of the doors that lined the corridors. In fact, I had no idea what was in the rest of the house at all – each room could be filled with empty boxes, or popping candy, or severed heads for all I knew. Robyn's words on the moor chalked themselves on my brain – her face hadn't exactly filled me with confidence.

When I saw a 'How To' guide on dissection lying open on Bryony's desk a lump of bile rose in my throat.

We both sat down on the edge of the bed carefully, testing the water.

Bryony saw me looking at the book on her desk and turned to me knowingly.

"What?" I asked.

"I'm going to de-squeam you."

"*What*?" I scoffed.

"I've never met anyone so squeamish before! You need some hardening up."

I put my hand to my face, smirking. "Oh, god . . ."

"You're asking for it."

"What is this going to involve exactly?"

She scrunched her mouth to the side, thinking, and reached down the side of her bed. "Take a look at this." She slammed a book down in front of me and thumbed through the thick pages.

She pointed to a shiny red diagram of someone's skinless arm. "This is a flexor carpi radialis muscle. It runs up the side of your arm and flexes your wrist.

"Eww."

"Here," she said. Before I knew it she'd grabbed my arm, pulled up my jumper and rested two fingers on my forearm. Her touch was cool and smooth. I held my breath.

"God, Cate!" she gasped.

"What? What is it?" I yanked my arm away to check for boils.

She hesitated then said, "Your arm!"

I pulled my sleeve back down fast.

"There's – there's nothing of it. You're so thin," she said.

I held my wrist and felt a scowl shadow my face. "I'm *fine*."

Her eyes were wide. "Have you been to see a doctor?"

Her words felt painful. "I can't help my natural body type."

She looked from the book to my arm and back again.

"Well. Maybe now isn't the best time for de-squeaming. I should have shown you a horror film. Sam has loads."

"Your brother?"

"Yeah, my older brother. He used to do *The Exorcist* impressions round my door."

I winced. "Don't."

She laughed. "It's OK, I'm not too much of a witch."

"What?"

She spoke slower. "I said I'm not a bitch."

I cleared my throat. "Oh, yeah, I know." I pushed the book away from me, hoping someone would decide to burn it soon.

"You don't think it's kinda cool?" she wheedled.

"What?"

"The human body stuff!" she laughed.

"Umm . . ."

"Not even just a little bit?"

"OK, OK, it's all right," I allowed. "It's just that any normal person would have shown me their holiday pictures and not a book of death and gore. I'd rather not think about what's going on inside me. It's too messy in there already."

There was the flash of concern on her face. It was like watching a deer realise she was being stalked. Deer don't see in pictures, just movement. You sometimes saw them just past the Slip and you had to freeze. If you pretend you're a tree for long enough they just go right past you. Fading out into the trees.

I bit my lip.

"Bryony? Do you go out to the moor on your own?"

She nodded slowly. "All the time. It's peaceful."

There wasn't a single sound besides our breathing. "Do you not know how dangerous it is?"

"Nowhere's dangerous if you know where you're going."

"You've been here less than a month."

She shrugged. "I've been here before. Visited anyway. And besides, I trust my instincts. Don't you?"

I looked at her, so sure of herself. How did she hide everything from her face? Years of hanging round with Tawny had taught me the basics of reading body language – and I thought *I* was good at hiding. But she was something else.

"You know," I whispered, "one wrong foot and you're in the river."

She shrugged. "Nope. I'm careful. Call it family intuition." She waggled her eyebrows but an ancient, deeper part of me didn't feel convinced.

"It was weird out there the night we found Robyn," I said, dipping my toe into a strange conversation that I hadn't been sure I'd wanted to have. "It was like you knew the way. Intuition?"

"I was just following the footpath, Cate."

"Robyn was so scared when she saw you."

Bryony looked at her bedspread. She was silent for a few moments, composing herself. "I think a lot of people listen to gossip and hearsay in Long Byrne. People start to think they see things in people that aren't really there." She looked me straight in the eye and I held her gaze.

"Robyn is very young – she might not always act like it, but she is."

There was silence for a moment but Bryony's word seemed final.

"OK," I said, with a new resolve.

Bryony talked to me about the moor and the lapwings, the croak of the pheasants and how the wind whistled low through your hair as you walked. Her eyes glowed with it. She turned on her laptop and stuck on a stupid song we'd both listened to when we were kids. We did the dance from the music video and collapsed in giggles on the floor. I hadn't laughed like this with anyone other than Tawny in years. When I finally glanced at the clock, it was nearly 11 p.m. I wondered if Mrs Hollingworth was trying to get to sleep in some distant wing. She probably wasn't having much luck tonight, not that I'd heard anything from her at all. Did she even *exist*? I hadn't seen any signs of life in the Hollingworth House other than Bryony. But I pushed the thought to the back of my mind and was happy waving my arms – or my flexor carpi radialis – around. Whatever it was.

We decided it was time for bed. The zip on the sleeping bag Bryony had lent me wouldn't do up all the way and there was a chill gnawing at my toes. I closed my eyes but the print of the thin floral curtains patterned the insides of my eyelids and I couldn't relax. Night seemed to bring the Hollingworth House to life.

Floorboards creaked. A pipe clunked in the ceiling, rattling the lampshade. I couldn't sleep – not that I usually slept. If I was at Tawny's I'd have to lie there for hours and hours, counting breaths, sheep, witches on brooms, pretending to be asleep if she woke up in the middle of the night. I'd soak in her Tawnyness: the powdery smell of spilt makeup and burning hair where she'd left it too long under the dryer. The smell of her berry shampoo.

I had way too much time on my hands.

But here, I felt restless. It was like something was pulsing in the room around me; thrumming through the floorboards, making the dust judder and shake in little measured beats. Like the Hollingworth House was taking its first breath of night air. Maybe if I stayed still it would settle on me and I'd get a real, true sense of the place, just letting it wash over me.

I inhaled slowly.

When I was little, Mum used to brush her hair one hundred times every night. All those coppery strands glimmering together in the bedroom lamplight. The Victorians did it; she showed me pictures of women with long wavy hair that reached their knees. I couldn't imagine any of them ever cracking a smile. Mum would finish her brushing and then do mine – fifty times because I was half the size. I pictured Bryony, perched on the pastel-blue window box, stroking her hair into the brush. The sound of it snagging and pulling free was soothing as I imagined the ghost of her there. Did she really do that? The image was so clear for a second, then it blurred somehow and I couldn't see it.

It was an old image.

Maybe it was something Jane Hollingworth used to do each night.

But this was Bryony's place now.

The earth from her boots, her toothpaste, a sweet woody perfume that I couldn't quite put my finger on. The photos of her blond brothers, her leather bracelet.

I breathed it in.

Suddenly, Bryony moaned in her sleep.

I kept my body very still, trying to imagine all my blood stopping, just grinding to a halt so my stomach wouldn't gurgle and I couldn't wiggle my toes.

I held my breath, feeling myself get very small; the darkness pressing in on me.

But Bryony didn't stop. She groaned and muttered. The same sound again and again, like a robotic doll stuck on repeat. My chest stung from holding my breath. Was she OK? Should I wake her up?

The air above me trembled. Her pale white hand fell down from the bed and landed on my shoulder, like a stopped pendulum. In the blue light from the curtains it appeared ghostly.

I let it rest there a while until I realised it was shaking. The feather charm on her bracelet quivered and knocked the bones of her wrist as it if was possessed. I felt panic bud in my chest. Then she gasped and I realised she was crying. Small sobs that made my heart twist. I couldn't tell whether she was still asleep or not.

I reached up and took her hand.

It was smooth and cold. Laced through mine, her knuckles felt sharp.

After a while the shaking stopped. The room grew quiet.

I strained my ears, hoping to catch the sound of deep easy breathing as she slept.

But the room was silent.

She might have been awake.

I listened and listened. I must have lain awake for hours and fell asleep holding her hand.

The Hollingworth House had its stories.

The twisting corridors, the cellar where they brewed their potions. There might have been a torture chamber in there for all we knew. Not many people have been allowed through its doors since.

But it wasn't the house you had to watch out for."

In Search of the Long Byrne Witches, P.J. Hebden

Chapter 15

It was so bright my eyes stung.

The silver light seeped around the corners of the curtains like the white frill around a postage stamp. Outside, the air was so still you could hear the church bells over in Stoutbridge. I definitely didn't miss the roar of the city. My phone had died and I couldn't see a clock – but whatever time it was, it was the latest I'd slept in for years.

My hand ached slightly from being slotted between her knuckles, but I realised with a jolt that Bryony wasn't in the room with me any more.

I sniffed and realised something smelled *good*. On the desk was a hot mug of black coffee next to a warm hunk of bread and marmalade. Imagining the feel of the bread pressed flat and glued to the roof of my mouth, or stuck like sponge under my tongue made my throat clench. Marmalade seemed like a million years ago too. I really wished I could eat it, but like with all food, I imagined worms in it, all the insects crawling all over the plate so that I could pretend it would taste like rubbish.

No way.

"Just try it."

I spun around.

The room was empty.

"Bryony?" I asked the door.

I was met with the clatter of a downstairs pipe.

Shaking my head and realising I must have imagined those words, I carefully wrapped the piece of bread in yesterday's socks. I would dispose of it later, undetected. My Chicks would have a field day.

I caffeined up then washed and dressed. I couldn't hear anything stirring in the house. Maybe Bryony was down in the basement with her auntie. I could imagine them sitting together in rocking chairs, working their fingers around needles and cloth and chisels by candlelight. Would there be a cauldron in the cellar?

"Oh, stop it," I muttered, shaking my head.

But the thought was always there. The Manor had once been home to Jane Hollingworth. Her neck hadn't been snapped for nothing. There could be anything lurking behind the closed doors of the Hollingworth House.

I went along the corridor, letting my feet drift noiselessly over the runner. The smoky smell of potpourri came up in little tufts from tubs on the window ledges. Doors lined the corridor which stretched the length of the house – a long gallery that would look out over the back garden if you could see through the mottled glass. Every door was like a pair of folded arms.

It wouldn't hurt, would it? I could have a peek around, right? I stopped outside a varnished wooden door. Two knots in the wood stared back at me like curious eyes. I tried the handle.

Locked.

Damn.

I tried a few more but they were all out of bounds. I wandered downstairs, running my hand along the smooth banister, and felt like royalty descending the stairs to dinner.

"Hello?" I called, but there was no answer. I took a tentative step into the living room for the first time. It was pristine, the smell of fresh polish tickling my nose. I tried to avoid it but that Evil Eye stared out at me from above the fireplace, etched into the sandstone like a watchful CCTV camera. I wondered what it had seen. What did it see in me?

I crossed my arms over my chest.

A movement outside the window caught my eye. I went over, my feet disappearing in thick, unused carpet. There was somebody peering around the corner of the frame.

"Robyn!"

"Cate!" Her eyes flickered, voice muffled through the glass. "What are you doing here?"

"I could ask you the same thing," I said grimly. "Stay there."

I sped around to the front door and opened it. Robyn was standing like a rabbit in the headlights, her hands holding the straps of her rucksack on her shoulders. She looked like someone had hit her in the face with an anvil.

I stood in the doorway. "What are–?" I decided to change tack. "How are you feeling?"

"Oh, much better thank you." There was a forced spring in her voice and I wondered if it was the same phrase she used every time Sandra asked her if she was feeling anything more like herself.

"Good. Good. Look, I'm really sorry I never came to see you; I didn't know whether I'd be allowed. I thought . . ." I trailed off, not even bothering to make my excuse sound convincing.

"That's OK. I understand," she shrugged. "I was a bit crazy."

I nodded. And showing up at the Hollingworth House made her seem even more so. Although, she wasn't the only one who'd been peeking in at the living room window recently.

"What's that in your bag?" I asked.

She hoisted it further onto her back. "Nothing."

"Looks heavy."

"Just stuff."

I bit my lip. "You're here to see Bryony, aren't you?"

Her face darkened back to zombieland. "*No.*"

I raised an eyebrow. "Right . . ."

Robyn tried to catch herself. "I mean . . ."

I folded my arms. "Look, Rob, something's obviously going on here." I sighed. I felt harsh, but what did she have against Bryony? "Maybe you should come inside."

"No. No, thank you."

"It might put your mind at rest. There's nothing here to be worried about." Did I believe what I was telling her?

Robyn's eyes swept the driveway. As she stood before me on the bright Hollingworth path, her hair pulled back making her neck look like a strangled chicken and the hollows under her eyes seem like sculpted agate, I didn't know what to think. Her backpack seemed to engulf her. If a breeze had rolled through she would have trembled.

"I don't know . . ." she said.

"C'mon, Rob. You should be resting. You're obviously here for a reason."

She blushed fiercely until her face looked bruised and battered.

I raised an eyebrow. "Come in. Maybe you'll find what you're looking for."

"Maybe," she whispered. I moved aside and she came into the house like a cat taking its first tentative steps into a new home. I watched her absorb the sea of peach and magnolia. "Not exactly a witch's lair, is it?" I said.

Her little face suddenly steeled. "You never know what people are hiding underneath."

There was a beat of silence where the house held its breath.

"She's not a witch, Robyn."

Another beat.

"Then why are you under her spell?" she snapped.

"*Excuse* me?"

Robyn stuck her chin out. I noticed her hands quivering on the handles of her backpack.

My voice sounded high. "Is that why you were out on the moor the other day? Trying to suss her out? Find her broomstick? Is that what's really going on here, Robyn?" I didn't realise how angry I was getting. This all seemed ridiculous.

"Someone's got to watch her."

"You're mental."

Her eyes flickered over to the mantelpiece. The Evil Eye stared sardonically at this thirteen-year-old detective.

"Is that how?" she whispered in the direction of the Eye. "Is that how she's got you?"

I shook my head, disbelieving, not taking my eyes off her. Robyn was losing the plot. She'd lost it.

"Witchcraft," she spat.

"Just think what you're saying here, Rob. What you're accusing Bryony of. She's done nothing wrong. All she did was move here." It was an effort to catch the tremor in my voice. But Robyn rounded on me, her features livid.

"The Evil Eye? Seriously? They have the Evil Eye on their fireplace. Cate – let's get out of here. Please. Come with me." She gripped her rucksack again and over her shoulder I saw the top of a book in the bag. My eyes narrowed. I'd recognise those yellowed pages anywhere: *In Search of the Long Byrne Witches*. This was too much. I almost growled.

"You know the Evil Eye watches out for evil, too? It wards it off."

"But why do they have it in their living room?"

"I don't know! It's an old house. People were superstitious years ago!" At least that's what I'd told myself. "It doesn't mean Bryony and her family are witches."

"Yes, they are."

"Oh, for fuck's . . . look, Robyn, you need to get this out of your head. It's getting ridiculous now. Why are you so interested in Bryony?" I felt my voice rising hysterically and hated it. "Why would it even matter if she was a witch?"

"Because there's nothing left to stop her from putting you under her spell. Once they have you, they'll take you away from me."

I looked into those wide earnest eyes, the ones that had read all those musty pages, dark words. Robyn had cracked.

And then we both heard it. The crunch of gravel on the path.

I felt her eyes on me and I didn't dare look at her. The air suddenly seemed still enough to hear my own heartbeat. Instead, I heard the beating of the Hollingworth House. Something shifted.

A crunch.

My chest froze. Bryony was approaching the door.

They said you never heard a witch coming. She was already in your mind, hushing your whimpers, smoothing down the stood-up hair on your neck.

She knew just how to let herself inside.

The Lunar Rites of Lancashire, Melanie Hargreaves

Chapter 16

I wasn't meant to be here. The living room suddenly felt like a secret place. All this history. I realised I had my nails in my mouth.

We looked at one another.

"Go. *Go!*" I hissed. She didn't need telling again. Robyn rushed to the window, nudged it open and launched herself out onto the same verge where I'd watched Tawny a whole lifetime ago.

Bryony walked in holding a carrier bag.

"The butcher's wasn't open yet," she said. "But I got some— oh."

"Hey." I felt suddenly light-headed and embarrassed. I edged my eyes towards the window but Robyn was out of sight.

Bryony came into the room, keeping her eyes on the frilly valance around the sofa, as if checking for a dead body under a bed. I felt her hand in mine again from last night. I gulped.

"Sorry, I thought you were Auntie," she smiled. She wore a khaki-coloured jacket and dark fitted jeans. Even in something so simple she looked like a model and I felt my neck reddening.

"Just me," I said. "Did you sleep OK?"

Bryony rolled back her shoulders. "Yeah, really well." I didn't want to tell her about her disturbed night. "This room is stifling, isn't it? Shall we go for a walk?"

"Sure, if you want."

We put her shopping away in the kitchen. She still smelled of the cold outside, like copper and leaves. Fingers red from the chill. I went to get my bag and met her in the hall.

"Not freaked out by the witch house then?" she said.

My nerves sprang into action. Had she heard Robyn escaping? "No!"

"I'd be freaked out. Auntie likes to keep that old relic on display." She jerked her head to the stone etching about the mantelpiece. "She can get really intense with the witch stuff." She rolled her eyes. "Like she says, it's in our blood."

"Do you believe it?"

"Yeah – I can shoot cobwebs from my wrists too."

"Where is your aunt, anyway? I've not met her yet."

"Oh, she likes to keep herself to herself."

I grabbed my stuff from upstairs then we went out and walked down the path onto the road, past Alder Farm and down to the Slip. My eyes darted around, hoping Robyn had completed her getaway – there had been no vials of holy water left along the path, which was a plus. She'd gone. Bryony swung her arms to keep warm, while I clenched and unclenched my fingers in my pockets around the hidden toast. Marmalade oozed steadily through the sock.

It was a clear day. If you stopped to peer between the gaps in the trees you could see the dark church steeple in Stoutbridge, and, beyond it, the mountains on the Pennine Ridge were a misty grey-blue. Our footsteps fell in line with each other as we headed out to the moor, picking our way through the summer-scorched gorse until the sound of the river had forced its way to us. I shuddered. It took me a moment to remember how I'd got here. I'd just been following Bryony and we were further out on the moor than I'd been for a long time.

She brought us to a halt and looked around. "This is where it happened, isn't it?"

My stomach flipped. "Where what happened?"

"Where they killed the witches?"

I kicked a rock and it clanged on my boot toecaps. "Yeah, they think so."

"I come here a lot. You just get a feeling about this place," she carried on. "You know, when someone's died somewhere."

Then why would you come here? I said to myself.

"I heard once about this old man who died sitting up in bed and no one found him for weeks and weeks." Bryony's eyes looked bright and I found myself staring at them even though I just wanted her to stop talking "When they got to him, they had to peel him away from the wall and where his head had been was this greasy yellow stain."

Bryony flared her eyes, like Tawny relishing the death of a tragic heroine in one of those old gothic novels. It didn't suit her.

"Another family moved into the house and didn't get round to decorating for ages. So when the kids went to bed and stayed up reading at night, they put their heads right on that yellow patch. Death-grease and old bits of skin."

I could tell she wanted my reaction. It didn't feel right. This was Tawny's domain – stories with dramatic effect. Bryony's shoulders were tensed, coiled and waiting.

I shrugged hard. "You're drama-central today. How's lead actress working out for you?"

She blinked, suddenly smaller and more Bryony-like. Her muscles unwound, like a cat giving up chase on a bird.

"Sorry. Bad things can happen anywhere. That's all."

I frowned, wanting to tell her she was getting cryptic and childish. I didn't like it one bit. But her mouth didn't have its usual firmness and I backed off: I wished I could press it with my thumb to get it back in shape.

She looked out across the moor. Her long hair ruffled in the wind, feathering out along the edges, and I could smell her usual Bryony scent. There was a crust of mud along the rim of her wellies. I felt like I knew Bryony differently than other people. I knew her hair tossed in silver-gold loops as she took long strides across the heather. I knew the sound of her muttering in her sleep. I desperately wanted to reach out and take her hand again.

She didn't belong to Tawny right now. She was all mine today.

"It's beautiful here," she sighed.

"Yeah."

"All these rowan trees. They say they're for protection."

I looked at her quickly. "Yes, that's what my mum told me, too."

Bryony's voice sounded far away. "They were planted after the witches were hanged." She didn't look at me.

I blinked. "Oh, yeah?"

She raised an eyebrow. "I thought you were some kind of witch expert."

I wanted to yell indignantly *I am!* But instead I said, "So, how do you know?"

"I thought everyone knew. People would make crosses out of them, or smear the berries on themselves to purify their flesh, like rubbing salt in wounds."

"Not poisonous then?"

"Nope. Not unless you're an evil spirit." She frowned. "It's what they made bonfires out of when they burnt witches in Europe."

I winced.

Bryony rolled her eyes and gave a dry laugh. "Don't worry, my aunt just likes to tell stories. She used to tell me them when I came to visit as a kid. All that stuff about what they did to those girls when they were in prison."

"That's dark, Bryony. She shouldn't have told you stuff like that."

She shrugged. "Our family's got a lot of history, like any other. Except ours is a bit more morbid. I've got to admit, Mum and Dad weren't too keen on the idea of me up here, after everything that happened at home. But I pushed for it."

My body became hyper-alert. Was she about to tell me what had happened at home? I struggled to keep my voice nonchalant. "Why didn't they want you up here?"

Her green eyes looked dark as a gust of wind blew her hair in May Day streamers around her.

"Come here," she said, a smile rising on one cheek. "I want to show you something."

"What?"

"Another way they kept evil out."

She fiddled with something on her coat. It was a small silver brooch tucked behind her lapel. She pulled the fabric back to reveal it nestled there like a toad in its hole.

"The Evil Eye," she grinned menacingly. The badge watched me lazily out the corner of its eye and my insides clenched.

I thought of what Robyn had said. The Evil Eye was a symbol of evil but also one of protection. I wondered which one Bryony kept in her jacket.

I tried to arch an eyebrow shakily. "I thought you said that was a load of crap."

She laughed. "Auntie said I should wear it. Wish it warded off knobheads."

"That would be useful," I agreed.

She unpinned the brooch and held up her finger. I wondered why it had taken me so long to realise what she was going to do. I'd seen all the Hollywood movies: you prick your finger, you make a pact: blood brothers, blood sisters, and you're for ever bonded and could sometimes hear each other's thoughts from all the way across the world. Tawny had wanted to do it once but we chickened out after raiding Sandra's sewing box for a needle. She changed her mind and we'd played our pillow game instead.

I imagined the small pop of skin as Bryony pressed the point of the brooch into the tip of her finger, like pushing a safety-pin through your shirt when a button pinged off. The tiniest bead of blood appeared from the hole, a miniature cork that had been stopping her vein.

"Like this," she said. She held out her hand, the bead of

blood balancing there – a dark plate on a waiter's arm. I clenched my teeth but instead of handing me the pin too, she turned towards the rowan trees next to us and made a sweeping motion with her hand. Two long elaborate strokes against a thin trunk, rubbing a thin streamer of redness onto the tree. I blinked the sun out of my eyes. The bark seemed to gleam where she'd first touched it.

"You put a big fat cross across something so Jesus would protect you," she smiled wickedly.

"Is that it?" I thought my voice sounded disappointed.

"Not impressed? I'm bleeding and everything!"

I never asked you to. I laughed half-heartedly. "Where did you learn that?"

"Auntie knows every charm, counter-curse and superstition in the book."

We carried on walking. "Do you think any of them work?"

"I doubt it." She shrugged. "Dad's a doctor. Mum's an accountant. I wasn't brought up to think like that. My brother on the other hand . . ." she rolled her eyes.

"He's into it all?"

With some effort she held up her wrist, as if it was pushing through a force field. The leather cord she wore all the time dangled its silver feather in the wind. "He made me a good luck charm for my exams last May. Typical him."

"Is he back in London?"

"Oh. No." A spasm of pain crossed her face. "Euan's not here any more. Killed himself."

It hit me like a branch in the chest.

How had she not told me something like that? I hadn't

told people about Mum, and yet somehow everyone knew. Maybe people really could read stuff like that on you. Not Bryony though – she'd slipped through the net, aloof and untouchable. I reached out and squeezed her arm, feeling like I was breaking every rule in the book.

She seemed to ignore my touch and sucked on her bleeding finger.

"See?" she said. "You're de-squeamed."

She quickly folded her thoughts away, like tucking a secret letter into her pocket.

"You don't have to do that with me, you know," I said shyly. "The hiding."

She shrugged again. "I know."

"When did it happen?"

"About four months ago – just before school finished. He always had these big ideas on life and death and pretty much everything else. A real little philosopher. It just all got too much for him."

I waited and she began to open up.

"They called us the Twins," she smiled sadly. "He's a year younger, but we look so alike. I used to shove on one of his beanies, stuff my hair inside and see if I could get away with being him. I almost did, but Dad always caught us out. He's got a sixth sense. He's a Hollingworth, after all."

She was lost in a reverie. I tried to picture them all together in that big London house. Bryony, Euan and Sam, all huddled together under a collection of horror movies and books: those two smiling boys from the Paris photo. I tried to imagine Euan suddenly gone.

I stayed silent. I had a feeling that this was the first time she'd spoken about it with someone. She went on.

"He got so excited about things. The doctors asked if he'd been on pills, doing drugs, that kind of stuff. The police searched his room, and then mine. But he was just Euan. My little brother. He wasn't crazy, he just saw things."

My heart suddenly missed a beat. *Saw things?* I tried to keep my expression blank. "What kind of things?"

She looked at me, slowly turning her head like she was taking a panoramic photo.

"He wasn't crazy, Cate."

"I know," I said quickly. "I'm sorry, I didn't mean . . ."

"He wasn't a witch either."

"I never said—"

Bryony looked off into the distance and I thought I saw things flashing in her eyes, the outlines of things reflected that weren't really there. She spoke quickly. "He saw how people really were. All their goodness and kindness, and then how everything around us corrupted them. He hated how even when you took the Tube to somewhere green you could still hear the constant drone of the traffic and smell the engines of all those manmade things. He hated it. He didn't understand how people could live like that. And I suppose he didn't want to."

Her eyes burnt into mine like I'd accused her of something terrible. "That's what he could see, Cate. Nothing more."

A blush rose fiercely to my neck and we walked in silence for a few beats. I gulped down a lump of bile that had been rising from my growling stomach.

"We should head back."

Bryony shoved her hand in her pocket. "I bet you wish you'd stayed at Tawny's last night instead of mine."

"What? No!" I said. "Why would you say that?"

"Well, it seems like all we talk about is death! Tawny would have you talking about something that makes you laugh. She's a lot of fun."

Wait, was Bryony jealous of Tawny? I tried to wrap my head around the thought. Someone like Bryony being jealous of anyone made my mind whirl.

"I don't care about that. I love Tawny but sometimes it's important to talk about stuff other than school and films and dance recitals. Remember when I said I liked talking to you?" I was breathing hard now. I wondered if she could tell. "I really meant that."

"Me too," she whispered.

We looked at each other for a long beat and I thought my heart might fall out of my chest at her feet.

She shrugged, a taut smile appearing around her lips. "Let's go."

We took the same route, letting the sounds of the river wash over us. I was glad that the path was narrow so that I could stand behind her and slow the rumbling in my chest. The way back seemed quicker and I was glad of it. I dipped my hand in my pocket and crumbled the crust of marmalade bread between my fingers, leaving a trail behind us, although somehow I didn't think we would want to find our way back. The gate to the Slip reared up in front of us and the relief swept through me.

"I'd better be heading back," she said.

I tucked my windswept hair behind my ear and stepped in front of her to cut her off. "Bryony, wait. Any time you want to talk . . ."

"Thanks." She said it firmly, although she still didn't look like herself under the shadow of the trees.

"And my Dad's a philosopher. An academic one, anyway. He's not so bad. Maybe him and Euan would have got along."

Bryony smiled, genuinely this time. "I hope so. Thanks, Cate. Thank you." She turned and headed purposefully towards the village. I slowed my pace to let her make her exit. Even when fleeing, she walked methodically, considering all eventualities in every step.

So Bryony had come to Long Byrne to escape from something. I didn't blame her. Long Byrne was a half-forgotten place in the middle of nowhere; maybe it was the perfect place to hide your past.

I turned my key in the lock. The wet weather had made the door swell. I gave it an extra shove and stumbled into the heat of the hall. Dad's door was open and I could see a fire burning in the grate, a pile of pine cones neatly arranged in a dish on the coffee table. It was like Alexa was preparing an early Christmas-card scene. It looked peaceful.

"Where the hell have you been?"

My head snapped up.

Dad rounded the kitchen door and Alexa stuck her head out nervously behind him.

I froze. "What's happened? Is everything OK?"

"You didn't answer my question."

"Out. Why? Is it the Chicks?"

"No, it's not the bloody hens." Dad glowered; the wrinkles on his forehead were dark crevices. "We've been worried sick! Your phone's off, no note – we've been turning over your room, ringing round everyone we know."

"What!" My voice was shrill. "Why were you in my room? I was out with Bryony!"

"Who on earth's Bryony?" Dad grew several inches taller. "We rang Tawny but she said she hadn't seen you and we didn't want to worry Mrs Brown after what happened with Robyn."

"This has nothing to do with Robyn—"

"We've been up since dawn." His glasses flashed. "That helper boy didn't turn up, so the cows were screaming to be milked—"

"I don't suppose you could have done it," I hissed.

"—while you were off gallivanting wherever you please!"

"I was with Bryony. It's no big deal," I shrugged but my shoulders were shivering. I hadn't had enough coffee yet and my head was spinning. "I didn't think you'd care. I'm here now, aren't I?"

"Don't you talk to me like that, young lady."

Oh, that was too much. "Talk to you like that? When was the last time you even *spoke* to me? If the cows hadn't started up, how long would it take you to even realise I was gone?"

"Caitlin Aspey—"

Full-name treatment. But I couldn't stop now; I was on a roll. "How long does it *ever* take you to realise? Maybe if you listened to me once in a while or took your nose away from that stupid screen you might know where I was and who I hang out with!"

His forehead lines came down one by one in a cascade. "I don't appreciate that tone, Cate."

"Well, you don't appreciate anything, do you?"

It sounded stupid, and we both knew it didn't make any sense, but I saw him crumple. I grabbed the stair rail and heaved myself up three steps at once. From up high he looked so small and skinny.

"And just so you know, Bryony is one of the best people you'll ever meet. If I *was* going to run away, it would be with her."

I slammed my door so hard the ceilings shook. We spent the rest of the day cooped in our individual rooms like dolls locked in separate boxes.

Long Byrne really was a good place to hide in.

On this night, and in this place
We call upon an ancient grace.
Bring us light and love, all weathers
And let our friendship never sever.
You are mine and I am yours;
Sweet darkness, let our love endure.
Juniper, skullcap, rose, vervain,
We shall never break the chain.

The Witches' Spell, written in 1622

Chapter 17

It was weird seeing Robyn back at school again. She had that gaunt look of someone who'd seen their dog put down, or spent too long indoors playing video games. Tawny gave her a little shove through the door for good measure. She told me the doctors had sat Robyn in a room with Sandra for nearly two hours and bombarded her with questions.

"It was like they were testing her for MENSA when, really, she's just a little teen psycho. She should team up with Rillington. A right pair of crazies they'd make." Tawny flounced off to Textiles with a shake of her head.

I spotted Robyn in the corridor on the way to class and tried to nab her but she was being swarmed on by a bunch of Year Eights.

"Robyn! It's great to have you back."

"Oh my god, Robyn, hi! Did you get my card?"

"Hey, Robyn Brown," they yelled. "HEY!"

But she kept her head down and slunk past, her skinny legs working overtime. She looked haunted.

"Oi!" they called after her. "What a bitch."

The first week of October smelled like turned-over earth and damp wood. Back gardens billowed white clouds of bonfire smoke that hovered over the cobbles, so our hair smelled like the fifth of November. People's secret stacks of dirty magazines and scribbled notes turned to ash in the cold air. The ice-cream van had stopped bothering to entice us with its clunky rendition of 'Greensleeves', but Rillington refused to turn the radiators on; we'd probably start to feel our toes again the week before Christmas. We layered up and were allowed to wear hats in class, even stupid Arctic ones like Matty Bridge's.

Most mornings, the sky was red and I sang the old rhyme under my breath. *Red sky at night, shepherd's delight. Red sky in the morning, shepherd's warning.* One of Mum's favourites. I wondered what we were being warned against.

Bryony had become the star of the school. People copied her simplistic style with cheap knock-off panic-buys and Kayleigh Whittard had dyed her hair blonde. In spite of this, all the fame certainly didn't make Bryony popular. I heard rumours that she was doing some guy from the rugby team up in Stoutbridge and had tried to seduce Mr Burroughs even though he was old enough to be her handsy uncle and wore hairspray in his beard.

"Bet she loves getting her fingers tangled in *that*," one of the Year Eleven girls screeched.

I started waiting for Bryony at the Alder Farm gate and she'd smile at me as she rounded the corner. There was a shared understanding between the two of us now. We'd both been through a tragedy that other people just couldn't understand, no matter how hard they tried.

"Hey," I said.

"Hey," she breathed back at me.

We'd rub each other's hands through our gloves and stamp our feet until our shins hurt. I loved the mornings.

There was less than one month to go before the big re-enactment day.

Rehearsals took over everything.

Rillington expected me to be there, against my protests, in order to make sure that people stuck to their lines. But I could hardly make my voice heard from the audience, so it seemed pointless to me. The panic of it started to wake me up even earlier each day.

It was Thursday. 4.50 a.m. I rubbed my feet together like a cricket under the covers, to stay warm in the pitch darkness.

The yard was quiet and my boots squelched loudly in the mud. A chill lined the air. Over the hill, the edges of the Hollingworth House glowed a dim lilac, like it had its very own aura.

There was so much to do. I wished Robyn was there. I felt a sudden wave of guilt, but I shrugged it off. I hadn't spoken to her at all since I'd seen her at Bryony's – there didn't seem to be a lot more to say.

A lad in Upper Sixth had taken Robyn's job on the farm – Joe Blakemore – we weren't cutting him a bad deal: fifty quid for four days a week plus breakfast, albeit one of Alexa's inedible concoctions. It gave her someone to perve on as she did the morning dishes anyway and, besides, it gave me an excuse to stay away from home more often. Dad was avoiding me and I didn't exactly want to speak to him either.

I opened up the cow barn then stooped into the henhouse

to collect the eggs. My Chicks were so peaceful, shifting groggily and letting me put my hand underneath their warm feathers. The eggs felt so fragile in my hand – sometimes I wanted to leave them there and let the hen pretend it would be a mum in a few weeks' time.

I frowned. Something wasn't right. Slowly, I counted the softly murmuring hens. Eight – nine – ten. Ten. Where was the eleventh?

No glossy black feathers in sight.

"Where are you, girly? Don't go playing tricks on me." I ducked outside to scan the yard, but no sign. The other hens blinked blearily at me from the half-dark. They'd better give Glossy a peck when she came back from walkabout.

My phone buzzed in my pocket. A Chick squawked in surprise.

Tawny was calling.

"Did you get the email?" she said.

"What email?"

"Honestly, do you ever use the internet? Classes have been cancelled, baby!"

I gave a triumphant laugh. "Why?"

"Something got stuck in the Science Block vents again. The whole school reeks of a McDonalds slaughterhouse."

I balked. "Gross, Tawn."

"Oh come on, going to puke up your breakfast?"

I didn't say anything.

"Rillington said we have to go in for rehearsals though."

"Seriously?" I wished I could Tawny Sigh. "I'd rather be back in Year Eleven doing maths."

"Stop raining on my parade. Get ready, OK?"

Tawny had never been up so early in her life. I suppose that was thespian dedication. Or maybe it was just the Long Byrne crazy showing through.

Rillington had a tight regime day of read-throughs and footwork planned out. It was like she'd mangled some rabbits in the ducts solely for this purpose.

"That was ... adequate," she sighed. "I think we should be ready to do this in costume now."

"Dress rehearsaaaaaaal!" Tawny sang.

I'd been backstage before – the smell of sweaty feet, talcum powder and greased metal clung to the curtains. Abandoned good-luck cards littered a cork notice board from years gone by and the dressing room reeked of menthol fags where Mr Lawrence came in for a quick puff before fourth period.

"I'm home!" Tawny trilled, flinging herself onto a stool and flicking her hair out in front of a long mirror that actually had lightbulbs around it like in the movies. We sidled into the dressing room after her. "We need a good-luck ritual. Bryony, any witchy tips? Got a rabbit's foot on you?"

Bryony's mouth twitched. "As long as you say something in rhyme, that should do the trick."

Tawny cackled with glee. "C'mon, Cate, that's your domain. Give us a rhyme for luck."

I shrugged. Making an idiot of myself was not something on my To Do list for the day. But even Bryony was looking at me expectantly.

"I don't know. I'm all out."

Tawny tutted. "Pathetic. You're the crappest witch ever."

Bryony saw me falter and she turned away, playing with a plaster on her right forefinger. Her lip gloss (à la Tawny) made her look like one of those pasty models in Teen Vogue. There was a line of kohl across her top eyelids.

I frowned. Seeing her like this, it was like our talk on the moor had never happened, and I couldn't wait until the next time we could walk to school together.

Tawny flipped open a palette of theatre paint that she'd brought from home, all thick and gloopy. She swished a brush round in the rouge and turned to her protégée. "Bryony! Dahhhling!" she drawled. "I'll make you a star."

Bryony grinned at her hands in a way I'd never seen before. She looked like a girl being asked to dance for the first time; shy and expectant. She stepped forward to sit in the glow of the mirrors and lightbulbs, and craned her face forward.

I couldn't keep my eyes off them.

Rose and Jane, together in the darkened room.

Tawny expertly cupped Bryony's chin. With large circular motions, Tawny made her white cheeks into those of a china doll. She slicked an easy red line around the nibbled lips, transforming them into something ripe, like they were ready to slide around a fresh apple.

Still holding Bryony's jaw, Tawny leant in as if to count the thin black lines of her irises.

"Beautiful," she whispered.

I watched intently. Bryony breathed out and I imagined that single breath creating steam on Tawny's hot cheeks. Her lips were parted slightly and I saw that Bryony's eyes were fixed on Tawny's.

None of us moved, letting the moment settle on us like leaves blown in the air. Something had happened. I wasn't sure what. But it was there in the room with us.

"Girls!" a voice screeched from the top of the stairs. "That's enough preening and twirling. Some of us would like to get some work done today." Rillington huffed and stormed off.

Bryony pulled her head back and stood up sharply. Her stomach was close to Tawny's face. The room inhaled raggedly and we all scrambled for the exit. I was the last to get out.

I suddenly realised I was panting.

Rillington scowled. "What on earth were you doing back there? For goodness sake, Hollingworth, you're not in a brothel. Wipe that tat off your face." Bryony nodded sullenly and scrubbed her hand back and forth against her lips.

"Right," Rillington clasped her hands together and turned to the hall. "Now the show can really begin."

Rillington had me on mood-lighting duty. Whenever Tawny and Bryony were going through their lines, I plunged the place into darkness for effect. If Rillington chipped in, I had to light the place up so everyone could see the tick in her forehead.

I turned light switches off and on. On and off. I got myself into a pattern of clicking so that all I thought about was the light and the dark, and not Bryony's stomach lying almost flat to Tawny's face.

Up on stage, everyone was really trying their best. The Groupies had known their lines and cues after a single read-through. They'd gone home and sat in their rooms, by candlelight (of course), and whispered my words between them again and again until they got yelled at for staying up so late.

They wanted to dazzle.

But it was Tawny and Bryony who were perfect.

They were mesmerising.

"The moon is bright tonight," said Tawny, tucking a strand of hair innocently behind her ear. "Is it time?"

Bryony came to stand beside her, walking the entire length of the stage so they were pressed shoulder to shoulder, looking at an imaginary point in the sky. "One more day, my love. One more day. Then we shall flee this place."

"No, please, let's go tonight." Tawny's face contorted to a plea. "There is light enough to guide our way. We can be far away by dawn."

"Wait," said Bryony, her voice rich and melodious. I had given Jane the stronger character and her hand fluttered to Rose's waist, drawing her closer. "Everything has to be perfect. The time must be right, and then we can go together."

"And then we can bind ourselves together?"

"Yes."

"And what will it mean?"

Jane spoke slowly. "The binding spell will mean our souls can never be parted."

Tawny's eyes were round and gleaming, her mouth set in determination. After two beats, the pair separated on stage with a lingering glance.

My stomach twisted as I watched Bryony's fingers trail the width of Tawny's back as they parted.

Next, Rillington wanted them to do the scene in the jail,

right near the end, and everyone got into place on stage. Tawny crossed her wrists behind her back and sidled over to the Year Ten boy playing the guard, and said, "Hold me tight." He looked like he was about to keel over.

The scene began. Bryony was motionless on the floor and Tawny was yelling, "Unhand me!"

The guard stuttered out, "If you say so."

We all watched closely as he called the Evil Eye to help protect him against the witches' magic. I'd come across the charm in a book when I was younger. I knew all those evenings in the village library would come in useful at some point. It was a nice little authentic charm from the period and I felt proud of adding it in, even if the guard boy was messing it up.

"I ca-call upon the Evil Eye. May it cast its gaze upon you, witch, and strike you down!"

Out of the corner of my eye, I saw Bryony's hand shift to the collar of her jacket and grasp onto something there, even though she was meant to be unconscious. I watched her as her knuckles grew tight. What was she doing?

Was she clutching her own Evil Eye?

I frowned but no one else seemed to notice. Rillington's eyes were on Tawny, who was doing a great impression of someone who was being scared out of their wits.

In fact, I was feeling a little scared myself.

Whatever she was doing, I had a strange feeling.

By 4 p.m., people were messing around with their phones. Girls with bright-pink painted cheeks sat with their legs wide open, too bored to even care. Rillington stood up and I flooded the place with 1970s fluorescent glow.

"Right, god knows that's enough for today, folks." She rubbed the bridge of her nose. "Josie, take that pointed hat off, *now*. We'll get back to it on Monday and see if we can . . . bring something together."

Tawny's voice rattled along the roof-tiles of the high street.

"I don't know what she's on about. We've had two minutes with that script and I think it's bloody decent. I mean, OK, so I couldn't pronounce some of it, but she knows I'm borderline dyslexic. It's a common trait among actresses, you know? Isn't that right, Cate?"

"Sure, Tawn."

"Wasn't I saying to you this summer about how all the best actors take ages to learn their lines and stuff? It must be in my blood."

I had so much homework to do. Miss Draycott was going to slaughter me. I'd watched her massacre Matty Bridge the week before when he'd handed in an essay on half a side of A4 and I definitely didn't want to be in her firing line. I was going to compare notes with Bryony on the way back up the lane – maybe she'd had some spark of inspiration I was missing.

"I'm heading home."

"What? It's four thirty!" Tawny laughed. "I've already asked our leading lady to stay over."

Staying over? The three of us? I bit my lip, thinking about the dressing room, and my stomach squirmed with jealousy. The dreadful pull of homework made me feel even more nauseated. "Maybe tomorrow, Tawn. It's been a long day."

She threw up her hands. "Fine. Bryony?"

Bryony dropped her gaze. "I'm still up for it."

I could have actually thrown up. I looked from Tawny to Bryony, their faces half shadow, half light, making up one full moon where we stood under the high street's lamps.

"O-OK. See you tomorrow?"

They turned and started walking off, so synchronised it felt rehearsed, their feet giving off one single echo with each step against the bricks. An old dream flickered in my mind like a torn flag. Bryony and Tawny down the Slip . . .

I began walking home and cursed my Psychology essay to the pits of hell.

The house phone went just as Alexa's soaps were starting up. I heard her huff over the theme tune in the back room, so I took the excuse to get away from Freud and ran to the upstairs phone.

"Hello?"

"Is that you, Cate? It's Miss Rillington."

"Oh, hi, Miss."

"Just to let you know school will be open tomorrow."

Joy. "OK, did they get the vents fixed?"

She sighed. "Yes, we found the problem. Looks like a hen had got in."

I felt my face drain.

"Probably dragged in there by a fox. It was quite a mess, anyway. All clear now though. See you tomorrow. The big day looms!"

I hung up the phone and ran to the yard. I counted my hens under the harsh light of my phone. Ten – still ten.

I went into the bathroom and swiftly puked up my guts.

Over the years different types of people have said they've seen things down the Slip. Early-morning dog walkers and primary school children whose older brothers had told them stories to give them nightmares.

Long Byrne had heard it all.

Strange sounds, ghostly wails. Sometimes groups of adolescent girls camped out there at Midsummer, hoping to catch a glimpse of the two girls pulling at their nooses like starched collars. Sometimes a rambler would get lost on the moor and come back as pale as porridge, startled by the sounds of a black grouse, saying they'd seen the Devil out on the Witches' Moor.

The after-effects stayed here for generation after generation.

The History of Long Byrne: Demons on the Moor,
Dr C. Munir

Chapter 18

"What do you mean, you don't know your cue!" Rillington thundered at Tawny.

"I mean I've had a French oral exam to practise for and if you want me to start chanting spells halfway through it, you've got another thing coming, Miss."

"Enough cheek, Brown. I can easily cut you from this."

"You think?" Tawny raised a menacing eyebrow. The room tittered. Rillington ruffled her papers. "Let's carry on then, shall we?"

Everyone was at least half in love with Tawny. She'd made Rose into the best flirt in Long Byrne. Even when she hopped offstage she stayed in character, mingling with the Year Nine Angry Peasants and winking to make them blush.

It was typical Tawny and they lapped it up.

"Oi, Pad!" she shouted across the lunch room. "Don't worry, maybe Rose swings both ways. You can have Jane's sloppy seconds." She did an exaggerated wink.

Pad blushed crimson and the whole canteen screamed with laughter.

When I nudged her sharply, Tawny only turned to me with her big grin in place and said, "Fuck off."

It was 4.30 p.m. and already nearly pitch black outside. I was wearing my biggest hoodie – the green one I wore when I was sick or had spent all night choking on bile over a dead black hen. I'd wedged myself in the corner of the room, my arms around my drawn-up knees. Matty Bridge had been showing me how to light fireworks on the field for the past half hour, in preparation for the big day. He seemed to like the pyrotechnics much more than a sane and normal person would.

The fireworks were going to go off right at the end during the hanging scene. For a bit of the old Tawny glamour, I'd given the moment a bit of creative licence, imagining the witches to fire lightning from their fingers to frighten the crowd just before they were brutally murdered. A jumpscare.

Tawny would like that.

I was trying to take in Matty's 'safety' instructions but I had just kept seeing black feathers.

How could this have happened?

I wished I could sleep, but a day's worth of caffeine buzzed through my veins and made my head spin. I imagined the thick sludge of three years' worth of coffee granules lurking somewhere in my liver. Thoughts that I wished would stay asleep stirred and nudged at me.

I hadn't told Dad or Alexa about the hen, because they'd never notice the difference and I wasn't on speaking terms with Professor Aspey anyway. I hadn't told Tawny because she wouldn't care. But I hadn't told Bryony because something inside my head told me not to.

I watched Tawny fan out her hair on stage. She'd said acting was in her blood – I dreaded to think what ran in my veins. And as for Bryony . . . I didn't know.

Tawny came to sit by me after her scene, Bryony in tow. Rillington was busy herding Year Tens into a straight line.

"Don't you think you're pushing her a bit far?" I said. "She's only trying to help."

Tawny scoffed. "I hate it when you get all brown-nosey over Rillington. She gave you a pep talk one time and now you're her golden girl?"

"*No*," I scowled. "I just think everyone needs to stick together to make this work."

There was a beat of silence.

"Oh Cate, get a life, why don't you?"

I looked at Bryony, who kept her eyes firmly fixed on the very interesting parquet floor. She'd barely met my eye in days. Maybe she felt like she'd let something slip she shouldn't have. I pressed my tongue hard against the back of my teeth.

Tawny stood up and grabbed Bryony's arm. "Come on, lady love, let's show 'em what we've got."

They went running back to the stage, leaving me sitting in the corner. Bryony didn't look round but I hope she felt my eyes scorching her.

The hall suddenly felt very cold.

The hair rose on my arms; a feeling swept over my skin, rippling it the wrong way. I wildly wondered if this was how Robyn had felt that night in the hencoop.

I started to get up but quickly sat back down, the room spinning. The stage suddenly seemed like a gaping hole, pulling Bryony and Tawny towards it while I was stuck in the corner. I screwed up my eyes and shook my head. When did things get so blurry?

Everything in the room seemed to dim.

A strange scene whirled around me like I was being sucked into the stage too. I put my head in my hands, trying to silence the intrusive thoughts, but I couldn't stop them.

Jane and Rose were best friends. BFFs. That was how I'd written it in the script. They did everything together and people didn't like that. They said their friendship was unnatural. The work of the Devil: two girls, sharing their food and beds and kisses on the cheek.

It wasn't right. But Rose and Jane didn't care . . .

. . . until Rose started looking at a boy she met while out picking loganberries on the moor. His name was Richard Westwell – a name I'd picked out from the village register – Dick. She swooned when he walked down the street with a bale of hay strapped to his back. Loved how his muscles looked when he had a pig under his arm.

Rose went after him like a puppy dog.

Jane's eyes narrowed. She could see Rose falling away from her – a leaf drifting out on the river. Jealous and angry, Jane confronted her and the pair quarrelled, out in the village centre. Everyone saw, everyone heard them screaming at each other like banshees, or something possessed.

That was when the whispers started.

They watched the girls like hawks. Things started to happen in the village. Bad things. Diseases and a bad crop. Things they used to blame the fairies for. But Jane and Rose were real, they were real girls, and they had waves of anger rolling off their shoulders.

One night the girls were nowhere to be found. The villagers went up to the moor. Their usual spot. And then . . . we all know what they found up there.

I looked at them on stage together.

Rose and Jane.

Jane and Rose.

Bryony and Tawny.

I didn't feel so good.

I found that I couldn't move. I was entranced by the two of them. The way they moved together. They looked so beautiful, so synchronised.

Up on that dark mouth of the stage, they might have been made for each other.

Something in me bubbled over, scolding my chest to the core.

I tore myself out of the chair. I had to get out of there.

"Hey, Cate!"

I turned. Tawny had her hands cupped to her mouth.

"Where are you going?"

"I just – I just need some fresh air. I'll be back in a bit."

"Well—"

"Keep your voice down, Tawny, we're not on the playing field now." Rillington glared.

Tawny cackled, but I saw Bryony bite her lip and slide down from the stage on her own. She came towards me and I felt my skin goose-pimple. *Go away. Not now.*

"You sure you're all right?" she whispered softly. "You look really pale."

"I'm fine. I just need to breathe." I yanked at the neck of my hoodie.

She nibbled her lip but her eyes were already flickering back to the stage. Back to Tawny. "OK. You know where we'll be."

The air outside was piercing cold. I didn't have a scarf and my feet felt like weights crashing to the floor.

What was *wrong* with me?

I took a deep breath. Was this what a panic attack felt like? I wasn't sure. I hadn't felt like this in a very long time, not even before I fainted after skipping breakfast and lunch. It felt like my mind was spiralling out of control. But, this much I knew:

Bryony and Tawny were the new stars of Long Byrne. Bryony's film-set blondeness versus Tawny's dark swinging hips. The hips I knew so well. Now there was the two of them, together . . .

I saw the way the way that Bryony looked at Tawny. Tawny, who she thought was so "fun". Who she thought everyone wanted to be around. Tawny, who did her makeup and sat barely an inch from her face.

Did Bryony belong to her now?

My mind reeled.

I steadied myself against the bus stop outside the school, the light of an orange street lamp frilling out around my feet. The wall was jagged and dug into my bones like a pitchfork. I wished I had fingernails as I chiselled off moss from the crevices of brick with the nubs of my fingers.

Without warning Bryony's hands came into my mind.

Their bitten-down stubs that still looked elegant somehow. My focus was slipping in and out. From all the coffee? From not eating? From something else? I thought I saw the lamplight expand and contract around my feet. A big orange pupil or a pulled noose.

I couldn't go back in like this ... it felt like I used to get after Mum. Like I was seeing things and hearing voices. But who could I tell about that? They'd think I was crazy. Best to block it out with magazines and loud laughter. Keep it all away.

But right now I had nothing. The only thing left to do was wait for Tawny and Bryony to finish rehearsal.

I thought of them saying my words to each other:

And in this secret place, I pledge myself to you.

I pledge myself to you.

I was still thinking about it as the doors creaked open behind me and the cast and crew trickled out. I'd been outside longer than I thought. A knot of enthusiastic Year Sevens were wearing mobcaps and chattering to each other. The standard Year Ten Goths slinked out sullenly, glaring at the chavvy farmer lad playing Dick. Definitely not to their taste.

The crowd dispersed and the school door was still and dark. Perhaps Tawny and Bryony were getting told off by Rillington, or having their dresses fitted? Tawny would be flouncing around the hall, doing pirouettes and arabesques so her skirts flared out around her.

Minutes ticked by. I chipped some old grey gum off the bus stop with the toe of my boot. The school looked at me with blank eyes and my whole body ached with cold.

Then everything went quiet.

Just like in the hen house.

From very far away I heard the pad of feet. I peered over my shoulder and couldn't see a soul on the high street. People were inside in their slippers, propped up watching TV with Digestives and a brew.

Not me.

A high-pitched, stifled laugh came from the side alley where Kayleigh Whittard had lost her knickers once.

The giggling got louder and I shrank into the shadow of the bus stop. Bryony and Tawny came out of the snicket, their arms linked at the elbow. Tawny's was looped through like she did with me when she was parading in front of the boys on the playing field. Like I was her chaperone and they should be jealous.

They spoke in a low whisper, snickering in the orange streetlamp. Their faces looked clear and unblemished in the glare, even their laughter lines were wiped away like a clean slate. They could have been any age in any time.

From where I stood, by the stone wall, I saw Tawny slip her arm away, even though Bryony seemed to want to cling on. Bryony was explaining something and Tawny said, "OK, yep. OK," even though I couldn't hear the words.

I thought they'd leave, go on up the high street, but they lingered. Tawny reached up and caught a lock of Bryony's hair between her thumb and forefinger. It might have been twisted gold.

So she *did* belong to her now.

The heat rolled into my face. I snagged my head away. *I shouldn't be seeing this*, I said to myself. I'd barged in.

I shouldn't be here.

I squeezed my eyes shut tight and took a deep breath. Someone was having a bonfire two streets away.

Tawny and Bryony.

Bryony and Tawny.

Rose and Jane.

When I turned around, they were gone. I could just make out Tawny's swaying gait up the high street, like every road was a red carpet for her and her alone.

Bryony was already nowhere to be seen.

By lunchtime the next day, I was ready to tear my hair out. Tawny and Bryony had been screaming through my mind all night and I was functioning on double my normal dose of coffee, which I didn't think was possible. To make matters worse, Dad had come to me that morning saying that he didn't feel like I was pulling my weight around the farm since Robyn left. I'd told him that I wished I lived anywhere except Long Byrne. It was his fault we were staying here living out some pathetic countryside dream.

Two weeks until Halloween.

Rillington had me on prompt duty. But Tawny wouldn't ever forget a line. Bryony looked like she'd rather be seen dead than failing. She kept her chin up high and her eyes bright over rouged cheeks. Tawny never seemed to leave her side.

"Right, let's call a timeout," Rillington grumbled. "Get yourselves in shape for scene three, people. I need a drink..."

Tawny caught my eye and heaved herself down onto the

edge of the stage. She pulled off her mobcap with dramatic flair, letting her hair fall all around her. I watched Bryony give me a small smile – the first in days – and lower herself gingerly to the floor.

Tawny fanned herself with her hand. "I'm knackered. Me and Hollingworth were up all night going over lines," she grinned.

My head felt crowded. I wanted to wipe that smirk off her face.

"Maybe you should both go and have a lie-down together," I muttered through my teeth.

"What's up with you?"

"Nothing."

"You look pissy, Cate," said Tawny, putting her hands on her hips. "Not had your coffee yet?"

"It's *nothing*," I hissed. "Except, I can't concentrate with you two eye-fucking each other the whole time."

The whole room spun round to look at us. How had my voice got so loud? Tawny's mouth dropped open.

"What did you just say to me?"

I was completely in for it now, I knew it. I felt Bryony's eyes waver on me but I couldn't let go of Tawny's face. My voice shook. "I said, maybe if you two could stop fingering each other on stage, this might actually be a decent play."

Tawny's hands were trembling by her sides. "Get the fuck out of here, Cate. You're embarrassing yourself."

I glowered. "The only embarrassing thing here is you."

"Get. Out."

"Fine!" I snatched up my stuff from under my seat. The bench toppled, the thud echoing around the hall. "I knew you'd mess this up, Tawny. I knew right from day one."

And then I was running.

Glamour. The witches had it.

They could cast a spell to make the viewer see something that wasn't there. They called it a Glamour.

"The witches would will it, summon up the pictures out of their bones to cloud the vision of their enemies. They'd see hidden doors in the forest, the ghosts of their dead loved ones, the Grim Reaper's hand outstretched over their heads. A witch could make you believe anything they wanted you to.

Just a pinch of glamour. A touch of flair.

They could make you live in a world of dreams.

In Search of the Long Byrne Witches, P.J. Hebden

Chapter 19

I don't know how it had happened. It was dark, late, and I walked along the street feeling sick with myself. Dark thoughts swarmed in my head, pushing up the lining of my skull. Tawny's face, livid and flushed overriding everything.

My phone buzzed in my pocket.

Can we talk?

Bryony. I thought of her standing in the wings, her phone clutched in her hand. Was she waiting for my reply right now? Was Tawny next to her?

Long Byrne was too small for us all.

I didn't know what to do, or where to go. If I went home, Dad and Alexa would be there, oozing their eyes all over me, still watchful and waiting for me to "disappear" again.

It wasn't *my* fault I'd not made other friends. Tawny was a full-time occupation. All those other birthday parties and sleepovers – missed and forgotten about. No one ever invited me any more. No one wrote to me with rainbow-coloured envelopes. In their eyes, I was property of Tawny Brown.

I did the only thing I could think to do.

There was a clump of stones in my fist. After a couple of failed attempts, one hit the window with a shudder.

A light came on behind the curtain.

"Robyn!" I hissed.

Her face swam to the window and her hands cupped the glass to find the thrower. She opened the latch.

"Cate?"

"Can I come up?" I asked.

Her shadow swayed on the window ledge, disappeared and a minute later I heard the key turn in the front door.

"Tawny's not here."

"I know. I wanted to talk to you."

Her eyes swept the floor, half in darkness against the yellow glare of the hall. Her pyjamas had pictures of kittens on them.

"Look," I scrabbled for words, "I'm sorry for how I acted when I saw you at Bryony's. That wasn't fair – I should have tried to understand."

Robyn nibbled her lip. What had happened to the girl I knew from the farm? Under the soft folds of her pyjamas, her arms looked like sticks. I'd seen her crank a rusty tractor into fourth gear – it seemed like those muscles were gone for ever. Even when she spoke it was like listening to a ghost. I shivered.

"Mum's spending a lot of time with me," she said. "We play a lot of Scrabble now."

I tried to laugh. "Bet you wish you'd never run away now, huh?" I winced. A silence stretched out. Why had I said that?

"Mum's been very good," was all she said, in a small voice. I nodded and could tell she wanted to close the door. I scuffed my feet on the step. Tawny and I used to write our names with chalk all over the stone path – hearts, yellow dragonflies and wonky hopscotches – and then watched it wash away in the summer rain. Robyn had sat on the top step smiling or reading a book while we shrieked.

That was so long ago.

"Robyn, what happened? I'm sorry. I just want to know: why did you run away?"

She shook her head. "Someone had to."

"Had to what? Do what?"

She looked up and met my eyes. I barely saw Robyn there. A shiver ran down my spine and set my legs to 'run-mode'. "I thought I could keep Bryony away from me; from you and Tawny too."

"Why? How?"

"I've seen her with Tawny. I've heard her in Tawny's room in the middle of the night."

My stomach recoiled. "Rob, how did you think you could keep Bryony away?"

She finally met my gaze. "I read about it. You can perform a ritual."

"A ritual?" I grimaced. "What do you mean?"

"A ritual, like a witch's spell. But you needed an animal sacrifice – animal blood to bind someone's powers."

My stomach made an iron thunk as it dropped. I was going to throw up. "Wait. What?"

"I know it sounds crazy but—"

"My dead hen," I reeled. "That was *you*?"

"What? No, Cate, I—"

I spluttered. "You killed her!"

"It wasn't me! I didn't do anything. I—"

My face contorted. "So that's why you were in the coop that time. What is *wrong* with you?" I felt my voice rising. Robyn went to shut the door but I threw my shoulder at it, surprised by my strength. Her eyes widened. "I just don't get it though, Rob! You put my Chick in the school vents? Why?"

"That wasn't me, that must have been her!"

This was ridiculous, I could feel the anger rolling off me in waves strong enough to blast open the door. I pushed with all my might.

"Why are you always hanging around her!" I yelled. "Leave her alone! You've got everything you could want – you've got all the attention on you now – you've got your Mum, you've got Tawny!"

"What?" Her eyes flared and I thought they looked black. "I don't want the spotlight! I'm not like them, Cate. I'm different – I'm like *you*!"

I laughed and it came out like a snarl. But she stepped forward imploringly.

"I'm in Tawny's shadow, I'm quiet, and I'm sick, too."

We both breathed hard into the silence, then her breath turned ragged like there was something trapped in her chest. "I just want to keep you all safe." Her shoulders heaved up and down, a buoy held afloat by her frail and feeble lungs. Our eyes flashed at each other.

Was this little girl really like me? This quaking thirteen-year-old? This killer? I narrowed my eyes. "You're nothing like me."

It hovered like a threat. Robyn's bottom lip quivered.

I'd gone too far. We both had. The light from the hall silhouetted her, all bones and angles.

"But don't worry, Cate," said Robyn in a whisper. "Bryony will take Tawny first. Not you. Tawny is always number one."

I turned and ran away from her.

My knees knocked together. I was shocked by the ominous sky. The moon was waxing, ready to double in size and multiply like a maggot. Dark air scudded around it, prodding and poking, making the whole night seem to quake and pulsate. I headed straight home with my shoulders hunched up around my face. I felt the hot thrum of tears down my cheeks.

Why had I even gone there? What the hell was wrong with me?

But, more importantly, what the hell was wrong with Robyn?

That night, I dreamt.

"Cate. Cate."

The night was dark, too dark – I couldn't even see my hand in front of my face. A cold wind got in through the gaps in my ruined shoes and whistled in and out of the seams. The grass felt slippery under my feet.

Someone struck a match and Robyn's silvery face floated before me.

"Robyn? What are you doing out here? It's dark. Your mum will be worried," I said.

"She doesn't know where I am. You won't tell her."

"I . . ."

"Follow me."

"Where?"

The matchlight suddenly disappeared, replaced by a line of lanterns swinging creakily from the old horse chestnut branches. The Slip winds howled and caught on my jacket. No matter how closely I clutched my arms, I still felt it in my bones. There was no reply when I called her name.

Instead, a black and white cat stalked out ahead in front of me. The lamplight caught on its pink-padded feet and I followed.

Ginger led me straight down to the moor, making me duck and weave to follow his footwork. The lanterns were rusted and scraped against the bark.

Out on the moor something was moving.

A mass. A dark mass of shapes and pulses on the ground. It was like insects, a swarm. And in the middle of it all was a blonde figure standing tall.

Her long hair clung to her waist, sticking to the mud on her dress.

The sound of chanting filled the air.

"Bryony! Stop! What are you doing?"

But she was in a trance, her head fallen back to face the night sky. I could see the tip of her nose. The black and white cat cowered behind my ankles. The noise was getting louder and louder. I covered my ears.

Then the blonde girl threw up her hands to the sky and the swarm went with it, making a heaving storm cloud of black air that streamed towards the village.

And with it, all I could hear was screaming.

***

The next day I knew something was wrong before I even left my room. My mind spun with the arms and legs of dreams, feeling them over in my head. Chicken guts and bloody feathers. What had Rillington done with her little body? Thrown her behind the playing field? It was a good job it wasn't a Friday – I didn't fancy anything in my head coming true. The air outside was thick, like you could bite into it and rip a chunk right out of it. I milked the cows, glad of their warm sturdiness against me, breath curling damp and white from their nostrils; I showered and grabbed a Thermos of coffee before heading to the door.

"Cate?" Dad met me in the hall. I winced. "Can I speak with you a moment?" It was the first time he'd spoken to me since our fight.

"I'm going to be late."

"Cate."

There was something in his tone that made me stop cold.

"Sandra just called. It's Robyn."

Oh god.

"They found her down the Slip this morning."

"What?"

"She's up at the hospital in Hillbury."

I gasped, my body crumbling. "She's all right? She's alive?"

He nodded. "She's alive."

"Who found her?"

He ran a hand over his balding spot. "That's just it. It was your friend Bryony."

"Bryony?"

Of course it was.

Dad twitched his glasses. He seemed to be mulling something over in his head, like he did with all his big questions. "God knows what she was doing out there at three in the morning."

God knows. No one knew. My blood turned cold. *Witch*.

"Thanks, Dad. Thanks for letting me know." I turned the door handle.

"Cate—"

"Yeah?"

"You know, I . . ." His mouth scrunched up.

"Dad?"

He smiled sadly at me. "Have a good day, OK?"

"OK."

I paused and let him have a slurp of my coffee before I left. That should set him up for the day. He turned back to his study door, Robyn's weight on his shoulders, and all I could think was one thing:

She deserves it.

I was called up to Rillington's office during first lesson. Everyone's eyes followed me as I scuttled out of the classroom. Gossip spread like crabs in Long Byrne.

Her eyebrows were knitted in 'that' look I was so used to.

"Come and take a seat, Cate."

There were two mugs of coffee on the desk. One jet black, one milky and gold.

There was a saucer of chocolate digestives next to her clipboard.

"Please take one." That was an order.

I took up the biscuit and dunked it in my mug. It wouldn't

fit in. I felt like a baby putting coloured blocks in different holes. I cracked the digestive in two, then let it go soggy before lifting it out just in time and cramming it in my mouth before I could talk myself out of it. It made me want to gag.

Rillington shifted in her chair. "I wondered if you'd like to talk about last night, Cate?"

The biscuit caught in my throat. Had she followed me to the Browns'? Had she heard the fight?

"Something seems to be bothering you. You said some rather hurtful things about Tawny Brown and Bryony Hollingworth last night."

Rehearsal. My stomach unknotted. I was being paranoid.

"Nothing's bothering me." I shrugged, keeping my face still. "We just had a fight. It'll be fine."

"Yes, but the rehearsals haven't progressed as quickly as we'd hoped so . . . we need to keep our friends close to keep the play on track."

What about our enemies?

"I'll try, Miss." I could see her applying her pop psychology to me again. "Can I go now, Miss?"

Rillington patted her desk. "Do you like living in Long Byrne, Cate?"

I was startled by the question. "I suppose so. It's OK sometimes. Boring as hell though."

"Even with the witches?" she half-smiled.

"I find them interesting." I knew I sounded so lame, but she was staring into my head with those bright-blue eyes and even my brain was blushing. I wondered what else she could see.

"Is everything all right, Cate dear?"

"Yes," but the noise caught in my throat. Pathetic. "Yes, I'm fine."

She nodded, seeing through me in an instant. Her eyes were soft in the feathery glow of the skylight.

"Sometimes we all need to cover up what's going on inside for our own sanity. But we don't always need to lie to people we trust." She reached out and nudged another biscuit towards me. "I'd like to think we could be friends."

I nodded, slowly. *Friends? With Rillington?*

"You can talk to me."

My face felt stiff, trying to hold back all my thoughts. There was just too much to say. I wanted nothing more than to ask if I could sleep there tonight, hidden in the school cellar with a hot-water bottle. I thought of my nightmare-filled room and shuddered. I opened my mouth and the words came out croakily.

"It's just that I don't remember when things got so complicated."

"Which things?"

Where to begin? "Oh, just about everything."

She smiled warmly, with sad eyes. "It creeps up on us all, I think. College can be a difficult time. It's a big step up from high school. Perhaps we've just got to ride the tangle until it smooths itself out."

Maybe. But college wasn't everything.

There was Robyn, alone and spooked in her dark room holding Ginger like her life depended on it. Now she was in a hospital bed. There was Tawny and her hand on Bryony's arm. Dad in his lonely study. Alexa in her kingdom of nail varnish and soap operas. Then there was Mum. There was always Mum.

It suddenly dawned on me that Miss Rillington was looking out for me. How had she become the warmest person I knew? I wonder if she even realised. My hands had stopped shaking.

I thanked her for the coffee and got self-consciously to my feet.

"Caitlin, you're welcome here any time. It's actually quite nice to have the company."

"Thanks, Miss."

When she closed the office door and I was turned out into the corridor, I realised there were tears in my eyes. Pathetic.

I shoved them away. Farmer Cate Aspey didn't cry. She could mend a tractor in a rainstorm, chop firewood in the dark. Hard as nails.

Yeah, right.

School might as well have been the Tawny Show. I knew I should go right over and apologise, but how could I? Tawny was surrounded by new admirers wanting to know all the details about Robyn. I knew I did. No doubt Sandra had brought Tawny to school kicking and screaming, but even though her face looked a little pinched around the edges, there was a glow in her eyes.

She was revelling in it.

"Tawny! How are you? You're so brave coming in."

"Is she allowed visitors?"

"God, Tawny – I can't imagine what you're going through."

And beside her throughout the whole thing, Bryony

stood like a shadow. Attached and necessary, head held high – the victor.

Tawny had won her. The stars of the show. Together for ever.

It had all worked out just like Bryony had wanted it to. With a jolt, I wondered which spell had been cast to pull that one off. Had Bryony used magic to make me say those things in front of everyone in the play? Had she made Robyn go crazy too? Lured her out to the Slip? Or had Robyn made herself this way?

Had I made myself like this?

They were blocking the English corridor with their throng of admirers, so people had to sidle along the walls to get past. I realised Tawny was in full makeup. She'd actually thought to spend half an hour on her face while Robyn fought for her life.

I saw her see me. Her chin rose up – prevailing Queen of the World. There was no way I was apologising to that face. I tried to straighten my shoulders but my chest felt like sandstone. Could she see the hate rolling off me like spilt oil?

Tawny slinked her arm around Bryony's waist as slowly as possible, looking hard in my direction. "Come on. Let's cop a quick feel before class." She winked at her crowd and then Tawny steered Bryony through the narrow corridor towards me.

She turned her head and gave me the look I'd been fearing. The Tawny Sneer.

She shoved past, her elbow jabbing my rib like a crowbar. The knock felt like she was trying to bash my skeleton out of my body.

"You'd think she'd *ask* about Robyn," Tawny said to Bryony. "She's the one who made my kid sister think she was invincible. Now she's hooked up to a monitor." I expected her to choke up. Perfectly rehearsed. Fit for the stage. She said it so the whole corridor heard and turned to shake their heads at me in the funnel of her wake.

Bryony looked over her shoulder, firmly clasped to Tawny's arm, and mouthed, "I'm sorry."

I nodded, thinking, *Witch witch witch.*

I nearly skipped Psych. Being anywhere near the Bryony-Tawny duo was not an option – even just one half of it. But I couldn't skip class; I just wasn't that person.

Bryony pushed a note towards me. *Can we talk?*

I let her hang for a minute, she deserved it. Then I scribbled back:

The Slip, after school.

OK.

She didn't speak to me for the whole lesson, even when we had to partner up on a worksheet about Jung. That bright blonde barrier of hers stayed there, solid, stiff, between us.

I was relieved.

But school without Tawny and Bryony was blank. I didn't know what to do with myself. You absorbed everyone else's conversations instead to keep your head from falling apart. Sitting under the stairs at break, I found out from passers-by that Mr Lawrence was messing around with Mrs Tyburn – scandal – and Kayleigh Whittard had a new piercing but wouldn't say where. I found out that Robyn was being observed for signs of hypothermia and the doctors kept asking her questions to make sure she wasn't a psycho. Debatable. I remembered those questions from when Mum died. The nurses in their scuffed trainers, shunting me from one room to the next. They were going to keep Robyn in for 'as long as it took'. That sounded like the ominous sort of crap spouted by Year Eights who painted their nails black and wore their fringes over their eyes, but it made me shudder nonetheless.

Fine, Robyn had run away. That was becoming the new norm. But what had Bryony been doing at the Slip before dawn?

After school I went to meet her. She looked immaculate even through the October drizzle and after six hours of classes. She raised her eyebrows when she saw me leaning up against the horse chestnut tree.

"I didn't think you'd come," she said.

I put my teeth together. Robyn's words flashed up around me like neon signs against the trees.

"What's going on, Bryony?"

She folded her arms, suddenly stern. "I could ask you that, too. You didn't need to make stuff up about me and Tawny. You knew she'd turn it against you."

"I meant with Robyn."

Bryony's mouth set.

"What do you mean?"

"You found her."

"In the nick of time too."

"It was pitch black and three in the morning."

She shook her head. "You didn't see her. She was muttering and shaking – saying she'd seen stuff out on the moor. She screamed when I tried to get her up. She thought I was some kind of monster." Bryony's brow hardened. "She's a little girl. She shouldn't have been there alone."

"And what were *you* doing out there?"

"Don't you start. I was collecting for Auntie."

"Collecting what exactly? Frogspawn? Eye of newt?"

"Stop being ridiculous." Her eyes narrowed. "This is *just* what Tawny meant."

My neck burnt. Tawny knew everything about me. How much had she told Bryony already in the space of a few days? I decided I didn't want to know and charged on.

"But what's going on with her, Bryony? I've known Robyn for years and she is the sanest person I've ever laid eyes on – not to mention the cleverest. You come along and she's a quivering wreck, afraid of her own shadow!"

Her face went blank. "Cate, if you're suggesting what I think you're suggesting then I'm going to walk away right now."

There was a new confidence to her. The kind you got from standing on the stage, seeing above people's heads, seeing things they couldn't see.

"Bryony," I breathed. "Robyn's more than Tawny's kid sister to me, she's my friend. Or *was* my friend. She'd never mentioned the witches before, but a few weeks ago, things changed."

Bryony's face was hard. "Cate, I thought we were going to talk this out. I thought you wanted to be friends. Now here I am, listening to this bullshit." She took a sharp breath out through her nose. "I was out down the Slip because Auntie wanted me to collect some berries because she loves to bake and I couldn't sleep so it seemed like a good time. Sleep's been difficult lately, you know, since my brother topped himself. I thought you'd get that, of all people."

I blushed fiercely. "Look, Bryony . . ."

"Yes?"

"We're friends, aren't we?"

She frowned. "Yes . . . I thought so."

I spoke measuredly. "I'm just looking out for Robyn; you'd look out for your brothers too, wouldn't you?" It was a pretty low card, but I played it anyway and Bryony's face fell into thought.

"You know I would," she said. "I really hope Robyn's OK. I just don't think she knew what she saw last night." She shook her head. "You don't know what you're seeing in the half-dark sometimes." Even under the trees I saw her face redden slightly. "Tawny said you sometimes used to touch her when you thought she was asleep. Like, stroke her or something."

My stomach clenched. "Did she?"

"I said she was just being silly," Bryony garbled. "Sometimes things are different at night. You can't be sure what you see or feel. I sometimes think I see Euan, but I realise I'm dreaming."

I nodded. So Tawny had already started the grand reveal. I could picture her smug and safe, surrounded by the audience of film star photos in her room. She'd be painting her nails, sucking the chocolate off a Lion Bar, laying out my secrets for Bryony, one by one, like cheap necklaces on a market stall.

Happy now, Tawny? My blood seemed to be scorching my veins.

I pushed down my anger. "I'm sorry. I shouldn't have said those things in rehearsal – I didn't mean them."

"I know." She didn't meet my eye.

"If you hear anything about Robyn, will you let me know?"

She said she would. We walked back under the trees about five feet apart. Thick splodges of rain had started to fall on the canopy of leaves, sounding like thunderous applause around us. Bryony had an umbrella and I flipped up my hood, preparing for a soak.

"I'll see you tomorrow," she said. "I need to go to the shop for Auntie while it's still open." She ran off, her expensive shoes clipping on the cobbles.

I didn't go home. I knew exactly where I was going to go. Back to the scene of the crime.

The records said after Rose and Jane fought and screeched,
it rained for seven nights with the power of the curse.
It washed the birds from the trees. Their broken wings
gushed down the roads, down to the Slip where the rats had
a feast.

The History of Long Byrne: Demons on the Moor,
Dr C. Munir

Chapter 20

Shilcock opened the door, looking thin and yellow in a baggy turtleneck. I launched myself into the hall. Water splattered everywhere.

"Evening, Cate. I think I've heard Tawny. Could you tell her to keep the volume down, love?"

"Will do, Mr Shilcock."

"And . . . wipe your feet, please."

I barged past him, thudding all the way up the stairs and into Tawny's room. I felt the bedroom door shudder as it hit the wall. Tawny was perched on the window ledge with a handheld mirror, and her eyes flew up.

"Jesus, Cate!"

"Can I see her?"

She sighed haughtily, turning back to the dish of candles in front of her and getting out her tweezers. I stood dripping.

"Robyn's not here, she's in hospital. I thought that was common knowledge by now. Even to you."

She hooked a rogue eyebrow hair over the pincers and tugged.

"They've not let her home yet? Is it serious?"

"Feel like I'm at a witch trial here, sweetie," she rolled her eyes, her voice flat.

I didn't know how Tawny could even see her reflection properly in the dim candlelight.

"They're keeping her in overnight, idiot. Mum's there now."

I made a move towards the bed. Without looking away from the mirror she said, "Don't sit there, you'll get it wet."

I stepped back and hovered by the door, all the momentum in me lost as the rain continued its onslaught outside. Why had I ever said those things?

"You're staying?" she said pointedly.

I tried to shrug. "If you want me to."

There was a pair of my underwear on the back of the chair – black briefs with pink stars I'd inherited from Alexa – and a wad of English notes I'd left the week before splayed under the desk, out of place in Tawny's Hollywood haven.

A silence stretched out and the nubs of my nails pressed between the bones in my palm.

"I'll just . . ."

"No. *Stay*," Tawny said, her head snapping round from the mirror. She held the round compact to her face and from where I stood I could see her twice, the white curve of her cheek snowy against the dark window. Her eyes held my gaze and I found I couldn't recognise the emotion there. I used to know every flicker of her body – how she rubbed the hem of her skirt when she was nervous, or how she could only wink her left eye. I used to tease her about it all the time.

My head ached.

"What's going on with us, Tawn?"

"You tell me." Her voice was icy.

She stared. I saw the miniscule motion in her face as her

jaw set. I hated this. "I'm sorry, Tawn. I am. You don't have to be mad at me. Can we just talk?"

"You see, I would, Cate. But I don't know when you became such a liar."

I half expected thunder, but the rain just kept coming down, dark and heavy on the four-paned window.

"What are you talking about?"

She scowled. "Oh, come off it. You're so self-righteous."

"What are you talking about?"

Tawny threw up her arms. "You're completely obsessed with her and it's doing my head in. You've been seeing her behind my back. Putting things in her head. It makes her feel like crap."

I stood gaping.

"What, Robyn?"

"*No*, you complete *idiot*. Bryony."

I froze. "What has she told you?"

"Pretty much everything I need to know. Cate, you're jealous of me and her. You're like a bad drunk."

My body was so tense I felt that one tap and I'd break. "You're messing with me. I haven't done anything."

She raised a freshly-arched eyebrow, still red around the edges. "What? Oh, come on. You haven't been able to keep away since you found out she was a Hollingworth."

"I—"

"You don't dream about her?" she spat. "You don't think she's beautiful? Your perfect little witch?"

"You're out of line."

We glared at each other, breathing hard.

"I think you'd better leave, Cate."

I didn't move. "Rehearsals are tomorrow night. We'll have to see each other."

Tawny shrugged.

Inside I cowered. This was Tawny. My best friend. "She's got to you. You were never like this before Bryony."

She turned back to the mirror. Bored. "Don't bother showing up, OK?" Her eyes were blank windows in her white face. Slowly and carefully, I backed out of the room. I wondered if she'd watch herself crying in that mirror when I left. Screw up her face like she did in auditions and watch the first big salty blob pearl up in the corner, then force it down her cheek.

I turned.

"Oh, and Cate? Stay away from my little sister – your witch crap is going to kill her."

Her steady gaze shook me and I was quaking as I went down the stairs. The smell of old coffee made me nauseous. I started to run but tripped on a black and white blur – Ginger arched his back and hissed as I stumbled out the front door.

No Tawny. No Bryony. No Robyn. I didn't have anywhere to turn.

I thought of Bryony. I imagined her shaking her head, so disappointed in me, ruining our friendship.

I ran up the lane, my head spinning, heaving with rain. I remembered those Health Ed. classes they'd put us through. "You need 1,400 calories a day for the mind to keep going. Your body will keep functioning. Your metabolism, your vision. All the parts will work, even if they're a bit clunky, but that is the bare minimum." Take in any less than that and the whole ship starts to sink. System failure.

I'd never taken any notice. I couldn't remember the last time my body worked properly. How many calories had I eaten today? How many meals had I replaced with coffee? When was my last period?

I slowed my pace to a jog. The rain lashed down all around me, making me see in blurred lines. Someone was up in front of me, walking down the lane slowly, her head down. I slowed down, squinting.

"Bryony?"

Her long blonde hair swung behind her.

"Bryony? Hey!"

But the girl turned around and it wasn't her at all.

The girl wore a long dark dress that skimmed the floor. There were drooping flowers behind her ear. She turned slowly to face me fully.

Those flowers should have died a long time ago.

I looked up and the moon was a gaping mouth.

"Bryony?" I whispered.

That girl was definitely not Bryony Hollingworth.

It was Jane.

And then I fell.

There are many examples of witch hysteria across the globe, several examples of which still go on today. The most commonly remembered case is that of the Salem Witch Trials of 1693. In several instances, the 'witchcraft' or evil-doing is linked to a certain town or place – hence the flourishing tourism industry of the once-unknown village in Massachusetts – and has resulted in copy-cat occurrences in the same area.

One such illustration is little known outside of the county of Lancashire, England. The locally famous Long Byrne witches (see Appendix 4b) inspired a series of events involving adolescent girls and young women spanning several centuries. In 1958, more than 300 years after the hanging of several girls out on the Lancashire moors, a twelve-year-old child smothered her sister to death after witches appeared to her in a dream.

Further examples of this pattern of shared abnormal psychological experience can be seen across the world and reveal a phenomenon perpetuated by the psyches of teenage girls.

Witch: An Epidemic, Paul Hann and Lena Puzinsky

Chapter 21

Let's just say, for argument's sake, you're twelve years old and maxed out on the legal dose of Diazepam. The white hospital sheets feel like greaseproof paper against your arms. The white bars are cold and chipped from where some other crazy kid had tried to gnaw herself free.

You're not restrained by any of those woolly cotton armbands you see in the films – they only do that if you've got sharp nails and look like you might gouge someone's tonsils out. Maybe you want to, but the drugs are kicking in and there's a weight settling in around your eyes, threatening to pop them right out of their sockets. There might as well be a fat guy sitting on your chest. Besides, you wouldn't want to go for anyone with your dad sitting right there, looking so sad and so tired from pacing in the waiting room all night long with the nurse who you'd soon call your stepmother.

There's a lingering stench of bile on your breath, even though they scrubbed your teeth for you, zipping the hard brush back and forth against your gums until they bled, and your windpipe is on fire where they widened it with the beige rubber tube.

Dad's been crying. You've never seen your dad cry before.

You hope you never have to again. You don't want to watch all those tears welling up in the wrinkles under his eyes, the dark smudges like crow feathers resting there.

A bold picture of a ship hangs on the wall, like it was someone's lifetime ambition to produce hospital art.

"Hi," you croak.

"Hello, love."

He's telling you he can't face going back home, back to all that noise and the people asking after you again and again, and the mail that will slot through the door still addressed to her. You had to return it all to sender – stamp by stamp – letting them know, "Mrs Aspey has passed away."

So you realise you're moving to the middle of nowhere and it's all your fault. Your mum is dead and you've overdosed on as many paracetamol as you could find in the medicine cabinet, when you should be at home in the city with your tatty old teddy bears lining the shelf and the purple name plate you made in Year Two still hanging on your door.

That should be how things are. But they're not. And you don't know how you can ever get yourself back on that track of history. You don't know how things can ever be the same again.

Not knowing is like a curse.

I wondered if Bryony had sat in those painful hospital chairs after Euan. The crackle of the intercom breaking the silence and the steady whoosh of wheels as trolleys were trucked by, one after another. An endless stream of casualties.

I wondered if what she'd told me about him was the truth.

I wondered if Bryony was really Bryony at all.

I opened my eyes but everything was blurred. My head felt like someone had chiselled it open and welded it back together clumsily with cement. My bedside torch was on and someone had put a hot-water bottle by my feet.

"Dad?"

Someone sighed.

"Do you want to give your old man a heart attack, Caitlin?" He was next to the bed in my small cottage room, looking like he hadn't slept for a solid year.

I was about to open my mouth to protest but then he gave me that sad smile. I tried to return it.

"I could try a bit harder if you wanted."

"Nah, sweetheart – you just keep at the rate you're going."

I tried to raise a hand to my forehead, but my arm was so heavy. *Ow*. "What happened?"

"Oh, the usual. You must have fainted in the lane. Alexa's bandaged up those grazes. A car saw you in the middle of the road at the last minute and brought you here. Frank Mitchell, it was, said he recognised you from the playground." It shocked me how hopeless he sounded.

"Pad's dad?"

"You've been out for a while, love. Maybe you could try . . . eating something?" He said the words like he was suggesting a glass of lemonade to an alcoholic. I nodded mechanically.

"Probably best if you stay off school today," he said.

"Today? I've been unconscious all night?" I tried to push myself up to a sitting position to find my phone but the throbbing in my head knocked me back down.

"It's about half four in the morning. Joe's doing your rounds. A good lad, he is, Joe." Dad sighed.

I felt a toxic mixture of embarrassment and fear, like my body wasn't my own and might do things I'd forbidden it to do. "I can't believe I passed out."

He smiled. "I've got to admit, I like it when you're a bit livelier."

I laughed but it came out as a rasp.

"Do you remember how it happened, sweetheart?"

I gulped, not wanting to answer that one.

"Dad . . . I'm sorry for how I've been acting lately. It's just . . ."

"I know. The anniversary – it's hard on both of us, love." He ran his hand through the little hair he had left. "She's in the past now, but that doesn't mean she's gone at all."

I nodded, not knowing how to tell him that wasn't what I meant at all. I didn't need 'the people we love never truly leave us' speech.

"But we'll muddle through, won't we? Then everything can get back to the way things used to be." He took my hand. "You know what, though? You're doing so well at college. You've got this play coming up too, I hear? Joe told me you'd written the whole script by yourself. Your mum would be so proud of you."

I swallowed salty tears. "Thanks, Dad."

He squeezed my fingers and the sadness in his eyes was a gate that barely held his emotions back. I heard a sniffle of anger in the hall.

"Oh, she's up, is she?" I said.

The air grew cold.

"Yes," Dad gave me a stern look. "Alexa?" he called, a note of warning in his voice. Alexa came around my door. The room was suddenly far too crowded. Her lipstick was firmly in place and she'd had chance to spray a fresh mist of perfume before she'd sauntered in. She didn't look like she'd missed an ounce of beauty sleep.

"What, Mark? Can't I be just the slightest bit angry? Just look at how worried she's had us."

"Lex . . ." he tried again.

"She's sixteen years old; she shouldn't have been out there alone in the dark. She shouldn't be in these dangerous situations, making us tear our hair out all night again. Think what happened to Robyn Brown. And now you! What is going on with you girls?"

I saw red. "Don't you dare bring Robyn into this! What *should* I be doing, *Lex*?" I mocked, forcing myself up to sit up. "Smoking joints behind the barn? Messing around with boys? Would that be better?"

"Caitlin!"

"Well, I'm not, OK? I was literally just walking home and I fainted. It's not my fault, all right?"

"Cate." Another warning from Dad. "You're being ridiculous, you know that's not what Alexa meant."

"You're right, you're right. *I'm* ridiculous. I'm sorry I'm such a disappointment to you. The walking teen suicide."

"Cate," Dad winced.

"I don't need any of you taking care of me." I glared into Alexa's eyes. "I'm fine."

The room crackled.

"Fine," she grimaced. "But I hope you know your father's been up all night at your side, Caitlin, and don't think it's the first time. Just remember that." She turned and exaggerated every step as she trudged down the stairs. You'd think she was actually a farmer's wife, stomping off to rub down the cattle.

Dad and I sat in silence. I wanted to stick my chin out defiantly – Tawnyesque, but I couldn't muster the energy. The look on Dad's face made me want to bury my own face in his shirt and stay there for a very long time.

He sighed. "Cate, what's going on here? Something's changed with you."

My eyes stretched wide and tight. "I'm fine. Nothing's changed."

He looked at me carefully, weighing me with his pupils, but there was a defeated man behind them. "Caitlin, I'm not prepared to lose another person I love."

My chest splintered. I held his gaze. "You're not going to lose me. Nothing's changed."

He gave me a hug before I had time move away.

"OK, sweetheart. Nothing's changed."

But everything had.

Dad backed out of the room like he did when I was a little kid who wouldn't go to sleep, turning the light out as he went. I lay in the dark, my stomach churning with guilt. I hadn't even stopped to think of what Dad must be feeling. Would we have a memorial service? Head to the river? Would we visit the place up near Hillbury where we'd spread her ashes? The dawn hadn't split through the hills yet and the yard outside was quiet. My Chicks would be pecking at their breakfasts – all of them, bar one glossy black hen.

All I knew was this: something wasn't right. And Bryony Hollingworth was the start of it all.

I slept all day and most of the night. Clouds flickered across the curtain. Faraway traffic beeped and whispered across the moor. By the time darkness fell I was wide awake and craving a caffeine fix. It gnawed at my gut.

I lay still for a long time then crept to the stairs. It was before dawn – long before it was safe to boil the kettle – but there were voices downstairs. I checked my phone. 3.11 a.m. The light was on in the study and I crept downwards until I could hunker down on the bottom step of the staircase.

Alexa sounded like she had a bad cold.

"She's sixteen, Mark. She doesn't realise the effect she's having on that girl. You can see how Robyn idolises her – they're both skin and bone."

"Lex, sweetheart, you know the trouble we've had with her eating—"

"I'm just saying that someone needs to talk to her. She can't see how much Robyn looks up to her – Tawny's best friend. Cate's practically been a big sister to her."

"I know, I know . . ." He sounded exhausted.

"Look, I know it's not my place, but after what happened to Cate's mum . . . what- what happened to Lydia; Cate's never quite recovered, has she? Do you think it's getting worse now the anniversary is coming up?"

I put my hand on the banister, closing my eyes and

drawing in a breath through my nose. I pulled myself up and went silently to the door.

"But what can I do, Lex? We've tried the pills, the hospitals, the therapy. I just don't know what to suggest next." I hated that he sounded so hopeless. Why couldn't he sound more like my dad?

I took another deep breath and walked in.

The room was heavy with soft plants and shaded lamps. Alexa jumped. There was a crumpled tissue in her hand. Dad had his arm around her shoulders. His wrinkles looked like the lines on a piece of A4, waiting for answers.

He half stood up, ready for a crisis. "What is it, Cate?"

"Dad, can you take me to see Robyn?"

She barely made an impression on the covers. It was like someone had covered a poor meal with a cloth – if it hadn't been for that dark little head poking up over the top of the covers I wouldn't have known a thirteen-year-old girl was in that bed.

Sandra lay curled by her side. A black smudge of mascara stained the white sheets beneath her head. Her hair was swirled around Robyn's hip like an elaborate sash. Even in sleep, Sandra's toes were pointed; the perfectly poised dancer from her past.

Tawny was perched on a rough plastic chair, her head on the end of the bed, her hand stretched up to hold her sister's.

Eyes closed, their dark hair spread out across the blank canvas, I realised for the first time how alike they all were. The Browns on a stark background of white. I stood in the doorway, suddenly feeling naked without flowers or chocolates to offer. Not so much as a handful of grapes. I could almost hear the parking monitor ticking away outside and Dad drumming his fingers on the steering wheel. People had always said how much Mum and I looked alike – they'd look at photographs and gasp. I didn't see it, even if I wished it was true. I couldn't imagine Mum with the same brittle wrists, the same concave stomach or the lank hair that hovered around my shoulders. Mum's hair was a luscious brown streaked through with gold in the summer. I'd liked to bury my face in it and feel it tickle my nose.

But she was gone. I didn't have that family any more.

I turned to go.

My knee caught the clipboard at the end of the bed. It flew across the floor with a whooshing sound.

Shit.

Sandra shifted in her sleep. I turned to sprint.

"What the hell are you doing here?"

Tawny's voice sounded ominous. I stood rigid under the doorframe. "I wanted to see how she was doing."

"It's really funny, that, y'know, Cate," she gave a laugh like rusted nails, rubbing sleep from her eye. "She was awake before and we were having a chat."

"Oh?"

"Yeah, 'oh'. She was talking about you, saying how you'd come down to visit her at ours the other night. How you were yelling and screaming at her. And, you know what, Cate? It sounded like you tried to bash the door down while you were at it."

"That's a lie." My face drained.

"Oh, really?" Tawny got up and thrust her hands onto her hips. "Strange, I've never known my kid sister be a liar. What have you been saying to her?"

"Nothing. Since when have you cared what we talk about?"

"She's my *sister*, Cate."

"Nice to know you're such a happy little family." I folded my arms. Words were just coming out of my mouth and I couldn't seem to stop them. Tawny snarled. It wasn't the usual Tawny affair, it was something deeper; an animal lift of the lip. Something in my chest cowered.

"You stay away from her," she said.

We stood across the room from each other, hands clenched like around the leash of a ferocious dog. Or a chicken's neck.

I looked at them all again, their dark hair, their pale faces under the fluorescent light. "You can have her. You can have them both."

Tawny face contorted, "Both? What do you mean?"

But I was already gone. She called me back but I was flying. I fled through the corridors, trying not to focus on the blip of machines; holding my breath until I was outside, smoking nurses blowing their fumes into my mouth at the doors.

The sun was coming up as I reached the car. "Drive. Please, can you just drive?" I asked him and we went home.

Charm for protection:
'Stay away, stay away,
Ne'er return.
Stay away, stay away,
Or you shall burn.
Stay away, stay away,
Spirits abound.
Stay away, stay away,
The Lord says you'll drown.'

The Lunar Rites of Lancashire,
Melanie Hargreaves

Chapter 22

Mrs Maldew had trays of gingerbread in the window – some were hard enough to crack your teeth but they tasted gorgeous. There were rows of sugared pumpkin, toffee apples and jelly bats. The perfect Halloween treats. Each year she tried to pass off Matchmakers as magic wands. We all went along with it obligingly and hexed each other up the high street before snaffling our treats at school. Matty Bridge had a sugar high all day and flicked toffee wrappers at Miss Draycott's back.

I imagined Tawny chewing on liquorice sticks, pretending they were fangs. She'd done it every year since I'd known her and she'd chase me down the Slip screaming, "I vant to suck your blaaad!" before collapsing in giggles.

I wondered what she was doing right now. Would she be with Robyn? Would she read her the problem page from a magazine or paint her a Get Well Soon card to prop up against the fruit bowl?

It rained hard and water flooded in big syrupy Vs down the roofs. We watched it pooling in the broken gutters. People gathered under stripy shop awnings and whispered about the re-enactment. The whole town was chattering. What did they expect – a public hanging? Were people really so excited about it? When you went past the Post Office on the way to school, old men would cackle at you and try to prod you with their walking sticks. Little kids nicked twigs from the bonfire pile and ran about with them lodged between their legs like brooms.

Long Byrne really set the mood for Halloween.

I slunk out of school before rehearsal. Dad had made me go in, even driving me to the school gate. But I wouldn't have stayed for any extra-curricular activity even if they had double espressos on tap.

I couldn't believe how quickly the month had gone.

Rose and Jane – Tawny and Bryony – were everywhere I looked. The teachers let Tawny wear her witch skirts in class. She swanned about in them every day "in character".

But even with everything, Bryony was still speaking to me. I went along with it although everything was murky between us now. Maybe it was sick curiosity. Every time I looked at her, my stomach oozed.

There was one week left before the re-enactment.

Nerves were showing, making everyone snappy.

I had been roped into helping paint the scenery – out of peoples' way – but my arms felt so heavy with exhaustion and caffeine that I wasn't much help. I climbed up the step ladder with one hand on the steel railing as if gravity had just grown ten times stronger. Rehearsals carried on around me as I wielded a blue paintbrush; I heard everyone's voices but didn't turn my head to look at them. All I wanted to do with my head was put it on a big fluffy pillow and never get up again.

I tried to concentrate through one of the biggest scenes.

"On this night, and in this place—"

"We call upon an ancient grace."

"Bring us light and love, all weathers—"

"And let our friendship never sever."

I knew the words by heart: the hungry look on their faces, the white cloth that bound them to each other. I waited for the next line but . . . it never came.

Tawny's blood-chilling scream made me shudder on the ladder.

I turned my head, the world suddenly feeling very blurry.

Tawny had sprung up from her kneeling position with Bryony on the floor and was frantically waving her arms around.

"Get it off me, get it off me!"

I saw a flash of blood. Was she hurt? I started to climb down but the assembly hall lights cloyed at my eyelids. I took another step and then I was falling.

My cheek smashed the parquet floor.

This time, everyone screamed.

"Cate!" Miss Rillington gasped and was at my side shortly before Tawny reached me. I was as shocked to see her there as she was to be there. Through my hazy vision I watched her remember herself and take two steps back but not before I saw the blood dripping from her hands.

"Tawny, what—" I mumbled.

"Cate, shush, it's OK." Rillington fussed. "Are you all right?"

But my eyes were trained on Tawny's hands. There was blood. And black chicken feathers.

I pushed myself up to my elbows and spun to where Bryony was still crouched on the ground like she was just waiting for her line in the play. The feather charm she wore at her wrist caught the light and I saw that it was also stained a deep, burning crimson.

She slowly looked up and over to us but her eyes lay on Tawny. There was something akin to hunger there.

The room vibrated.

"Do you need a doctor, Cate?" Rillington asked.

"No, I'm fine, I'm fine." The world was still spinning around me.

"Why don't you go home? It's all the excitement. Do you need anyone to pick you up?"

I looked at Tawny but she was pretending to be busy with her nose in my script.

"No, I'll be OK, thanks." I got shakily to my feet and left, casting a glance back at the scene behind me. Everyone was slowly heading back to the bloody scene. I wanted to stay, to find out how my poor dead Chick had ended up on Tawny and Bryony's hands. But Rillington said, "Get some rest, Cate."

Tawny glanced back over her shoulder at me and I saw a streak of fear there before it disappeared into a grimace.

Life without Tawny might as well have been no life at all.

At 8 p.m. I waited for Bryony by the horse chestnut tree with my torch balanced on a branch and my hood yanked around my ears. We'd arranged it beforehand but things felt different now. The dark sky looked overcast through the trees. I wanted to go home. I rubbed my arm where it had smacked the floor and thought of the look on Bryony's face as she stood over the mess of blood and feathers.

The expression had made her face look like a skull.

I knew I had to speak to her.

She came bounding towards me down the mud-pocked track. Her cheeks were rouged and her eyes lined with kohl. She was shining.

"Where were you?" I said.

"Sorry, had to stay behind!"

"Well, why didn't you text me?" I cringed after I said it. So needy, but the panic in me was growing to fill my whole chest.

"I'm sorry." I saw her glimmer falling off right in front of me. "I didn't realise the time. I think we're ready for the big night!" she added, grinning despite herself.

I was too cold to care. "Right, sure."

"OK, Cate, I'm sorry," she said in her low voice. "You could have gone home."

The ground seemed to shake beneath me.

"Are you all right?" she said.

"Never better," I muttered.

I thought of Robyn in the hospital. I thought of my hen slumped dead in a hot metal vent. I had so many questions.

"What the hell just happened in there?"

"What do you mean?"

"Obviously the blood."

"Oh," Bryony rolled her eyes. A Tawny move. "Must have been someone playing a prank. I don't think it was real blood. One of the Witch Groupies trying to spook us before the big event."

I shook my head.

"No?" said Bryony with more than a hint of a smile.

"No." My voice was firm. "I think I know who it was."

"Please enlighten me." Bryony's voice was sardonic and my brow crumpled. This felt so unlike the Bryony I knew; the one who had grown in my heart for weeks and weeks. This was someone else. This was –

"Bryony?" I asked. "You remember that day up on the moor . . . how did you know that my mum killed herself?"

Her jaw set and her eyes went blank. "Like I said, I thought it was obvious. People talk."

"Not even Tawny knows what really happened. I told people she had heart failure."

"No one believes that, Cate," she scoffed.

I folded my arms over my chest, keeping my own heart from leaping around like an angry cat in a cage.

"I know what death feels like," she continued. "I've seen the way it looks inside a house, and your face is full of it."

All my blood drained to ice. "What do you mean?"

"Well, it's just hanging there, isn't it? Like cobwebs. Everywhere you look, you can see it. Your dad, completely obsessed with work. You, not eating. It's all part of it."

"Wait, what? Me not eating?"

She raised an eyebrow. "Oh, give it up, will you. I've not seen you eat so much as a cracker since I've been here. You're really ill."

I felt my jaw drop. "Shut the fuck up, Bryony."

"Not admitting it to yourself yet? How long has it been, Cate?"

I stared at the ground.

"Oh my god, you thought I'd read your mind, didn't you? For fuck's sake," she glowered. "You still think I'm some sort of witch."

"Don't be ridiculous ..."

"I'm not. *You* on the other hand ..." She spun on her heel and her long skirt fanned out around her.

"Where are you going?"

"Home."

She turned back and there was that Tawny Sneer balanced on her chin. She'd honed it, spending all that time alone with Tawny in her room.

"Please don't be like that. Stay," I said, starting towards her. I couldn't believe I was begging.

"Did you know that to keep functioning," she said, "the body needs to eat approximately every four hours?"

I stopped. "Thanks for the info."

"To keep functioning *normally* anyway."

"Why are you saying this? We need to talk about the blood."

She raised her eyebrows.

"I'm *fine*," I insisted, feeling the ground tremble slightly.

She shook her head, her face softening. "Cate, when was the last time you ate something? A slice of toast? A bowl of soup?"

I shrugged. "Let's leave it, shall we?"

"You're wasting away." She came close to me and put her hand on my shoulder. I hoped that under the calm exterior she wasn't wincing as my shoulder blade pierced her fingers through my hoodie.

She looked at me with wide green eyes. Then slowly she bent down and kissed me on the cheek.

Even in the black air of the Slip, the whole world seemed to brighten with colour. One moment I was repulsed by her, the next I couldn't get enough. Her lips were firm and smooth. Had they kissed Tawny's cheek? Had they kissed her mouth? She pulled away and stood up tall.

Don't stop.

I squinted up at her, but I pulled back and gasped. In the light of my torch, her eyes clouded, her teeth looked razor sharp.

Bryony?

Or was this Jane?

I stumbled, recoiling, smacking my back onto the chestnut tree.

"What?" she said. She stared at me hard. Her gaze was piercing, my head throbbed. Could she see inside my head? A Hollingworth witch?

"Do you look like your mum?" she said quietly, as if from a distance.

I thought I'd heard the wrong words at first. "What? Why?" I spluttered. "Why ask that?"

She shrugged, the easiest question in the world. "I'm curious. Genetics, it's interesting." But there was something shrewd in her eyes, and the razor grin was back on her face.

Did she think she was being funny? "Stop trying to piss me off and just tell me what you're after. For god's sake, Bryony, I thought we were friends."

Her eyes glinted, steely. "How did you try to kill yourself?"

Had she been playing with me this whole time? Making me feel close to her and then tearing me apart? My mouth gaped open. Where was this coming from? "I never said that I did."

"Oh, come off it. It's written all over you. Sob-story mum, moved to a new place, new stepmother, eating disorder. You've got every reason to try to kill yourself and I know you, Cate; you're not one to put up a fight."

I was plummeting. "How do you know what I'm like? You've known me six weeks. Who even are you?" My eyes were saucers, like I'd never seen her before.

She scowled. "I'd known my brother for sixteen years and I thought we were exactly the same. Sam's older, he does his own thing. But Euan and I, we were *different*, and the same all at once. But really, I had no idea what he was thinking, did I? Now he's dead. Swinging from an attic beam. And Cate," she narrowed her eyes, "it's not how long you know someone, it's how deep you can push yourself inside their head."

My eyes flared wider.

Witch.

It was all true. Robyn was right. I felt like I was shrinking beneath her. *You're not in my head. You're not in my head.* She smiled and it was not Bryony's smile. I didn't know where it was coming from.

"Had any dreams lately?" she whispered.

I stared at her. With a flash of fear I thought of Jane in the country road.

She laughed, and it was a harsh spit of sound. "Oh my *god,* you actually dreamt about me! Go on, what was it about? I'm flying round your head, am I?"

When had she become so cruel? *This isn't her,* I told myself. *This can't be her. This is someone else. Not my Bryony.*

"Shut up."

"Oh, go on," she leered. "You can tell me."

"I don't need this. Not from you." My chest felt tight. "Did Tawny put you up to this? Why are you being like this?"

Her eyes were manic. "Like what, Cate? Go on."

"Argh! Just leave me alone." I pushed past her. My mind felt foggy.

"Yeah, try and get away. What was the dream? Did you have a good feel, like with Tawny?"

I kept walking. My feet slid in the mud. I kept going. My head felt strange; fuzzy, like in rehearsal.

"It's almost Halloween," she called after me. "Who knows what the witches will bring."

I hit a hard wall of fear and stopped dead.

"What did you-?" But when I turned around she was already walking away. Up the Slip. Up to the hanging ground. Up to the river in the middle of the night.

A Hollingworth witch.

I began walking at double the pace, trying not to fall on the exposed roots. I was at the kissing gate which marked the entrance when I turned back.

"Break a leg," I yelled.

I hoped Jane would snap more than that.

They prepared for their magical ritual days in advance. Drinking thistle tea and rubbing their dirty bodies with ointment made from goose fat. They burnt sage in the air around them to sweat out the elements from their skin. You had to be pure for a ritual.

Saint-like. Devilish.

If you weren't prepared, there was no telling what might happen.

In Search of the Long Byrne Witches, P.J. Hebden

Chapter 23

The day came.

Halloween.

I didn't sleep any more. How could I?

All the cast members looked like they'd just crapped themselves. The Witch Groupies rehearsed their lines in an eerie chant that whispered through the corridors like noxious smoke. You could spot their faces around school, faintly green and shrivelled-looking. All except for Tawny.

She was on fire. In assembly Pad Mitchell kept trying to sit her in his lap, "for good luck". She laughed, "Not a chance!" But threw me a triumphant glance as if Pad were a puppy I'd wanted in a shop window, but she'd jumped the queue.

I wanted to tell Tawny about what had happened down the Slip, but I couldn't get close enough to infiltrate her golden aura. When I'd plucked up the courage to call her, I was met with a woman's voice saying the number had not been recognised. Blocked.

I'd spent the entire week slinking about the school like a ghost, Bryony's words imprinted on my eyelids every time I closed my eyes. Robyn still hadn't come back to school and it wasn't worth the risk going up to the Browns' house to talk to her. Had Tawny told Sandra I'd filled her daughter's head with witches and things that went bump in the night?

Psych class was dangerous too; there was no way I could face Bryony or my slipping grades. The best thing to do was escape around the back of the science block and stay there for an hour or two.

"Is that you, Cate?"

Rillington marched around the corner doing the rounds under a large golf umbrella, smock swinging. I winced. I hadn't been there five minutes.

"Skipping class, are we?"

"Family emergency, Miss."

She pursed her lips. "Surely that's something Mrs Waddington should be made aware of?"

"Yes, Miss . . ."

"Cate . . ." She paused. "Maybe class could be a distraction today. Don't you think?"

She meant the anniversary. But that was the last thing on my mind right now. "I'm fine, I'm fine," I muttered.

Rillington sighed. "Go on, I'll sign your absence form at the front desk."

I felt my eyebrows shoot up my forehead. "Miss?" I said.

"But you'd better be on time tonight at the re-enactment or I'll make sure you never see the outside of a classroom again. Do you hear me?"

I was too gobsmacked to speak for a second.

"Yes, Miss. Thanks, Miss."

Then she did the weirdest thing I'd ever seen Rillington do. She winked at me and went on her way.

I stood reeling for a minute then sank down the stained wall at the back of the creepy P.E. block to wait out Psychology class under the rowan trees. People usually bunked off together and I wasn't sure what to do on my own. On the other side of the field, the big wooden stage had already been erected and draped with dark material. It looked as ominous as the Hollingworth House, which I'm guessing had been the plan. Workmen and blokes from the village were pitching carnival rides and testing the lights, bellowing unintelligible shouts to each other in the drizzle. I didn't have a brolly, but the water felt good and cool against my skin. The branches bounced, full of fruit and life as the rain rocked them back and forth. They looked like nothing could harm them.

I snatched my hand up, snapped off some smaller twigs and stuffed them in my bag. For protection.

"Thanks, Mum," I whispered.

My phone buzzed. Tawny never texted any more but every time my phone went off, my heart rate went into turbo.

It was Dad.

Sorry, I cant make it to the play tonight. Let me know you're ok. Very proud. Luv dad

I'd expected as much but he'd promised to be there as I left the house that morning. I knew he'd spend all night with folders open on his screen, poring over photos, her old stories and playing Fleetwood Mac – his and Mum's first wedding dance. I wished I could be there with him.

Sorry, Dad. The re-enactment was waiting.

***

At 6 p.m. the playing field reeked of vinegary chips and wet metal. There was just one hour left to go.

All the fête stalls had been resurrected behind school and stood like dishevelled second-hand umbrellas, but everywhere was bustling with activity. Someone was cooking caramel, the sugar fusing, gooey and golden, to the boiling pot. A portable candyfloss machine was whirring away by the rugby pitch. Miss Waddington handed out sticks to kids dressed as zombies and axe murderers.

Apple-Bobbing, Pin the Tail on the Werewolf, Shoot-the-Skeleton. The whole of Long Byrne was packed and buzzing with re-enactment excitement. Halloween was in full swing.

I'd read somewhere once that Halloween was when the veil between this world and the next, the afterlife, was at its thinnest. I looked out over the giddy, chocolate-smeared faces from the wings of the new stage and I couldn't help but feel tired.

Everything was set. It was going to be perfect. . . except for the rain.

No matter how many times I flexed my fingers or shoved them between my thighs, they just wouldn't get warm. The rain spiked down in sharp talons, scratching at the stage as the cast and crew huddled under the tarpaulin canopy. The rain bouncing on it made my head pound. If Rillington didn't look so pale I'd be wishing she'd choke on her umbrella for making me be here tonight.

"This cannot actually be happening," Tawny groaned. "I'm not going out there in this. I'm not, I'm not." Rillington turned up her lip, looking slightly feral.

"It's just a shower. Sorry to curl your hair, Tawny, but the show must go on," Rillington said through tight lips. "You signed the form."

"I didn't sign it in blood, Miss."

"Get your cap on and stop whining."

Tawny clenched her teeth and hissed, "If I snap my neck on those boards, I'm going to become a lawyer and sue the crap out of her."

"You'd already be dead," Bryony observed.

But Rillington had switched off from them and turned to me. She put her hand on my shoulder. "Glad you could make it, Cate," she said with a knowing look.

The whole place was a health and safety nightmare. There were still dark curls of sawdust on the stage floor – not exactly tried and tested. Screaming kids, sparklers and a good dose of rickety scaffolding. Brilliant.

Tawny and Bryony stood huddled close together, elbows linked. I tried to focus on something else, anything else, but I couldn't stop staring at the stars of the show – a lump of bile lodged in my throat. Bryony's eyes slid up to mine, blank and colourless. Was this Bryony in front of me, or Jane?

There was a *bang* overhead. Swirling rockets lit up their own smoke fifty metres high and even though we saw firework displays every year, everyone whooped and sighed. Even Matty Bridge's rugby team. I felt dizzy looking up and slammed my hand on the scaffolding to keep myself from falling.

"Do you know where the word 'bonfire' comes from?" Bryony whispered in Tawny's ear, white steam curling under her jawbone.

Tawny shook her head, tasting the question on her breath, already impressed by what Bryony was going to say.

"In Pagan times they used to light a fire for their goddess, to bring a good winter and light up the way. They'd stoke it with cattle bones to keep away the bad spirits. A bonfire, or 'bone fire'. Cool, right?"

My eyes snapped up to her face, but she was perfectly calm – that sickening Bryony serenity. *Or Jane.* I suddenly felt very glad we locked the barn door at night, in case someone tried to revive old traditions. My cows were safe – safer than my glossy black hen anyway. Nausea wormed its way through my intestines and my head throbbed, making it difficult to see clearly. I watched as Tawny threaded her fingers through Bryony's, pressed her thumb inside Bryony's palm then twisted her long fingers to hold the hand another way, like a prolonged kiss. Tawny turned her eyes up to Bryony and I saw they were shining in the way Tawny only ever looked at movie stars. Complete adoration.

My mouth fell open as I dragged my eyes to Bryony. Her face was triumphant, her chin held high. She lowered her gaze to me and smiled. It was the sharp, grizzled smile of a four-hundred-year-old witch.

My heart stopped. Was that it? Is that what this was all about?

Bryony had wanted Tawny all this time – wanted her to belong to her, maybe even bound to her.

Just like Jane and Rose.

I could hear the crowd gathered in front of the stage. Some people were clapping rhythmically as if the play was the only thing they'd wanted to see all their lives. They didn't know. No one else knew what was going on. Except maybe Robyn.

I had to warn Tawny.

There was no time left.

"Brown! Hollingworth!" Rillington barked over the rain. "You're up!"

"Showtime, baby!" Tawny winked at us all then turned to kiss Bryony on the cheek. She bounded away to the wings. There was a perfect pink lip print on Bryony's skin.

I stared at it, frozen to the spot.

Bryony looked incredible. Her eyes were rimmed with dark eyeshadow so they glowed, catlike. Definitely Tawny's handiwork. Her hair was curled and twisted in a golden rope around her shoulders. She flicked her gaze my way. "Everything OK?"

She actually looked concerned. A great actress. I steeled my stomach.

I didn't speak. If I answered her I'd be sick.

"I know it's the anniversary—"

"You should be on stage!" I cut in. *Witch.* My stomach lurched dangerously.

She clutched at a pleat in her dress, sinking her hand deep into it. I found my eyes resting there.

"Cate?"

I blinked, clutching my copy of the script, trying to train my eyes on it. Was Rillington watching?

"It'll be a success. The re-enactment. Just wait."

I looked at her, searching for more traces of Jane in her

face – the sallow skin, the high cheekbones – but now it was just Bryony, smelling like laundry detergent, sandalwood and rain, no matter how hard I looked.

But I knew she was still there.

I let my face harden.

"I don't care about the stupid re-enactment," I spat. "I should never have written it in the first place. Why would I want to do you a favour?"

Bryony looked at me shrewdly. "Me?"

I raised my head, meeting her dead in the eye. "You planned this all along, didn't you?" Bryony's eyes flickered to Tawny's back in the wings.

"Time to go, people!" Rillington's voice hammered out.

Bryony grinned and it was the smile that I'd feared. "And now it's showtime." She turned and the whole cast was swept away with her. Rillington stood between us and I could no longer see my best friend.

Tawny. I had to warn her about who Bryony really was.

I stepped out from behind the stage and moved towards the edge of the crowd. Rillington would be expecting me in the wings, but from the audience I'd be able to watch them and keep my eye on Tawny and Bryony for the next twenty minutes at least. Out in the crowd, people were getting restless and picking candyfloss from their fingers. I spotted Pad Mitchell leaning over the barrier, wolf-whistling at the bare platform. Pathetic. Girls clutching big polyester bears stood looking awkward on first dates while their partners shovelled candied nuts into their wide mouths. I hadn't realised just how many people were going to be there. My stomach did a little flip. Hopefully my name wasn't on the programme; I didn't want my name anywhere near this play.

Mum would be disgusted by it.

"Cate!"

Someone tiny was running straight at me.

"Robyn!" Without even thinking, I held out my arms and swept her up in a hug. I was worried to pull away but when I did she was smiling, curls held safe under an oversized hat.

"Hey," she said, breathless.

"What are you doing here?" I half choked. Everything that had happened came to me on a tidal wave and I took a step back.

"Good to see you, too!"

I took in her pale face and sharp chin. "Are you supposed to be here? I didn't even know you were out of hospital." My eyes checked the stage. Nothing yet.

"Oh, don't you start and all. Mum doesn't know I'm out of the house though. I left Ginger in my bed. Do you think she'll notice I've grown a tail?" She smiled easily like it was old times; like she didn't remember anything at all.

"Look, I have to . . ."

"The doctors said it was OK for me to go home, so long as I stayed with someone all the time. And look," she grinned, "I'm with someone now."

Somehow I wasn't sure this was what Hillbury General had in mind. I wanted to ask her more, but she looked worse than I'd ever seen her. She was a skeleton. I could practically count her ribs through her overcoat, and the purple smudges under her eyes burnt almost coal black now. I couldn't leave her.

"Well, I'm not letting you out of my sight." I put my hand on her shoulder. "Stay right here. You going to be OK watching this, though?"

She nodded, sticking her chin up. I'd almost forgotten she was Tawny's sister. "Yeah, the witches don't exist. I know that now. It's just a story, isn't it?"

Isn't it?

I couldn't answer her.

"I'm sorry, Rob. For everything, I really am."

She nudged me. "For what?"

"Everything." *You were right,* I wanted to say. Something was going on. The rumbling crowd around me; Robyn's body almost like an apparition in front of me; the mist of rain around us all. This couldn't be real. "Friends?" I asked, but my voice was barely audible.

"Of course," her eyes turned up in happiness.

"And . . ." Was I pushing my luck? "Robyn, I need to ask you . . . what happened? I'm so glad you're feeling better, but did you really think Bryony was a witch?"

She ran a hand across her cheek and dipped her head. "Hear me out, OK?"

"OK . . ."

She kept staring at the ground and I could almost feel her cringing. "I used to get this feeling around her. It started in school. Whenever she went past I'd get this tingle down my spine, a really creepy feeling, but like I was meant to talk to her, too. But I never knew what to say." She looked at the empty stage in front of us.

I reached out to clutch the side of her jacket. "Go on?"

"You'll laugh at me."

"I'd never do that, Rob."

"Yeah, right," she smirked.

I tried to laugh. "Go on."

She scrunched her forehead. Could she not remember? Had they pumped her full of pills at the hospital too?

"I found out she was a Hollingworth and suddenly she seemed like this . . . superstar. And I wanted to talk to her more than anything. That's when I started having nightmares."

I shuddered. "Nightmares?"

"I used to watch her go out to the Slip when I was on my way to the farm really early," Robyn went on. "She looked like she was off to do something important. One time, she caught me looking at her over the hedge. She stopped, stared at me for a minute and then went straight past like I was just some stupid little kid. I was annoyed at that. So, I followed her."

"Why?"

"She . . . there was something about her. I needed to talk to her." Robyn suddenly flushed.

A trickle of terror slid through my ribs. "Yeah, there is something about her, isn't there . . ."

"I followed her and she was . . ." Her brow puckered again.

I took Robyn's hand as Rillington strode onto the stage.

"She was what, Robyn?"

"She was out on the moor drawing strange symbols in the soil. She had stones and twigs all around her, feathers too."

My blood ran cold. Black feathers?

"I asked her what she was doing. But she yelled at me, telling me to leave her alone. It was like she was a completely different person, like she had different eyes or something. I don't know. At least . . . that's what's I remember. The doctors said things might get a bit hazy." Robyn put her fingers on her temples, suddenly looking overwhelmed. She felt so small against my arm.

"Cate, her eyes went a strange colour. I was scared. I wanted to stop her. I didn't know what she was doing. And I don't even know if there's anyone else living in the Hollingworth House. I think it's just her up there on her own . . ."

Witch, witch, witch.

"Have you seen anyone else there, Cate?" She looked at me with eyes like liquid.

No, no, I hadn't.

The air was sparkling darkly around me. Robyn's words had confirmed everything I feared. Bryony was a real Hollingworth witch, living in the Manor like she owned the place. Was there really a Mrs Hollingworth? Had anyone actually heard from her in years? There truly was witchcraft in Long Byrne and the curse was playing out all over again. Jane and Rose had really damned this town when they damned each other. Bryony might do anything. Or was it Jane?

Tawny.

The play was about to start. My whole body felt like ice.

"Good evening, ladies and gentlemen!" Rillington beamed. "And now, the moment you've all been waiting for.

"It was on this day of Samhain almost four hundred years ago, that two girls were hanged for their crimes out on Long Byrne Moor. Their deaths were followed by many others. But who were those girls? And what was their real crime?"

Something twisted in my gut and I drew Robyn closer. Who were they? Who *are* they? Tawny's skirt flipped impatiently from the wing.

"These are the questions we all want the answers to. So without further ado, I give you the *Witches of Long Byrne*."

The crowd erupted and Tawny and Bryony walked onto the stage. I grasped Robyn's hand tighter. My head felt light and my eyes were fuzzy.

They strode in time, their heads held high, looking at the air clinging above our heads. The audience hushed themselves into awed silence. Tawny looked like a fantasy with her face made pale and her lips done out in blood red. I could almost smell Pad Mitchell's breath from across the field. They made their way to centre stage and knelt down in unison. Tawny's voice rang out. It was the scene where Jane and Rose pledged themselves to one another – bound their souls together.

"On this night and in this place—"

"We call upon an ancient grace."

"Bring us light and love all weathers –"

They stared into each other's eyes. Was Bryony in Tawny's head right now? Could they see only one another?

The audience were mesmerised too.

"And let our true love never sever."

Bryony bound their hands together but there was no blood or feathers this time. They rose to their feet but

Bryony wasn't looking where she was supposed to be looking. She was looking at me.

I gasped.

Jane. I was right; Robyn was right. She was right about it all. Witchcraft was in Bryony's blood. The Hollingworths were witches and Jane was right on stage in front of us. And yesterday she had bound herself to Tawny – my best friend, Tawny – with a spell involving blood. I looked up at the sky and the moon was full.

It was all real. And it was Halloween . . . I had to protect Tawny. Tawny. *My* Tawny, who hated me so much right now. God knows what Jane had planned for her on the anniversary of her own death.

But it was like a train wreck – the play was in full swing and I could do nothing to stop it.

We watched and watched, the scenes unfolding before us. Jane and Rose braiding each other's hair in the big draughty kitchen. Jane and Rose linking arms on their way to market. Rose laughing at a boy's jokes while Jane looked on, enraged. Jane and Rose ready to scratch out each other's eyes on the moor. A cold sweat stood on my forehead. I watched Jane circle Tawny, speaking the words I'd written like a recited spell. And it was then, in the final scene, that I felt it. The whole crowd went quiet, not breathing, and all I could hear was the rain on the shoddy stage soaking into that fresh-cut wood. My heart started racing. It was happening again – all that dread I'd felt in the hayloft surging in my chest, making my heart beat like a whirring broken toy. I looked at Bryony in the silence and stillness and she was the only thing moving.

She looked right at me and smiled.

Then I heard her voice as clear as day. "She's mine," the voice said. My knees almost gave way. She had been in my head all along.

I tore my hand out of Robyn's.

"Where are you going? Cate?"

I ran.

"Cate!"

The girls were:
Mary Alice Nolloth
Jennet Smithe
Eliza Naylor
Alice Farwell
Hetty Hildrew
Isabel Middleton
Eliza Copps
Jennet Adams
Mary Rattenbury
Dorothy Evans
Alice Evans
Ellen Ambrose
Eleanor Middleton
Charlotte Lymm
Elnett Day
Jemima Leathorpes
Rose Ackroyd
Jane Hollingworth

The History of Long Byrne: Demons on the Moor,
Dr C. Munir

Chapter 24

I dashed around the back of the stage. I had to speak to Tawny.

Rillington wheeled around a corner. "Cate!" she hissed. "You shouldn't be around here. Get back to the wings."

"I need to find Tawny, Miss! You don't understand."

"There's no time for that now. The play's about to finish. You need to be there for the fireworks."

"But I—"

"And in this secret place I pledge myself to you."

I froze.

I could hear them chanting my words over the speakers. This was the final scene, just before they would be killed on the moor. I pictured them together, holding each other on the stage, clinging to one another, fingers splayed, nails clawing.

I craned my head but I couldn't see them. I could only hear the pistons of the carnival rides. I flung myself past Rillington, but it was no use; I couldn't snatch Tawny from the stage with everyone watching. Rillington had grabbed my hood to stop me and was trying to speak to me but I couldn't hear anything. The world seemed to be passing me in slow motion. I ran back down the stairs and into the audience.

There they were.

They looked at each other hungrily, their hands clasped tightly together. Bryony looked like Bryony, but only just. Was that a flicker I saw there? Who was she right now?

My eyes burnt with static and I looked out over the crowd to see if anyone else had noticed what was going on. Everyone stared up, enraptured. They couldn't see it. I looked back and forth between Bryony and the audience but nothing in their eyes changed. That's when things started to get weirder. I could hear something . . . A dull roar that hurt my ears and then . . .

"Cate!"

My name being shouted, over and over.

"Cate. Cate!"

I spun around, recognising the voice but not understanding where it could be coming from.

"Cate!"

"Mum?" I whispered.

That was a voice I hadn't heard in a very long time. And yet there it was, as clear as day, calling my name.

Where are you, Mum?

"Come and find me," she said.

It seemed like nothing else mattered in that moment. Mum was speaking to me and I had to go to her. It was like a dream but my eyes were wide open.

BANG.

I jumped, drawing a ragged breath.

Glitter poured down all around us as the firework fizzled. My gaze ripped back to the stage. It was the hanging scene.

Tawny rose gracefully onto the scaffold, her chin jutting out defiantly even in character. I'd missed my cue entirely. My head spun. In the back of my mind, I could hear an angry hiss that reminded me of Miss Rillington's voice but it seemed very, very far away.

"You'll be next!" Jane cackled, scouring the audience with an evil glare. "I'll curse you all! If I'm going to Hell, then you're coming with me."

Her voice cracked. I'd written the words, but I absolutely believed her.

It was almost too real and a panic rose up in me.

"Cate?" came the voice.

I jumped and spun around as more fireworks erupted behind me. Someone else – a gloating back-stager – had taken up my duties, excited that I had failed. Up on stage Tawny and Bryony were hand in hand on the gallows, smiles carved deep into their flushed faces. Everyone cheered in a roar that tore my eardrums. Someone threw a plastic rose at Tawny's feet; she picked it up and placed it between her teeth. High on the stage, she leant in to Bryony, their lips an inch apart and Bryony took the rose between her own teeth. The crowd went nuts. Pad Mitchell wolf-whistled.

"Get in!" he yelled.

"Come and find me," the voice said again.

I blinked. *Find you?*

"I'm out where it happened." I heard the words but they seemed to be getting further and further away from me.

"Mum! Wait!"

"Come find me, Cate."

"I'm coming!"

I turned around to head down from the stage stairs but Rillington was in front of me. "We did it, Cate! Well done!" She was grinning almost ecstatically.

"I need to go," I pushed past her.

"Wait, Cate! We need to celebrate. Cate?"

I had quickened my pace and I was already running through the crowd. I knew exactly where I was going.

I sprinted down the street then carried on until trees reared up in front of me. I squeezed my way around the kissing gate, and I was on the track. I squinted down the dark path, my head feeling light – the moonlight quavered. When *was* the last time I'd eaten anything? Did I have enough energy to keep going? Rain began to thunder on the leaves above.

Someone was up ahead.

"Mum?"

She was walking away up towards the moor. Her hips were swinging in her long dark skirt.

I stopped. *Wait, what?*

"Tawny? How did you get here?"

She spun around, her eyes large with surprise. "Did you follow me here?"

How did she get here so fast? Why wasn't she back on the green, celebrating with the others? The fayre was going to run late into the night.

"Don't be stupid. You shouldn't be here right now, Tawn." My voice trembled, coming out high and reedy through my teeth.

She sneered. "Checking up on me? For fuck's sake, Cate.

I'm not five – I don't need your supervision. I'm sick of you *looking* at me."

"I didn't follow you." *I was looking for someone.*

"Screw you.." Tawny yanked off her mobcap, turning away. Her hair fanned out in a perfect shining curve in the moonlight. I gulped.

"Where are you going?"

She bared her teeth. "What? Going to stalk me there too?"

"No, don't be crazy. I—"

"*I'm* crazy?" she laughed, flashing that feline grin. "I'm the one who's been covering up *your* crazy for *years.* You think people want to hang round you after your little meltdown in rehearsal? That really was the final straw." That snidey sneer on her face made my neck bristle and I realised how it suited her perfectly. "Without me there, everyone's going to see you for what you really are."

I trembled. She was going low. Something in me turned away from her. "Yeah?" I said. "You think people are going to like it when they hear what you and Bryony get up to?"

"What?" she spat.

"I know what you've been doing. I've seen the way you look at each other. I understand what's really been going on."

Her eyes looked weird under the stage makeup; too large for her face, like they were popping out of her head. My head ached and she hissed, "You're actually mental. I've done everything for you over the years. I was holding you together."

A curl of mania whirled in my chest and I folded my arms over it. "Tawny, wait, I'm sorry. I didn't mean that. I need to talk to you about Bryony. I think – I think she's got you under a spell."

She froze then stalked towards me; that wild look was fixed onto her face.

"Oh my fucking god, Cate. Just because you've got a dead mum doesn't mean you can go psycho."

I glared. How dare she bring Mum into this? I clasped my elbows to form an iron bar with my arms. "I'm serious, Tawny. I've been speaking to—"

"Who? Who've you been speaking to? Robyn?" she scoffed.

"Tawny, please listen to me. I know it sounds crazy, but—"

"No, Cate. You listen. We're done. You don't own me. We're completely *done*. OK?"

We stood under the trees of the Slip, with the rain thundering on the canopy like turbulence hitting the outside of a plane. I made my voice as low as possible so she couldn't hear my tears brewing. "Why are you out here, Tawny?"

She scowled. "Bryony and I are celebrating – she said she had something to show me. Satisfied? May I go about my business, Aspey?"

I ignored her. "It's dangerous. She's going to show you something bad. I know it."

"You're a psycho."

I ran forward and tried to snatch her arm but she pulled away. "Please listen to me, Tawn. I'm scared."

Tawny laughed. The sound split the thick air under the trees. "You've really surprised me, Caitlin. You'll go to any lengths to have her for yourself."

"Shut up, Tawny. Just listen to me." *Don't do this.*

Don't go to her. My head was so dizzy, Tawny threatened to fade away.

"You picture us, don't you? Oh my god, this is what's this is all about!"

"No, Tawny, you've got it all wrong. Just *fucking* listen to me."

She was three inches from my face. Her breath hot, white coils on my jaw. *Don't, Tawny.*

"Just like you wanted to fuck me."

My stomach jerked dangerously. She'd gone too far. The Slip melted away.

I launched myself at her.

I grabbed at her hair with my fingers, twisting them around the thick dark mass.

"Get off me, bitch!"

"You're the bitch!"

"Arghhh!"

Then we were tumbling.

"Get up and fight me," she hissed.

I found I had an extra reserve of energy I never knew about. My eyes sparkled, taking in everything: the air, the night, Tawny's livid face. What did she have that I didn't? A tiny voice inside my head said, *Bryony should have chosen me.*

"Come and get me," she snarled.

She was dancing through the tangled roots, somehow finding her way even in her long theatrical skirts that were stained with mud and leaves, but she didn't know the Slip like I did. As we ran, her skirts snagged and tore more on branches and I thought my legs would give way. I hadn't eaten all day, but somehow I stayed upright.

We ripped out into the open. It was pitch black except for the moon.

I felt feral.

Suddenly a crashing hiss was all around us: the river so loud I thought the ground was quaking. Tawny screamed over it. "Give it up, Cate! You think you can take me?"

"You want to try me?"

And there it was. The Tawny Sneer. "She'll never be yours. I won."

I was breathing heavily, a pain ragging at my left-hand side. "There's no one here."

"What's that supposed to mean?" she hissed.

I jutted my jaw, hoping I looked as menacing as I felt. "What do you think?"

"You wouldn't dare." I saw a flash of fear on her face before the actress in her had time to sweep it away, her eyes flickering towards the river. "What would your precious Bryony think? You ever thought about that?"

I found myself stalking towards her. For the second time I thought I saw panic cross her face. It didn't suit her. She looked like a rabbit being squeezed too hard by a child. "You wouldn't, Cate. You wouldn't."

I wouldn't. But she didn't know that.

I jumped at her and scrabbled so we both fell. The river coursed next to us. It was just like our old game with the nightmare dog, except I didn't have a pillow this time. We were both hitting rocks; the wet grassy tendrils on our clothes like cold fat on grease paper. I shoved her and she was pinned. I felt invincible. I slipped off my coat and pasted it over her mouth, just like in our old game.

"No!" I heard her cry.

But I was pushing hard. I had her now. The moonlight shook around us.

"No, Cate!" Her eyes were wide. The game didn't feel so fun any more.

Then I heard footsteps behind us.

"Get off her! GET OFF!"

"Bryony?"

I turned my head. Bryony stood behind me, and next to her . . . Tawny.

"What?" I gulped. I turned back to the floor.

Robyn was struggling under my grip; her small hands on my wrists.

"Rob?"

Everything was confused. The air was thick liquid. It seemed to be throbbing around me. What was going on? Robyn's eyes were wide and fearful below me. Bryony glared at me, sick with horror. Tawny was coiled and ready to spring.

I looked up into the sky and the full moon shone down; a glamour on us all.

What the hell was I doing?

The pause was just enough time for me to let go. Robyn pushed hard and stumbled with unsteady legs. But then I heard the thud. The shriek.

I heard the crack of her body on the water.

"Robyn!" someone screamed.

We skidded towards the river.

She was caught in the reeds; her skin sticky white in the black grasp of grasses. She looked like she was covered in PVA glue that hadn't set, and if I touched it they'd have to peel her away from me.

Her eyes were closed.

"Robyn! Rob!"

I tried to reach out to her, but the current was too strong.

Tawny flashed out from behind me, throwing herself over the bank, her hair flying in the water. She grabbed Robyn's hand and held on tight. I stood back.

"Cate, you bitch! What the *hell* were you doing to her?" Tawny gasped between breaths.

Bryony snaked forward and the two of them heaved Robyn onto the grass.

A dull black weight.

Just like how they'd found Mum.

We all stood there, sobbing hard against the black air.

Tawny's voice grated. "What did you do?" We stood there far apart from each other, shaking in unison. "Cate, what did you do?" She threw herself on her sister, putting her face close to Robyn's slightly open mouth.

"I – I—"

My lips were grasping around airless sounds. My head throbbed. What had happened? Words wouldn't form in the thick night around us. Something didn't feel right.

I looked at Bryony. She stood there looking at me; a small smile played on her lips, then it was gone. Did I imagine it? I wanted to scream at her. Why wasn't she helping? Why was she smiling? Why—?

Witch, witch, witch.

The smile was back in place.

Witch, witch, witch.

What had she done to me?

I gasped, wrenching myself back to the situation in hand. Robyn was still on the ground between Tawny and me.

"Is she . . .?"

"No. No thanks to you, you crazy bitch!" Tawny picked up a rock from the ground. "I'll fucking kill you."

The world flipped. In one line of my vision I saw Tawny rising with the rock firmly grasped in her hand. If I blinked, I could see Bryony laughing behind her, the river crackling in her voice.

Witch.

I turned and I was running faster than I'd ever run in my life. The pain in my side flamed through my entire body. My feet fell in thumps back to the Slip.

Robyn. Robyn.

What had I seen? *What had I done?*

My feet thudded on the ground. The leaves, thin as loose skin, slipped over themselves, catching me off guard. I could hear Tawny's feet close behind me, along with my ragged breath. My hands smacked wet mud and I felt my knee split beneath me.

The sound of the river pummelled my ears. Clawing the wet leaves, I eased myself up. Blood oozed through my jeans. I felt dizzy and sick. I touched the blood. My palm grew hot over it.

I couldn't be sure what was real any more.

"In this place, I pledge myself to you."

"Crazy bitch." Voices spun around me. No, just one voice.

"Bryony?" I whispered. I dreaded the reply.

But there was none.

I whispered, "Jane?"

I pushed myself up but it was hard. A rustle came from the hedges that marked the nearby fields. A chanting. I covered my ears, but the chanting got louder. A strange language I didn't recognise in heavy, repeating sounds. I couldn't see anyone in the dark. It was swelling, getting louder. It was bursting my eardrums.

"Shut up. Shut up, shut up, shut up!" I screamed.

Tawny came up behind me and knocked me back down in a single bound. "You're crazy! You're actually fucking insane." Her eyes flared and I saw the red rims in the dim moonlight. I'd cracked her. She lifted a rock in her hand.

"Don't!" I yelled.

I lashed out my hand, knocking something hard. I felt my fingers break. Tawny screamed.

She lay, half-panting, half-sobbing on the ground. She pulled up her skirt; the rock was embedded in her leg. I watched, horrified, as something trickled down her bare thigh; a black worm on snow. I couldn't keep my eyes off it; the way the blood streaked downwards, full of purpose. The sounds that came from her were animal and wild.

The world didn't make sense. Bryony's witchcraft had taken hold of me, amplified by the thin veils of Halloween. Maybe Mum would be close by.

Then, there she was, looming over us.

Bryony. Her blonde hair was in tatters in the rain.

Jane.

She was smiling.

Chapter 25

"What are you doing?" I was bent double trying to hold my knee together but the blood kept pumping out under my fingers.

"Get help!" I cried as Tawny writhed in agony. But Bryony was only looking at me.

"I'm waiting," she said.

"What for?"

"Waiting for someone to hear her shouts and come running."

"No," I felt tears coming, "but you need to help her now! Robyn, too!"

But Bryony only smiled and squatted down beside us. "You don't understand, Cate. No, what's going to happen is that someone will come running and I'll tell them all about your little rampage. I'll tell them all about how you tried to murder Robyn Brown and then stabbed your best friend." She tilted her head to one side like she was about to deliver sad news. "Then what do you think will happen?"

I kept my eyes focused on her, as much as I could.

"Then you'll get carted off to a little asylum. And you can leave me to finish what I came here to do." She flashed a grin.

Tawny was looking at her in horror. "Bryony. What are you doing? Help my sister!"

"Quiet," Bryony smiled and raised her hand. Tawny's body went limp automatically as if hit by a wave of water.

"Tawny!" I yelled and swerved my body towards her. But Bryony was already there, her hand pointed in my direction. There was a force pressing against my neck like I had an electric collar on.

Bryony smiled through it all. The hollows under her eyes looked more pronounced, like she was much, much older than she was.

"That's better," she said.

"What do you want with us, Bryony?" I croaked, my windpipe tightening. I grasped at my throat.

"I came back for her. I'd waited a long time."

"What are you talking about?"

Bryony shook her head so the tendrils of her wet hair moved like iron bars. "I came back for my Rose."

"You're insane," I choked.

"No, Cate. You are. After all, who's going to believe you?"

"Are you trying to tell me that you think Tawny is Rose Ackroyd?"

Bryony – or Jane – grinned. "She had to come back some time; we all do."

I cast a glance at Tawny lying unconscious in the dirt. Tawny, my best friend. Tawny, who I'd do anything for. Tawny, who was bleeding to death in the cold, Halloween rain.

"You thought she was yours but you were wrong." Bryony bared her teeth; a skeleton. Her hand was still raised, keeping me pinned to the floor. I pushed against it, trying to reach out for Tawny's hand but it was pointless.

"You're evil."

She went on. "I had you pegged as soon as I clapped eyes on you. A menace. Something to be removed from this situation. Do you think your cute witch obsession and strange illnesses could keep her hooked on you for ever? She always loved the drama, Rose did."

"She's not Rose – she's Tawny."

"You're wrong, actually. I knew who she was the moment I saw her." She grinned, looming over me.

"She's not a witch."

"Rose was never a witch, not really. That was always me."

"You're not Jane," I spat.

"No?" Her grin darkened. Bryony rose up to her full height, seeming to tower above me. "Oh, but I am. I am Jane and I came back to Long Byrne searching for Rose." She pointed at Tawny's limp form. "I picked Bryony's body as my own – you see, the spell works better when you keep it in the family."

I shook my head. "No."

Jane cocked her head. "Who was looking out for poor Bryony Hollingworth after her brother died? With everyone distracted, I was able to slip inside, control her mind, make her move back to Long Byrne. And when I got here, who did I find?"

"Tawny . . ."

She gave a laugh that could have been a bark. "You've got it in one. Tawny Brown. My poor Rose incarnate. I'd have known those eyes, those hips anywhere. Here she was, right in front of me. But unlike my Rose, she was surrounded by *people*.

"All I wanted was her and to be with her all the time, to convince her to run away with me back like we should have done four hundred years ago. But first I needed to get rid of everyone she cared about.

"A neglectful mum – that was no problem. Tawny's mother would hardly notice if she was in her room or not. Her sister, Robyn – an insomniac, not quite there in the head. She sensed something wasn't right but was easy to scare off with a few nightmares, some late-night trips to the moor, some ominous glances. Child's play. But then there was you."

All those feelings I'd had when looking at the Hollingworth House, all those knots in my stomach: they had all been leading to this. I glowered, mustered all the strength I had to show this being how much I hated her right now. I would kill her if she hurt Tawny or Robyn.

"You were different. But then again, Cate, I could see right through you from day one. I saw how you looked at me, those long lingering glances. You think Bryony didn't notice? You're too obvious for your own good.

"After I saw how you felt, it was easy to wrap you around my little finger and find out all your inner workings: your pain and your sorrow. Gosh, what a sad little girl we have here." She pouted then snapped her spiky grin back in place, each tooth like a dagger to my heart.

"Once I had all the information I needed to drive a rift between you and my Rose, that was it. She was mine."

Jane cast a glance of longing towards Tawny.

"I won, Cate. I got my prize, and now there's nothing left for you in Long Byrne. Once Tawny dies, her soul will come to me. Rose and Jane are going to live for ever. Unlike you. Go and join your sweet, wet mother, Cate."

"No," I muttered. My mouth felt half-filled with dirt from the sodden ground around me.

"Sorry, Cate," she shrugged. "That's just how it has to be."

No. This couldn't be happening.

Panic shot through me. Tawny. Dead. My Tawny. My mind flashed back to the smell of magazine pages in her bedroom, melting chocolate on our fingers. Tawny twirling in her vintage dresses. Tawny in her long skirts on stage.

The stage. The play. I had written about the witches. *I* had done it. I had written a curse to hurt them! There might be a way to stop this. To stop *her.*

Jane was stalking towards me.

Would it work in real life?

"I call upon the Evil Eye," I began. "May it cast its gaze upon you, witch, and strike you down!"

"What are you doing, Cate?" said Jane, a sing-song taunt underneath her voice.

"I call upon the Evil Eye. May it cast its gaze upon you, witch, and strike you down!" My voice felt choked, but Jane was panicking. Maybe it was working.

"Now, now. Don't go messing with things you don't understand."

"I call upon the Evil Eye. May it cast its gaze upon you, witch, and strike you *down!*"

"Don't do it, Cate!" A note of fear fell on my ears.

She flung out her hand and twisted it towards me, but nothing happened. Were her powers failing? Was I protected?

I kept saying the words I'd written again and again, Jane's protests growing louder and more ragged. An energy was building around me. A swirling, pulsing power, like I was encased in something hard like a snail's shell; something that no evil could penetrate.

I was protected. The Evil Eye had come to stop her just as it had when the prison guard spoke the words in the play.

"How dare you think you can stop me," she screamed. "You can't keep us apart! We are destined to be together. She belongs to me. You are nothing!"

If I was nothing, then why was my voice louder than hers now?

"I call upon the Evil Eye. May it cast its gaze upon you, witch, and strike you DOWN!"

She twisted her hand so that her wrist turned all the way around. But her gaunt face was filled with horror. My words echoed around the trees and a searing light burst through the Slip.

All I heard was her scream before I blacked out.

They didn't bury the girls in Long Byrne. The village didn't want them. Rose Ackroyd and Jane Hollingworth were dumped in unhallowed, unmarked ground like carrion, pecked at and choked on by birds. People would sit and whisper about them, hunched over their hearths, shaking their heads with sorrow, telling their story over and over again until it became a legend.

They shook their heads, 'What a pity.' 'Such a tragedy.' 'What a waste of youth.' People are always willing to find an alternative history if the first one didn't go to plan.

In Search of the Long Byrne Witches, P.J. Hebden

Chapter 26

There were pinpricks of light dancing above my eyes, but my arms felt weak and heavy as I tried to reach up and grasp them. An echoing Tannoy played around my head, making the lights judder. I slowly peeled my eyes open. A small screen blinked bleakly next to me.

"Dad?" I called, but my voice was a whisper.

He knew I hated hospitals. Why was I here? Why would he let them shove wires in me that tied me to the bed like this? But then it all came flooding back and the heart monitor next to the bed went crazy. *Tawny. Robyn. Bryony.* Where were they right now?

My leg and my hand felt heavy. When I looked down, I saw the plaster cast on my wrist. No pain, though. I must have been given a crazy dose of painkillers.

My vision was hazy, and I realised that I was in a single room with the curtains drawn. The only light around me came from a long rectangle of meshed glass in the door. In the half-light, I saw a drip coming out of my right elbow crease and felt sick.

"Dad?" I croaked again.

It was then that I heard voices in the corridor.

" . . . several hours. We know you're worried, but I can assure you she's in good hands. She's experienced a trauma and there's a lot of bruising around her neck that will need to be dealt with but we'll be here to get her back on track."

"Will there we more questions from the police?" *Dad.*

"I can't say, Mr Aspey, but I expect so."

There was a stifled sob I recognised as Alexa's.

"Shall we?" the unknown voice said. The door creaked open and someone flipped on the light, scorching my brain.

"Dad?"

There was a scuffling sound as he rushed over. "It's OK, Cate. I'm here."

"Dad!" I hated that I felt my lip trembling. "I'm sorry."

"Shhhh, shhhh." He pulled me into his chest and kissed the top of my head. "It's all OK now. I've got you."

Alexa shuffled into my view and put her hand on my unbandaged knee. She wasn't wearing any makeup around her bloodshot eyes, which made me blink in surprise. A woman with dark skin and a coil of black hair held back with a Biro stood next to her. She wore a white coat with a rainbow-coloured lanyard.

"Hi, Cate. I'm Dr Munir. How are you feeling?"

"I – I – don't know," I stammered.

"That's OK, Cate. You've had a big night."

"What happened?" I shook my head. I knew exactly what had happened. At least, I thought I did.

"It's OK, Cate." She kept repeating my name and it was mildly annoying, but oddly comforting. "I'm going to ask Dad and Step-mum to pop outside for a moment, if that's OK?" Dad looked perturbed, like he'd lost his notes just before a lecture, but he nodded.

"We'll be right outside, sweetheart. We love you," he said.

They closed the door behind them with a muffled click and then it was just me and the woman in the white coat.

"How's your leg?" said Dr Munir.

"Fine, I think."

"There'll be a doctor who'll come and check on it in a while."

"I thought you were a doctor?"

Dr Munir took a seat on the plastic chair next to the bed. "I'm a psychiatrist, Cate."

Ah.

"It sounds like you've had a very rough night."

Sirens came back to me in a flash. A single, chilling cackle. "What happened?" I asked again, even though I wasn't sure I wanted to know.

"Well, maybe that can all wait until morning. Right now, we just want to see that you are all right and have everything you need."

I felt pitiful, slumped in my hospital bed wearing a wrinkled paper nightgown. I didn't feel all right at all. Shouldn't I be in a police cell right now? After what I had done . . . With a jolt, I saw Bryony's face in my mind and shuddered. I was surprised when Dr Munir didn't pull handcuffs out of her pocket. Instead, she found a pen and brought it to a clipboard, making several red ticks in boxes I couldn't read.

"Doctor, where's Tawny? Is she OK?"

"Your friend Tawny Brown and her sister Robyn are on the same ward, just a few doors down."

I could have vomited with relief.

"And . . . Bryony?"

"Bryony?"

"Did you find her too?"

"I'm afraid I'm only aware of the Brown sisters. But I can ask some questions to the police for you, if you'd like?"

I didn't make any movement so she continued to write on her sheet. Where was Bryony? Had they caught her? Why hadn't she taken Tawny with her?

Had the Evil Eye claimed her just as I'd hoped it would?

"How have things been going, Cate? Prior to tonight. Any problems?"

And here were the questions. "What sort of problems?" I asked stubbornly.

"Things at school. Things at home. Things with friends?"

I shuffled so I was sitting more upright, but didn't say anything.

Dr Munir's eyes flicked down at an official sheet behind the one she'd been scribbling on. "When you came in tonight, you weren't really making much sense but you did say a few words that our residents caught. You were talking about a witch on the moor. Can you tell me a little bit about that?"

I found myself glaring. "I don't remember. I must have been dreaming."

Dr Munir noted a few more things down.

"Maybe let's not worry about that for now. We've spoken to your friends and found out some details. You don't need to go over those just now. We're just here to make sure you feel safe and so you get well again."

"Well?" The word seemed alien and we sat in silence for a few moments.

Then she said something that made my heart almost crack through my ribs. "I know quite a bit about the Long Byrne witches," she said.

I looked at her directly and my blood ran cold. "What?"

"The Long Byrne witches. It's the four hundredth anniversary of their death this year, did you know that?"

"Yes," I said, my voice a flat line. "Why are you still talking about witches?"

She continued, unruffled. "I grew up in Stoutbridge, just over the way from you. There were plenty of girls obsessed with spells and spooky things out on the moor. Do you know a lot about the witches, Cate?"

I nodded, the IV in my arm itching but I forced myself not to touch it. "Yeah, I guess." Inside, my muscles recoiled. Why hadn't anyone caught Bryony?

"I've been speaking to a few people tonight and they say that you were out on the moor. I wondered if you'd like to talk a little about that." Dr Munir had kind eyes, but many doctors did. I'd seen a lot of them over the years. I played with a wrinkle in the sheet below me. I didn't say anything.

"OK, then." She put down her papers and really looked at me. "I believe it's the anniversary of a very difficult event for you."

"Yeah," I said.

"Has it been on your mind?"

"Yeah . . . of course."

"Of course. It must be incredibly hard at this time of year.

I was sorry to hear about it when your father told me just now."

I nodded, but she didn't do the sad head tilt. Just stated it all matter-of-factly.

"You know, Cate; it's funny. Trauma in our lives left unprocessed can lead us to do very strange things. To see very strange things. Be in strange places at the wrong time."

I stared at her, wondering what she was going to say next. Her eyes were like warm, dark liquid and she stared back at me but didn't say anything. The room felt very small all of a sudden. I felt very small.

"When did you last eat a meal, Cate?"

There was a lot to talk about.

Dr Munir wanted to talk about food and caffeine and blackouts, and I kept her going, steering the conversation away from the witches. My mind couldn't focus and all I kept thinking about was Bryony bursting through the door or hearing a desperate shriek from Tawny from down the corridor. Oh, Tawny. Dr Munir talked about neuropathways and tests that I didn't understand, but I agreed to be put on a waiting list to see a psychotherapist and a nutritionist. After all, maybe this time it would work. There would be some forms to sign but it was the early hours of the morning and I was completely exhausted. She didn't mention the witches again.

"Can I see Tawny? Can I see them both?" I asked, my eyelids drooping. I'd made an effort, I'd joined in; I deserved some payback.

"I think I'll have to check with Dr Fitton in the morning, but you should be able to see them after that."

"OK."

"And, Cate?" she added. "You will heal from this. It might take some time, but what's past is past. Maybe it's time to put the ghosts to rest."

Dr Munir smiled and I watched her back as she left, and Dad and Alexa stepped in. Dad told me that Tawny had told the police that there was a man out on the moors who'd stabbed her in the leg, who'd broken my fingers and almost drowned her sister. I looked from Dad to Alexa. I just nodded silently, afraid to dispute Tawny's story. They stayed and I was so grateful.

My eyelids were drooping but I kept shaking myself awake. "I don't want to go to sleep," I murmured. "I'm scared." I was scared of the nightmares that were to come.

It seemed like hours later when I finally let myself be held by Dad and even Alexa as I drifted off to sleep.

There was no mention of Bryony's name.

Something made me jump in the middle of the night. I awoke to the sound of faint beeping, the smell of new plastic, and the rumple of hard sheets under my back. There was someone lying on the bed next to me and my body stiffened.

"Hey," she said.

"Jeeeeesus," I said, smacking my hand to my mouth. "What are you doing?"

"I always sleep better with you." Tawny turned over so she was facing me, her eyes at shoulder height. We breathed quietly into the hospital sounds for a minute. My voice was caught in my throat. How long had she been lying there?

My eyes darted to the door. Surely a nurse would have seen her come in and tried to stop her? But then again, the nurses didn't know what had happened. No one did.

"Tawny . . ."

Instead of rising to attack me, Tawny reached up and cupped her hand to my jaw. She held it gently and looked into my eyes. She didn't smile, but her gaze was watery. Relieved, even.

"Cate, what happened? I'm so confused."

I looked back at her. Was she acting right now? All the sleep had evaporated from my skin and I could swear the peep of the monitor beside me was reaching a crescendo. Tawny kept looking at me, her blue eyes catching in the fluorescent light of the corridor. Maybe this was just her and not a character.

I shook my head. "Me too . . ."

She sighed, pawed my cheek once with her thumb then turned on her back, her dark hair cascading off the bed. I realised I had raised my body up on my arm, ready to fly if necessary. I looked at her hand but it was empty. No concealed weapon. I knew she was strong, though – she wouldn't need a blunt object to do some damage.

"I couldn't sleep," she said.

"Right."

"Too many thoughts, you know?"

We lay in silence for a moment. This wasn't a normal sleepover. I had a sudden twist of longing in my stomach as I thought of us in her red room. I wondered if I'd ever see it again.

"How's your leg?" I asked croakily.

"Sore." She prodded the lump of wadding below her loose pyjama bottom. "But not broken or anything. I'll live. The limping actress."

I cringed. "And Robyn?"

"She's OK. Asking after you."

I was so relieved that Robyn was OK I could have cried, but I didn't take my eyes from Tawny's face. I nodded instead.

"Tawny . . . why didn't you tell the police what happened? What *really* happened?"

Her mouth opened slightly and she let it hang for a second. "It . . . it looks bad," she said simply.

"Bad?"

"There was so much blood." She shook her head. "You were screaming. You just kept screaming. I don't think you realised what was going on. What you were doing."

I didn't remember screaming.

"The police kept asking questions and it looked *really* bad. I couldn't tell them what had happened. I couldn't have them thinking badly of you."

I closed my eyes to stop the new tears that had layered there. We listened to each other breathe.

"Cate?"

"Yes?" I whispered. Tawny played with the dry material of the hospital gown at her hip. I heard it crackling between her fingers, creating static.

"Was it all Bryony?" she said.

I looked again at the door, half-expecting to see Bryony's face hovering at the window. Instead, a night porter moved past silently with a cart of old bedding. Tawny was looking at me, still except for the rise and fall of her chest.

"I don't know," I muttered. "I honestly don't know. She didn't take you with her."

The frown line appeared between Tawny's eyebrows. "What do you mean?"

I swallowed and my throat felt like broken glass. "She said you were meant to be together. Just the two of you. That she was going to take you with her. Did she not say anything like that to you?"

Tawny looked at the ceiling to consider this for a time that seemed like for ever. Then she slowly shook her head.

"No. Not at all."

"Oh," I said.

So much had happened in such a short space of time. Had I imagined the whole thing?

"It's OK," Tawny murmured. "I know you've not been well."

"Huh?"

"Since your mum died."

I didn't respond.

"So, you don't believe me?" I asked. I didn't know my body could ache more than it already did.

She seemed to ignore me. "This is a big time of year for you. The anniversary. But I'm glad you can get help now," she whispered and gave me a half-smile in the dark. "I don't blame you or anything, for what happened. They'll help you here."

We stayed very still; the only sounds were our breathing

and the monitor next to me. After a while, she shifted so she was facing away from me – a tight, little ball for me to curl around. I carefully lowered myself back down to the bed, staring at the back of her dark head. The minutes ticked by and I found the weight of the day pressing further and further down on to me until I could have been crushed with tiredness.

Then, so quietly that I half-thought I imagined it as we drifted off into a strange kind of sleep, she whispered, "You were always my girl, y'know?"

"I know," I said. "I know," slowly drawing my body around her. I always slept best with her there. But I knew this would be the last time.

In the morning, we decided to get our story straight. This was the official line:

Tawny, Robyn and I went to celebrate the success of the play out on the moor. We thought it was the appropriate thing to do. However, we were stopped by a man who said he was a hiker who'd got lost in the mist and couldn't find his way back. But just when we were pointing him in the right direction, things had got violent. He'd tried to strangle Robyn then chased Tawny and me away up the Slip. The moors make people do crazy things. He'd disappeared after his rampage and Miss Rillington had found us shortly after.

Our stories matched up to our injuries and half the police force in East Lancashire was out looking for a white male: about 5'10", stocky build, thick eyebrows and a navy blue raincoat.

I didn't contest it. How could I? Everyone around me told me I was doing so well, but how could I tell them the truth? They couldn't see inside my head. I couldn't show them the nightmares I had.

When they went to question Bryony the next morning, they found the Hollingworth House locked and deserted. When a warrant was obtained, they found empty drawers, a tidy kitchen with a well-stocked fridge, an abandoned scalpel – but no one had slept there for days.

Epilogue

Months later, Rillington asked if I'd heard from Bryony – she liked to take me aside in the school corridors and ask me how I was doing. I think she had a guilty conscience about filling our heads with witches. The doctors said my memory might not be great after what happened. Flickers, glimmers – grasping on to half-truths. It was the way the mind processes events it isn't equipped to handle.

But my answer to her was, "No, I haven't seen or heard from her since. I don't know where she is." What I meant was, I didn't know whether she was dead or alive.

All I hoped was that she was very, very far away.

After everything happened, I started getting the help I needed about Mum. It was about time. It's strange realising you're really quite ill when everyone else around you must have known for ages, like living on the dark side of the moon when all the people around you can see the glaring light. The psychiatrists tried not to show how angry they were at Dad and Alexa, although they did mention 'the signs of depression' more than was necessary when they were in the room. Lucy, my therapist in Hillbury, said that it wasn't my fault, that I wasn't to blame for being ill and for forgetting things a lot. That I was on a journey to healing. That this was a good thing.

I was going to get better.

I began to write more – not about witches, but about me. I wrote in a light-green diary that I could shut if my emotions got too much. But I had to admit that I quite liked writing about something other than death and horror and frightening flashes on the moor. I wrote about school and my feelings but most of all about Mum. Sometimes about food and which meals I had missed the most during my "hungry years". I had eaten a whole plate of spag bol a few days before and I documented the whole occasion in my new diary.

This was going to be a process but, after what had happened, I knew it was time to take care of myself.

At the start, Dad talked about moving away. He reeled off place names – the Isle of Skye, Australia, Timbuktu.

"But Cate wouldn't want to leave Tawny, surely?" Alexa said across the kitchen table.

Tawny and I had only spoken once since that morning at the hospital, and then only to go over the series of fake events from the night before. There was nothing more to say. Too much had happened. How could things ever go back to how they had been before? But sometimes in the corridors at school I caught Robyn staring at me from the corner of her eye. Only for a second – nervy and frightened like an animal caught in the air ducts – but it was enough. I knew which page we were on.

No one ever speaks about Bryony.

Long Byrne has a history of violence. I'm part of it now.

My past feels like part of the witches' curse but it'll get better though. Slowly but surely. I know that now. It'll take time but I'm willing to do the work and let the past fall away from me, like brushing off autumn leaves. Like peeling off wet bark.

But I can't do that in Long Byrne.

One wet spring day, I packed up my rucksack, already half-filled with magazines and balled-up socks – the bag I'd had ready to go ever since we moved here. Dad and Alexa were waiting for me in the front of the new Land Rover, the hatch down at the back. Alexa clutched her bag hungrily in her lap, wondering how it would look against the shiny black windows on the city high street instead of out here on the moors.

"We can come back and visit whenever you like, sweetheart," Dad said to me in the rear-view mirror, the university lights already twinkling in his eyes.

"That's OK, Dad. I'm done here." When he turned around to squeeze my shoulder, I smiled at him.

We drove down the country lane away from Alder Farm, the car bobbing up and down in time with the river that ran alongside us. I would never have to see it again. I would never see the Hollingworth House over the farm and I would never see my Chicks or my sweet cows again, but I would take that if it meant I never had to think about Bryony, the witches, or anything else that had happened in this strange place ever again.

The thing was, we should never have moved here after Mum died. We shouldn't have lived in a place where we could revisit our grief on a daily basis. It only added to the pain; kept us living in the past.

But I've made a decision and there's no turning back now: I'm changing my life for the better.

Long Byrne has a history of violence. And so do I now. But I refuse to keep reliving the past.

This time around, in my new life, things will be different.

I am breaking the curse.

Acknowledgements

This book has been a long time in the making. Quite a long time indeed!

It's so strange to think how much has happened between then and now.

I began *The Black Air* in 2013. Back then, I was going through some mental health difficulties similar to Cate's and was struggling to keep myself afloat. However, I found the long, dark winter nights writing this book to be an incredibly therapeutic time. I wasn't ready to speak about these issues aloud, but being able to type things out was my way of processing what I was going through. In this way, this book has been so helpful for my recovery. I hope that, in some small way, this book can help others too and let people know they are not alone.

But the idea for the plot first flowed out of my life-long obsession with the Pendle Witches in Lancashire. Growing up nearby, I was able to pester my parents to take me to the foot of Pendle Hill where, in 1612, a witch hunt broke out. The panic that spread across the local community around Barley, Blacko and Newchurch resulted in the deaths of twelve people at Lancaster Castle. I always wondered about what the young women among the group must have been through and how the story of their deaths has endured to the present day. This was my first foray into the world of witches and now, all these years later, I can say that I am a proud witchcraft practitioner myself!

I want to give special thanks to Emma Jones, April McIntyre, Nicola Semple, Charlotte Atyeo, Charlotte Rothwell and my family, who read this first. Thank you all for your kind words and encouragement over the years.

To Hazel Holmes at UCLan Publishing – who saw a spark in *The Black Air* – I can't thank you enough and I'm so glad this book is finally out there in the world.

IF YOU LIKE THIS, YOU'LL LOVE . . .

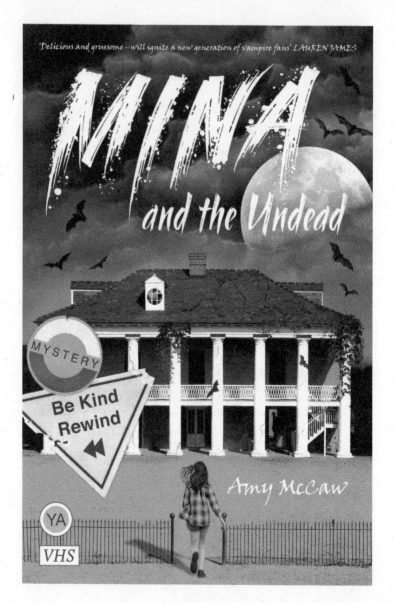

'Delicious and gruesome – will ignite a new generation of vampire fans' LAUREN JAMES

MINA
and the Undead

MYSTERY

Be Kind
Rewind
◀◀

Amy McCaw

YA

VHS

BRYONY
PEARCE

Black magic just met
its match . . .

RAISING

HELL

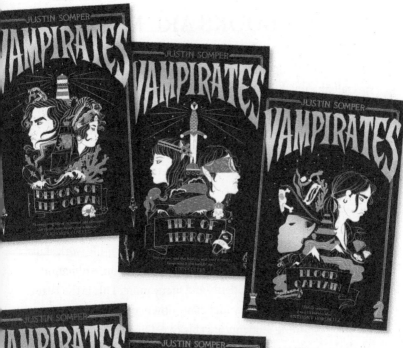
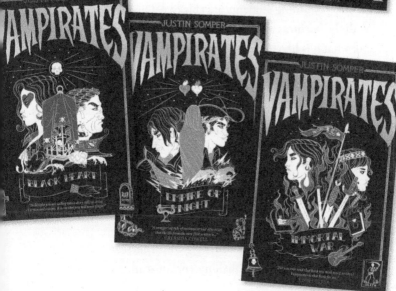

HAVE YOU EVER WONDERED
HOW BOOKS ARE MADE?

UCLan Publishing is an award-winning independent publisher specialising in Children's and Young Adult books. Based at The University of Central Lancashire, this Preston-based publisher teaches MA Publishing students how to become industry professionals, using the content and resources from its business; students are included at every stage of the publishing process and credited for the work that they contribute.

The business doesn't just help publishing students though. UCLan Publishing has supported the employability and real-life work skills for the University's Illustration, Acting, Translation, Animation, Photography, Film & TV students and many more. This is the beauty of books and stories; they fuel many other creative industries! The MA Publishing students are able to get involved from day one with the business and they acquire a behind-scenes experience of what it is like to work for a such a reputable independent.

The MA course was awarded a Times Higher Award (2018) for Innovation in the Arts, and the business, UCLan Publishing, was awarded Best Newcomer at the Independent Publishing Guild (2019) for the ethos of teaching publishing using a commercial publishing house. As the business continues to grow, so too does the student experience upon entering this dynamic Masters course.

www.uclanpublishing.com
www.uclanpublishing.com/courses/
uclanpublishing@uclan.ac.uk